HOW DEEP IS YOUR LOVE?

I put down the phone. I felt nothing.

For months, I'd been prone to crying jags triggered by everything from pretty sunsets to Barry Manilow songs. Now my best friend's fiancé had been shot dead and the strongest emotion I could summon was disbelief.

Failing at feeling sorrow for David, I decided to worry about Jana. That was a genuine emotion. Where was she? Why did the cops want to talk to her? I considered myself a hard-core cynic about affairs of the heart, but I knew that Jana loved David with the kind of love that lasts forever.

I also felt relief that the cops weren't questioning me. After all, I was the one who wanted to kill him.

last dance

miriam ann moore

AVON BOOKS NEW YORK

This is a work of fiction. Names, characters, places, and incidents either are the product ot the author's imagination or are used fictitiously. Any resemblance to actual events, locales, organizations, or persons, living or dead, is entirely coincidental and beyond the intent of either the author or the publisher.

AVON BOOKS
A division of
The Hearst Corporation
1350 Avenue of the Americas
New York, New York 10019

Published by arrangement with the author
Visit our website at **http://AvonBooks.com**
Library of Congress Catalog Card Number: 96-95175
ISBN: 0-380-79118-8

First Avon Books Printing: May 1997

AVON TRADEMARK REG. U.S. PAT. OFF. AND IN OTHER COUNTRIES, MARCA REGISTRADA, HECHO EN U.S.A.

Printed in the U.S.A.

RA 10 9 8 7 6 5 4 3 2 1

Dedicated to my husband, Matt,
without whom nothing is possible

1

It was a *New York Times*, bagels-and-lox Sunday afternoon.

I had finished as much of the *Times* crossword puzzle for June 5, 1978, as I was going to. I was trying to work up enough energy to do some writing or enough fatigue to go back to sleep. The TV set was on and I was halfheartedly watching "Firing Line."

I detest everything William F. Buckley stands for. I thought Gore Vidal had it exactly right when he called him a crypto-Nazi at the 1968 Democratic National Convention. I do, however grudgingly, admire the man's vocabulary. I used to play a game with myself during "Firing Line." If I could get through an hour of his plummy interrogation without reaching for my *OED*, it reassured me that I hadn't become a complete illiterate since leaving college. I was doing pretty well until he accused Senator Moynihan of being burdened with a pellucid agenda and I was stumped with five minutes to go.

I might have gotten it, if I'd been working with more sleep. Pellucid. I knew it must have something to do with clarity, but Buckley wouldn't stoop to anything so obvious. I was ready to get out the dictionary when the phone rang. I went into the kitchen to answer it.

"Hello."

"Babe."

Four months of seriously hot sex, and if he knew my name you couldn't prove it by me. Everything that attracted and appalled me about him was wrapped up in his pronunciation of that one word.

Then it hit me that something was wrong. Sunday was his day off. He always spent Sunday with his family, so how could he be calling me?

"Where are you?"

"At the station and I can't talk long, but I wanted to tell you."

"Tell me what?"

"It's bad news."

"I'm a big girl, Doug."

"I know it, babe. O.K., here goes. David Price is dead."

I thought about that for a minute. I wanted to see if I would start crying. Nothing happened. I asked the most important question I could think of.

"Is Jana all right?"

"That's what we'd all like to know."

"What's that supposed to mean?"

"Nobody knows where she is. Price was shot in the apartment at close range with no sign of forced entry."

"Oh my god! They don't think Jana . . . ?"

"Let's just say they'd like to talk to her real soon, and her turning up missing don't look too good. Do you know where she is?"

"No. Really. I swear I don't."

"Well, if she happens to get in touch, tell her it'll be a lot better if she comes in under her own steam."

"I will. Definitely. Uh, Doug, how come you're in on this. Isn't it a homicide case?"

"There's a drug angle. I gotta go."

I put the phone down. I still felt nothing.

For months, I'd been prone to crying jags triggered by everything from pretty sunsets to Barry Manilow songs. Now my best-friend's fiancé had been shot dead, and the strongest emotion I could summon was disbelief.

Maybe that was the problem. It was hard to imagine David Price being dead because he had always looked so perfect. I'd never been able to really picture him and Jana having sex because he wore his clothes so well that an actual body would have been superfluous.

Failing at feeling sorrow for David, I decided to worry about Jana. That was a genuine emotion. Where was she? Why did the cops want to talk to her? I considered myself a hard-core cynic about affairs of the heart, but I knew that Jana loved David with the kind of love that lasts forever.

I also felt relief that they weren't questioning me. After all, I was the one who wanted to kill him.

2

David Price was so good-looking it made me sick.

The first time I saw him was on a miserably hot afternoon in August 1977. I'd managed to survive desert heat in Israel quite nicely, but the slithery humidity of late summer in New York was too much for me. I walked out of my air-conditioned office on 57th Street and nearly fainted. Going into the subway with the rest of the maddening after-work crowd was unthinkable. The nearest door was a singles bar just off Columbus Circle. The gleaming metal exterior promised sanctuary.

As my body temperature returned to normal, I noticed the music. It was the kind of music that nobody played anymore. In that hangout I would have expected something canned and loud. Instead there was this soft, jazzy piano. I looked around and noticed a small stage at the back of the bar.

I walked toward the stage and when I got close enough to see the piano player I nearly threw up. Fine features, with no trace of effeminacy. Short hair that would look golden in the sunlight. Eyes as blue as a cliché. Lips just full enough to be heartrending. Delicate, long-fingered hands that gave reality to the phrase "tickling the ivories." He was wearing a tailored gray jacket with narrow lapels and a blue tie that matched his eyes.

Each detail felt like a blow to the gut. I doubled over, grabbing a chair before I could completely humiliate myself by hitting the floor. I got seated with an amazing lack of grace. The nausea was spreading throughout my body into a generalized dull ache. Watching him was like having a bad flu, but looking away would have been like an amputation.

He finished with a flourish and I heard a lone set of hands clapping. They turned out to be mine. He looked up. He smiled at me. When he smiled, it turned up the gorgeousness level one more notch. It was impossible not to smile back. It didn't even hurt.

"Any requests?"

My brain was seizing up like an old DeSoto.

" 'Blue Moon'?"

I picked it out of a memory. I used to listen to that kind of music with my parents. Two hours later I was still sitting there, staring and smiling and trying not to puke my guts out.

Here's what happened when I told that story to my shrink:

"Why do you think you responded so violently? Were you physically attracted to him?"

"Well, who wouldn't be?"

"Then why the nausea?"

"Because I knew I wanted him, and if I've learned anything, Karl, it's that girls like me don't get men like that."

That was a rare moment of candor. What I told myself at the time was that I wasn't looking for a man. In fact, since he seemed to be finished, I was going home. I was working on steadying myself enough to stand up when I saw him walking toward me, smile and all. I felt a sweat break out all over my body. It was a struggle to form words.

"You were great."

I sounded like an idiot and there was nothing I could do about it.

"Thanks. I haven't seen you here before."

His speech was curiously unmusical, almost flat.

"I haven't been."

"I hope you'll come back. Not everyone appreciates good music."

I decided not to mention that I didn't either.

"When are you here?"

"Just Tuesdays and Thursdays in the afternoon. They let me play here before the weeknight rush. Then *they* come on."

He looked with distaste at the rock combo that was setting up. They had rolled the piano off to one side.

"Do you play anywhere else that I can see you?"

"Nope."

"I guess it's hard to make a living as a musician."

"No. It's easy."

"But you said . . ."

"I said no gigs, I got sessions."

"You've lost me."

"I play on recording sessions. Disco records, commercials, radio-station jingles. I'll bet you've heard me a hundred times."

"So you do make money playing?"

"Yeah."

"Then why do this?"

"Gotta make sure I still got my chops."

I followed him as he hurried out of the club. The air was cooler, but I was flushed and sweating.

"What's your name?"

"David Price."

He waved for a cab. I couldn't stand to see him go.

"Can I buy you dinner or something?"

"I'd like to but I can't."

A taxi arrived like a flying carpet to take him away. I was left with the first thing I had noticed about David that wasn't perfect. That accent. The vowel in "can't" started somewhere back in his throat and had the Midwest all over it. Maybe women who grew up in Brooklyn shouldn't cast stones, but I hated that sound.

I went home and checked my tarot cards. I shuffled while

re-creating David Price in my mind. Just the thought of him reminded me of being in the hospital when I got really sick after my senior year of high school. When I laid out the cards, the first thing I saw was the Nine of Swords, the Prince of Wands, and the Two of Cups. In the most basic terms, he was a man of creativity, I was attracted to him, and I didn't have a chance. I'd known all that the minute I saw his eyes.

None of these glad tidings prevented me from showing up two days later. This time I brought Connie from Reception. The week after that I took Elyse from Records and Jeanine who did god-knows-what. They were all favorably impressed, although no one else reported the particular symptoms that continued to afflict me.

The female employees of Heartman Publishing had to join a long line. David, in his way, had quite a following. There seemed to be an endless number of well-coifed career girls sighing from their bar stools. I couldn't tell if any of them had gotten further than I had. Since I had no hope, I became an avid observer.

I came to realize that the smile was sometimes a prop that he flashed the way a con man shows everyone a roll of bills. After weeks of watching, I started to recognize the difference between a fake and the genuine article. There was a tightening in the jaw when a request displeased him or someone got too close to the piano when he was playing.

I always stayed for the whole two hours. I always took the opportunity to talk to him as he was leaving. I told myself that he liked me, that I was a friend, even though he wasn't interested in me romantically. I started writing a story about a piano player who falls in love with a writer.

"You're acting like you're in high school," Jana said to me, quite unnecessarily, one Tuesday as I was dressing for work. I mumbled back some profanity, but there was no point in arguing. It was exactly like being in high school and Jana didn't know a tenth of it.

"I don't think Gloria or Betty or Andrea would approve." She went on taunting me.

Jana was amused by my feminist vehemence as only a woman completely comfortable with herself could be.

"Germaine would understand."

"Yeah, but she wouldn't be pulling the scared-rabbit routine. If you really want him, go out and get him."

"Who says I want him?"

"Why else would you be putting on that makeup so thick?"

I put down the mascara and turned around. She was lying across my bed in a baby-doll nightgown with wavy chestnut hair spilling over her shoulders. It was no joyride for my ego to live with a roommate who made me break into Harlequin romance–purple prose every time I tried to describe her.

"Jana, what am I going to do? I can't go on like this."

"As my daddy would say, Get your ass in gear, soldier. When do I get to meet Prince Charming anyway?"

"Any Tuesday or Thursday between five-thirty and seven-thirty."

I'll come by your office tonight."

I had to go. It was very important to Heartman Publishing that I be in my office analyzing shit promptly at 9:00 A.M. Since this pathetic task was so lucrative, I tried not to disappoint them.

A whole day went by producing detailed critiques that I assumed were destined to go unread. Any job that paid half the rent on a two-bedroom apartment in the Village had to be held on to, no matter how crazy it was making me. That day the pickings were especially wretched. Another sex survey? Was there anything to be said on the subject after Kinsey? If there was, these creeps hadn't found it. I was busy crucifying their production when Jana came in.

I had tried very hard not to imagine what would happen when Jana met David. I felt like a scientist deliberately mixing two volatile chemicals. I was strung so tightly I could barely answer Jana's questions as we made the short walk to the Junebug.

"Just how handsome is he?"

"Gorgeous."

"Like Robert Redford?"

"Better."

"You must be deluded."

We walked in and I followed her eyes as she got her first look at him. There was an exhalation of the words "Oh my."

Jana Crowley was a waitress by profession and an artist by passion, but her greatest skill was the fine art of flirtation. She had never met a man she couldn't have. When I heard that breathy drawl kick in, I knew all was lost.

The Jana Crowley technique was an anthropological phenomenon worthy of preservation on film. *National Geographic* could have done a whole television special on it. I'd seen her in action many times and it never failed to amaze me. The essential factor was the way she could project the message "I don't care." All the self-confidence and independence I sought in the women's liberation movement could be contained in one of her smiles. No wonder she got bigger tips than any other waitress at Swenson's. You needed a stopwatch to time how long it took the prey to become infatuated.

I don't know how long it took for David, because I couldn't bring myself to watch. I sat at the bar, sipping a ginger ale.

Jana was noncommittal and vague on the way home. She said he was "sweet." She said he was "awfully cute." He played "real nice." I knew she had even less interest in that kind of music than I did. Then she said she'd like to draw him. Alarm bells went off in my head like a pinball machine.

If she came home the next night, it was after I'd gone to sleep, but she called me at work the next day. She wanted to meet me for lunch. As if I had time. Especially when I was reading a biography of Queen Victoria that seemed to go on as long as the old biddy herself.

"Why should I schlepp all the way back there? Couldn't it wait till tonight? What's so important?"

"David came to see me yesterday."

"I'll meet you in the park."

We sat together on a bench near the arch. Sweltering summer had been replaced by smoky autumn. Jana had her sketch pad out and was absentmindedly drawing. Even in the roughest outlines, I could tell it was David.

"So what happened."

"He came to Swenson's."

"Yeah?"

"With flowers."

"Flowers?"

My voice was a strangled scream.

"Roses. He asked me out for dinner."

"And?"

"And I went. Then he had to go to a recording session, one of those disco things. He said I'd probably be bored, but he asked me to go anyway. It was actually kind of interesting. I did some sketches of all the different musicians. When it was over he asked me to go back to his apartment."

"What did you say?"

"I said no."

"Why?"

"Well, it was late."

"And?"

"And I wanted to talk to you."

"You don't need my permission to have it off with David Price."

If I'd gotten anything out of a year in Great Britain, it was the ability to use that phrase with aplomb.

"Marti, I think it's serious."

"Serious, shmerious. He's divine, you're beautiful. You're attracted to each other. He didn't want me, so I served you up on a platter. Fuck his brains out. Have sex at high noon in the middle of Madison Avenue for all I care, but don't sit here and tell me it's serious two days after you've met him!''

''Calm down.''

''I'm perfectly calm.''

''No you're not. I know you're upset. I just want to make sure you won't do anything funny if David and I do get involved.''

''Funny? Funny how? Like dynamiting the G. W. Bridge? That kind of funny?''

''I mean like going back to how you looked before. And acting like a dyke.''

''Well, I still wouldn't kick Cheryl Tiegs out of bed.''

''Don't even joke about it.''

''Just tell me this, since you're so concerned about my well-being, did David mention me?''

''A little.''

''Well what does he think of me.''

She recrossed her legs to buy time.

''I know he thinks you're really smart.''

''Everyone does.''

''And he likes you. Don't get me wrong. He really appreciates you showing up all the time.''

''But?''

''But he said you were immature. He couldn't believe we were the same age. He thought you were twenty-three. You should be flattered.''

''Immature?'' I screamed. ''What makes him think I'm immature?''

''Well, since he can't see the temper tantrum you're throwing right now, I have no idea.''

One Saturday in December I was sitting in the kitchen, rereading ''Murders in the Rue Morgue,'' instead of contemplating the ever-decreasing list of people I wanted to send cards to, when Jana walked in. There was a glow surrounding her. I knew it was more than the melted snow adding a sheen to her hair.

''What's going on?''

''Read my cards.''

That meant something serious. When we first met, she had called the tarot "mumbo-jumbo" and assumed I was making everything up. A year after that, she was asking me for a reading every night, and I had to cut her off for her own good.

I went to my room and got the cards. I unwrapped the silk scarf that I kept them in and tied it around my neck. She took the cards and started shuffling. She looked positively luminous. It must be about David, I thought. She put the cards down and I started laying out the reading.

In the center were the Queen of Swords, the Prince of Wands (my old friend), and The Lovers. Definitely David. The right-hand path was cup-heavy with the two and ten plus the world. Love, happiness, and a sense of finality. He must have proposed. I checked her hand. No ring. The Two of Cups can relate to home and hearth. I took a shot.

"It looks like David asked you to move in with him."

"Marti, these things are so amazing. Do they say if I should do it?"

I glanced at the left-handed path. Ten of Cups, Nine of Swords, and Death. As I've told so many people, Death means change, not literal death, and never mind the blood dripping from those swords.

"Do you want to move in with him?"

"I want to live with him and marry him and be together forever. I didn't think I was ever going to fall in love like this."

"But you have?"

She nodded vigorously. I swept the cards off the table. I didn't bother to finish the reading.

"Then you should live with him."

They were all moved in by the first of the year. I suppose I could have found a roommate to help make the rent on the apartment, but I wanted to be alone for a while. Like the rest of my life.

So I had to give up a rent-controlled two-bedroom apartment in Greenwich Village. If that's not a motive for murder, what is?

3

Jana couldn't have killed David.

Not that Major Crowley's girl wasn't plenty tough, but the wounds she inflicted tended to be of the emotional variety. When things got really rough, her first instinct was to duck, cover, and run like hell. That's what she was doing the first time I met her. It happened at the airport in Tel Aviv.

I had finally given up on trying to argue with the girl at the El Al counter, an exercise in futility that was threatening to make a Jewish anti-Semite out of me.

Apparently the cheap ticket that had gotten me into Israel when I was full of enthusiasm to do my bit for the Jewish state wasn't going to get me out when I decided that I was sick of picking dates in the desert, hearing machine-gun fire, singing Hebrew songs, and being hit on by Israeli men. For this I left Berkeley?

It was no go with the El Al bitch in English or Hebrew. Instead of throwing an unseemly fit, I was planning to walk away with dignity and regroup. Instead I fell on my keister because someone was crouching amid the pile of luggage containing my bags, and I tripped over her.

Later on I would find it hard to believe that she'd been able to conceal all five feet, six inches of herself in that pile, but there she was. After I went sprawling, she was all over me apologizing and asking if I was O.K. as she dragged me toward the nearest ladies' rest room. I was still somewhat shocked and trying to figure out if I'd suffered anything more than embarrassment. I couldn't understand why she had one arm planted firmly around my shoulder and her head scrunched down in my jacket until the thought crossed my mind that she was trying to hide her face.

"So who's after you?" I whispered.

"Wait till we're inside."

After we were in the ladies' lounge, she actually waved me into a stall. Despite being rumpled and terrified, she was well-dressed and smelled faintly of something floral.

"This isn't going to stop anyone who's really trying to get you," I pointed out.

She shrugged.

"Yeah, well, I had to think fast. I'm lucky I got this far. I really need help. I hate to ask you but . . ." She smiled shyly.

"If this is an elaborate panhandle, you are barking up the wrong tree."

"The problem is not money. The problem is a crazy Arab."

"There's another kind?"

"He was being a perfect gentleman until the day before yesterday. Then out of nowhere he asked me to marry him."

"That was sweet, if you like that sort of thing."

"Except I got the idea he wasn't going to take no for an answer. Plus I think there may be some other women on board. Akhmad is very charming, but I do not cotton to that kind of treatment. Besides, I don't think I'd look that good in a veil."

That was bullshit modesty. She had *shiksa* beauty in spades. She'd look good in anything.

I was prejudiced enough to believe that any woman who hung out with a guy named Akhmad deserved what she got. Besides, if she really was in trouble, whence the presence of mind to be cracking wise? Maybe this chick was some kind of raving kook.

"Wait here a minute."

I left the stall and stepped out of the ladies' lounge to take a look around. It was a scene of barely contained chaos, but the main terminal of Ben Gurion Airport was always like that. Maybe it was worse than usual because there'd been rumors of another attack and folks wanted out.

Then I noticed a group of men in traditional Arab garb moving purposefully through the bedlam. The man in charge was tall, and the robes only added to his imposing presence. He was snapping orders and had the clipped accent of a British education. When he passed my lookout post, I caught a glimpse of sharp features, a walrus mustache, and penetrating eyes. If this was Akhmad and he was set on a new harem addition, then my buddy in the john was in a pickle, all right. Patriarchy at its most blatant.

I ducked back in. She'd emerged from the stall and was standing by a sink, trying to fix her hair. I reported what I had seen.

"That's him."

"Who the hell is he, the Sheik of Araby?"

"The oil minister of Qatar."

"You're telling me he's in OPEC?"

"Uh-huh."

"Those gouging sons-of-bitches!" I noticed some American Tourister mom–types looking at me disapprovingly, so I lowered my voice. "You run in interesting circles."

"Well, in a suit at high tea, he's just swell."

"It looks like his goons are all over the place, but I can probably get through to airport security."

"No," she said slowly. "I don't want the authorities to know."

"Look, I know it's embarrassing. I once banged this guy I met at a frat party. He turned out to be the president of the Berkeley Young Republicans. I would have died before telling anybody, but this is a heavy scene. We need airport security, the police, and maybe Haganah. Someone with guns. Someone with clout."

"I don't want my father to find out."

"Aren't we a little old to be worrying about what daddy thinks?"

"He's at the peace talks in Paris. If this gets out, it'll be a big mess. He thinks I'm in England."

I was getting exasperated.

"I've always assumed I was pretty bright, but I must be missing something here. You are trying to escape the clutches of this rich and powerful man who seems to have his own army out there, but you don't want me to contact anyone in authority because your father might find out that you've been consorting with swarthy strangers in the Middle East. Is that the picture?"

"Well you don't have to be quite so snotty about it."

"But you want me to help you?"

"You have to."

"And now the sixty-four thousand dollar question... Do you have a plan?"

She did and it wasn't half bad.

It was based on two assumptions. The first was that Akhmad's men, with their eyes out for a debutante-type in a floral print, wouldn't pay any attention to me leaving the bathroom, wearing jeans and an army-surplus jacket over a Mothers of Invention T-shirt, heading for the British Airways ticket counter. The second was that an overworked British Airways employee in a sea of brown faces wouldn't notice that much difference between two American female brunettes and wouldn't give me any trouble using her ID and traveler's checks to buy two tickets to London.

Jana Crowley, Jana Crowley, Jana Crowley, I kept repeating to myself as I walked the gauntlet. I had to remember the name when I signed the checks. The pounding in my heart nearly drowned out the airport din. This girl might be crazy, but she was trusting me. I didn't want to screw up. I sure as hell didn't want to get caught by this Akhmad character. Sooner or later he was going to eliminate all the other possibilities and simply storm the bathroom. Maybe he was just going to try the siege approach.

Big-time chutzpah for a guy in a country that he and his cohorts had vowed to destroy. Didn't anybody recognize him? Where's the army when you really need them?

"Jana Crowley." I muttered while standing on the line at the ticket counter. What kind of a name is Jana. How white-bread can you get? And who was her father anyway? What was he doing at the Paris peace talks? Those damn things had dragged on while the slaughter did likewise.

If we got out of this, Jana Crowley was going to answer some questions. I was starting to think the whole thing might make a great story, maybe even a novel.

One look behind the counter and I knew it was never going to work. Far from being some frazzled specimen willing to do anything to move one more customer along, there was a walking, talking advertisement for British manhood, resplendent in blue and white. I had the impression that as soon as he finished selling tickets, this gentleman would be flying the plane.

I ordered the two tickets, spelling the names out. Then I produced the traveler's checks and passport. He looked at the picture, looked at me, and looked at the picture again. Was doubt crossing his manly brow? I touched my hair.

"These home permanents," I quipped and tried to put a smile on my face that would tell that I wasn't a criminal, that I was just trying to help a fellow American out of a jam. Something in the way I smiled must have gotten through.

"Quite," he said, handing me the tickets.

I was so relieved, I was willing to give the imperialist bastards their whole empire back, including the United States. I even hummed a few quiet bars of "Rule Britannia" on my way back to the ladies' room.

We weren't out of the woods yet. Akhmad and his henchmen were still very much in evidence throughout the main terminal. What we needed was a good old-fashioned, rip-roaring diversion. But what? I didn't have any cherry bombs on my person, and I didn't think a mass sing-along of "This Land Is Your Land" would do the trick.

The bad guys called the question for me. Akhmad had just dispatched a robed thug to breach the fortress. He was approaching the rest room with a look of distaste mingled with a strong desire not to contradict an order from his boss. His reluctance gave me enough time to get there first, although not enough time to get in and tell Jana the play.

I stood by the entrance. As soon as he put a tentative hand on the door, I let loose with the loudest shriek I had. Then, in equally piercing tones, I used a Hebrew word, literally accusing him of eating unkosher food. In popular Israeli slang, it meant he was the most disgusting degenerate imaginable.

The poor schmuck was frozen with embarrassment. I repeated the statement using the closest equivalent terms in French, Spanish, and German. People were looking and pointing and whispering, but no one was moving except the slowly backpedaling henchman. He backed right into the cutest little old lady, who let out her own holler and smacked him with an oversized handbag. Then he stumbled against a veiled Berber woman, who alerted her husband and the diversion was on.

Shouting, running, scuffling. Akhmad's men were rapidly abandoning the area. I called into the bathroom.

"Jana, come on!"

We barreled out of the turbulent terminal, leaving a small riot behind. It would have been wonderfully dramatic if we'd gotten to the gate just as the engines were revving up, but since it was only reality, we made it with fifteen minutes to spare.

Showing remarkable restraint I waited until we were seat-belted in at 10,000 feet over the Mediterranean before I turned to her and asked casually:

"So how did you get into this mess?"

She had the smile of a child about to launch into a protracted version of "The Dog Ate My Homework."

"It's kind of a long story."

"We've got five and a half hours from here to London. Even if you were Marcel Proust, it couldn't take that long."

"Who?"

"Would you can the evasive maneuvers and cut to the chase?"

"You sound like daddy."

"Ah, yes, Daddy. In Paris, at the so-called peace talks. Let's start there."

She pushed a ringlet of hair behind her ear and smiled coyly.

"Well, if you really want to know . . ."

I shook my head with a mixture of admiration and amazement. What an overgrown nymphet; what a flirt. I soon found out that she would flirt with anyone, not because she was polymorphous perverse, but simply because it was her first line of defense as surely as mine was snide humor. She had an accent that ranged from Daisy Mae to the Queen of England, depending on who she was working on.

Once she realized I wasn't buying, she switched gears and leveled with me. At least I think she did. In return I lowered my shield of bitchy wit a few notches. Somewhere in the sky we became friends.

The first thing she told me, rather proudly, was that she was an army brat. She had lived in Kentucky, Nebraska, Mississippi, Düsseldorf, and Bangkok. Major Frederick Crowley would move the family whenever the army said it was time to go. School got perfunctory attention. Most of her real education came from her mother, a pure Southern belle. The plan was for Jana to grow up, marry a West Point cadet, and be an officer's wife.

Unfortunately for the plan, fate had given the lonely, only child a talent for drawing and a passion for visual art. She would disobey her father's braying commands to see statues or museums or monuments that were off-limits. In 1965 she'd actually managed to get into Cambodia to see the temple of Angkor Wat. She got some great sketches, but the Major nearly blew a gasket.

By that time, however, her respect for her father was being worn away. Major Crowley was increasingly assigned to diplomatic missions that involved men from intelligence. They were supposed to be faceless, but their ugly rodentoid features stayed in her artist's brain.

She'd finished high school without meeting Lieutenant Right, so she entered the University of Texas in 1968 to study art history.

"Houston, fine-art capital of the world."

I instantly regretted that one. Sometimes my mouth runs a few feet ahead of my brain. All that moving around had probably left her with an academic record somewhat less sparkling than the one I'd amassed being a grind in Brooklyn.

She said nothing, but gave me a slow once-over that concluded with a dismissive smirk. I might be smarter, but she would never consider me a threat where it really mattered. For two strangers, we sure knew each other's weak spots.

Jana had gotten a degree out of college but not much else. She wanted to make art, not read about it. The required composition course had left her with a distaste for all things smacking of literature.

She was no hippie, but by that time bumming around was no longer the province of dropouts and flower children. Jana went south of the border, working as a waitress in Mexican hotels, which gave her time to draw a lot of ruins.

Daddy still had hopes for a military match and snatched her back to Europe, where she was introduced to all manner of high-ranking military men, government officials, diplomatic envoys, and, of course, their sons. That was how the current imbroglio had started.

Her father's job at the peace talks was largely a matter of form. He was there to smooth over egos. This kept him from personally supervising his little girl, much less realizing that she had combined her mother's wisdom on the taming and manipulation of the male creature with a streak of independence. Thus ignorant, he'd sent Jana to stay with his friend, the ambassador.

The ambassador had a friend who was the attaché of the envoy to Sweden, and he was acquainted with Akhmad El Hassan. They all met at a garden party in Sussex. The next thing you know, Jana had accepted an invitation to see the pyramids along the Nile. Sunrise on a tropic isle was not mentioned.

At first Akhmad had been the perfect gentleman. Jana had been staying in his residence, which was nothing short of palatial, where he entertained in the grand style. Everything was copacetic until she came in from the pool one day around tea time only to find Akhmad in deep conversation with a rat-faced man in an ill-fitting suit.

This particular rat, she had last seen talking to her father in Bangkok, a few days before an extremely bloody coup erupted in a village in Laos. Meaningful glances were exchanged all around, after which everyone pretended that it all meant nothing.

The next day, however, her English-educated, perfect gentleman metamorphosed into the ardent suitor with hot desert blood. It seemed a propitious moment for an unabashed retreat. Just getting to Israel had required bribing guards and hitching a jeep ride with some passing soldiers.

It was a great story, but I couldn't help feeling miffed. I'd always considered my skirmishes with authorities during demonstrations to be the stuff of high adventure, not to mention my one experience in drug-running. (All right, I walked the pot across campus, but it was pretty exciting at the time.) Jana, by comparison, was leading a life that made *The Perils of Pauline* look like *Rebecca of Sunnybrook Farm*. It was discouraging, but at least I knew what we had to do with the information.

"As soon as we get to London, we need to call the American Consulate."

She looked at me as if I were the village idiot. I thought about it a minute.

"O.K. Yeah, if this guy is CIA, then the consulate is

probably in on it. We'll find a reporter, maybe someone from the *Washington Post*. They've got a London bureau, right? Maybe we could get in touch with Woodward and Bernstein."

Not even the village idiot. I must have grown antennae and become a Martian.

"We'll find a way to keep your name out of it. Anonymous tip. Just let them know that our CIA is conspiring with one of those Arab bastards and see what they turn up. And we definitely have to tell the Israeli ambassador. Oh, man, I wonder if it's an invasion in the works."

"What did you say your name was?"

"Huh? Oh gosh, we haven't even been introduced. My name is Martha Hirsch, but please call me Marti. Never trust anyone over thirty to name a child. What were my parents thinking?"

She held up one finger. Her wrists were thin. The physical delicacy was at odds with the brass balls she had demonstrated so far, except when it came to confronting her father.

"Now, listen to me, Marti. I'm not telling anybody about anything and neither are you. Is that clear?"

I opened my mouth to protest, then closed it again. I was full of arguments, but her finger stayed up and her green eyes left no possibility of discussion. I used to have a Spanish teacher who could shut up the noisiest classroom with a similar finger and a drawn-out stage whisper of "*Silencio.*" I *silencio*-ed.

Jana Crowley was a mystery. Maybe that's why I offered no resistance to her suggestion that we travel the English countryside together.

I had no desire to return to the country I thought of as Amerika. Nixon was gone, but nothing had changed. Besides, I'd always wanted to read Shakespeare's plays in the country of the mother tongue.

We stopped in London long enough for Jana to ascertain from the ambassador that her father was completely unaware of her recent adventures in Middle Eastern diplomacy. I bought a full volume of the plays, and we took off on the next train out of Victoria Station.

It was a hell of a year. I'd had comrades before, and lovers of both sexes, but never a real best-friend. We grew that close in a remarkably short period of time.

It was exhilarating to have no purpose or mission, except to keep moving and keep reading. Ten years of marches and movements can wear you down. I was surprised to find myself liking most of the people I met.

I knew in my heart that if I met the same people in America (excuse me, Amerika), I would brand them as rednecks, yokels, and hicks, but because their accents were English, Irish, and Welsh instead of Southern or Midwestern, I found them charming.

Jana and I knew that she could always wire her father for money, but we fostered the illusion that we were short on funds. Poverty gave us freedom.

We traveled by rail, foot, and thumb. At night we would go to the nearest pub and Jana would ostentatiously take out her sketch pad and start to do a drawing of me. Someone would take notice and then ask her to do a picture of them or their child or farmhouse or dog. That was always good for a few pounds or at least a meal, and sometimes a bed for the night.

If there were no art lovers, then I would unwrap the tarot cards and Jana would shill for my fortune-teller routine. Some nights I managed to amass a rather goodly sum, although the further we got into the rural countryside, the more I was afraid I might provoke someone into burning me as a witch for putting on too good a show. I do have a gift, but half the gift is intuition.

Jana quickly moved from skepticism to fascination, possibly with me as much as the cards. It was as if we were opposite magnetic poles, fighting the laws of nature by being pulled together. I wanted to understand her coolness, detachment, femininity, and power over men. On the other hand she was dumbfounded by my passion for politics, literature, women's liberation. She was amused by my feminist polemics on how we needed to be independent of men and overthrow the patriarchy.

We started debating the topic on the plane to London and were still flogging it to death a year later en route to New York. Her typical answer to one of my little rants was to look me straight in the eye and say calmly:

"Let's say you're having a fight with somebody, what's the worse thing you could possibly say to them?"

"I don't know. Fuck you, I guess."

"Right. Kind of nasty, but it's overused. It doesn't really pack a punch. But if you were a man, you could say 'suck my dick.' "

"So what?"

"Have you ever heard a man say that? Outside of the bedroom I mean."

"The kind of men I hang out with don't say that kind of thing in or out of the bedroom."

"Well, you hang out with the wrong kind of men. I tell you, Marti, after one of them has dropped that, there's this chilling silence. Either someone's gonna get killed or someone's gonna back down."

"Typical bullshit, macho posturing."

"When you can say it, then you'll have a leg to stand on."

"A third one anyway."

Jana and I remained entrenched in our positions on the battle of the sexes, but we did manage to change each other.

She wanted to know if I was really enjoying my reading of the Shakespeare plays, so I tutored her in remedial literature appreciation, using my cumbersome volume as the main text. By the time we were in Scotland, reading *Macbeth* within view of a suitably spooky castle, I was fighting her for time with the book. In self-defense I turned her on to Wilde and Shaw as soon as we got to Ireland.

When we left Victoria Station, I had suggested that we look in the cloakroom to see if there were any bags with babies in them, and she had looked at me blankly. When we arrived at JFK in New York, she looked over with satisfaction and said:

"Henry Higgins, eat your heart out."

We'd gone shopping in London before coming back, and my appearance was her victory. It had taken a year of reasoning and cajoling and playing up to my jealousy, but she had convinced me that I could fix my hair, put on makeup, and wear sexy clothing without betraying my whole gender. It wasn't easy. It wasn't even comfortable. If I had ever known how to walk in high heels, my brain had long since rejected the information.

During our first months back in the States, I walked around New York in my high heels and miniskirt, praying that I wouldn't run into any of my feminist cohorts from Quincy U. or Berkeley. By the time my feet stopped hurting, I realized that it didn't matter anymore. I still had all the right rhetoric for my political beliefs, but the feelings were gone.

The best thing about David getting killed was that it gave me something to care about.

4

I stayed in bed listening to my blue plastic doughnut-shaped Toodleloop A.M. radio: 77, WABC.

"Shadow Dancing." "Baker Street." "Too Much, Too Little, Too Late." "Love Will Find a Way."

Nobody called.

"Copacabana." "Bluer Than Blue." "Three Times a Lady."

I thought about getting up and trying to write.

"With a Little Luck." "You're the One That I Want." "It's a Heartache." "Emotion."

The same songs, over and over. That's what I loved about top-forty radio. It was always the same and it was always changing.

I thought about smoking some pot, but the crying jag started before I could get around to it. Maybe it was hearing the spoken part of "Miss You" for the third time that day, or seeing the lights of the George Washington Bridge through my window. Who was I kidding? There were no rational explanations. It was just another out-of-nowhere fifteen minutes of sobbing that left me red-eyed and gasping for breath.

I decided to call my shrink. Well, he wasn't really my shrink, he was my boss, or rather would have been, had he been paying me any money.

"Karl, it's Marti. Look, I'm sorry to bother you, but . . ."

"You've been crying again."

"That's not exactly a news flash."

"What was it th-th-this time."

"It was nothing. Just like always. And that's not why I'm calling anyway."

"So?"

"Have you heard anything about David lately?"

"David Price?"

"No, David Brinkley. Yes, David Price."

"Not since last week when you spent twenty minutes telling me about the suit he wore to some show at some gallery."

"Yeah, it looked great, but I don't know if it's appropriate for a funeral."

"Whose?"

"His."

"He's d-d-dead?"

"Murdered."

"By?"

"Person or persons unknown."

"And how's your friend, Miss Crowley?"

"Missing in action."

"And you don't think that's worth a few tears?"

"I got the call this morning. The jag just happened."

"You've read the book, Marti."

"I keep telling you it's not like that."

"And I've told you, you cannot get therapy by assimilation. You're invaluable to me, but you're not doing yourself any good."

"Boring. Get an editor."

"Have you written anything lately?"

"I'm a little stalled right now."

"Why don't you try writing about David Price?"

"What's there to say? He was gorgeous and he played a hell of a piano."

"Write about who would want to k-k-kill him. Write about why you fell for him so hard."

"I wouldn't call it falling exactly."

"I'm blind, Marti, I'm not brain dead. Are you coming into the office tomorrow?"

"I guess so."

"Good, I have some more tapes for you to transcribe."

"No problem."

"Will you be able to sleep?"

"As well as usual, unless the kid next door gives me trouble."

"All right then, I'll see you tomorrow."

Some phone-side manner. Well, I wasn't seeing Dr. Hammerschmidt for his nonexistent soothing qualities. I knew he was a genius, but as far as I was concerned, he was way off base about what ailed me. In fact, it was his fault I was crying in the first place.

I never cried in England, but that sojourn came to an end in 1977.

Major Crowley was making threatening noises from Fort Dix, Jana wanted to find out if she was as good an artist as I kept telling her she was, and I wanted to write. Amerika had just inaugurated a Democratic president. Maybe it was time to drop the hostility and the *K* and give the U.S.A. another chance.

We went to New York City. I had a fierce craving for a Sabrett hot dog. One more shepherd's pie would have driven me bonkers.

I called my parents collect from London to tell them I was coming home.

"That's nice," my father said. "What are you planning to live on?"

That was a new and troubling thought. My first instinct was to reiterate that I was a writer and that was how I was going to support myself. Not even my colossal ego could support that contention for long. I'd never actually sold my work. Making money hadn't even been an issue until the England trip. It was unlikely that the gypsy routine would make a dent in the cost of the smallest New York broom closet.

Silence ensued at $6 per minute. Finally, just when I thought he might have fallen asleep or had another heart attack, came the reassuring rumble:

"Don't worry. I'll get you a job."

"No, Dad, you don't have to do that."

"I don't want you should starve while you're writing the Great American Novel."

"I'm doing short stories."

"I've still got some contacts in the business. Call when you get back. Are you flying?"

"No, Dad, I've got a luxury suite on the QE-Two. Yes, I'm flying. And please, Dad, this isn't the time for the Mike Todd story."

"You're my baby. I worry."

"Right, Dad. I'll call you."

Good old Dad. Jana had the Major implying that he would send the Fifth Airborne if she didn't get back to the States, and I had Maury Hirsch making pronouncements from the comfort of his semi-retirement in West Palm Beach.

He was as good as his word; there was a job waiting for me when I got to New York. Jana did her part by making sure my wardrobe met her standards of how I should dress. Purchases from Bloomingdale's joined the goodies we had picked up in London. I reported for work at Heartman House Publishing attired in short sheath skirts with silk blouses and blazers.

When I'd mentioned a preference for longer, fuller skirts, my fashion consultant had weighed in with a heavy veto. She had determined, after a year of sharing rooms with me and presumably knowing what she was talking about, that my legs were my best feature and should be shown at all times. Pantsuits were absolutely verboten.

It wasn't worth arguing that my job at Heartman House didn't require me to be a fashion plate. All I had to do was read. Like all publishers, Heartman House was deluged with unsolicited manuscripts. In trade parlance, they're called slush. Someone has to read and evaluate them, just to make sure that the Next Big Thing isn't missed simply because no one's ever heard of him or her. That was my job: read and evaluate.

It was highway robbery. My half of the rent was covered, plus I'd have plenty of time for my own writing in the evenings. When I produced The Great American Novel, I'd be right inside the publishing world. What could be more perfect?

It was awful.

Suddenly I was plunged into a nightmare that should have been a "Saturday Night Live" skit. "Bad Unsolicited Manuscript" with Leonard Pinth Garnell. Pretentious coming-of-age stories, unfunny satires, moronic mysteries, science-fiction things that convinced me that certain people shouldn't have access to LSD and a typewriter at the same time.

I read and summarized. Then I went home and wrote. Within weeks I was consumed with paranoia.

What if I was as god-awful and pretentious and moronic as the stuff I was reading? It gnawed at me. I couldn't sleep. Then I stopped writing altogether, which was unprecedented.

The incendiary romance of David Price and Jana Crowley should have been inspirational enough to break through my paralysis, instead it aggravated my anguish. I felt like a failure at love and a failure with words, which had always been my friends.

Not writing was like being crippled, but everything I did write seemed to turn to shit as soon as I typed "The End."

I wanted to quit, but that would have been an admission of total defeat. I was still planning a McGovern victory party the day before the election.

In lieu of walking out, I got myself transferred to the nonfiction division, where I would no longer be faced with the refuse of other imaginations.

I soon had a new problem

It looked like any other unsolicited manuscript. The title was "The Persistence of Memory: Ticking Time Bomb in

Our Society.'' The author was Dr. Karl Hammerschmidt. I started reading, expecting some Kraut socialist's alarmist critique of surrealist art. What I got was so riveting that lunch time went by unnoticed, and so frightening that I had to shake off chills more than once.

The doctor was a psychiatrist, not a sociologist. His topic was something called Post-Traumatic Stress Disorder, which I had never heard of. Essentially it had to do with being freaked out by stuff that happened years ago, hence the time-bomb metaphor. His patients were all Vietnam veterans who were suffering various forms of psychosis as a result of their experiences during the war.

It was a rough book for me to read. I had to face exactly what some of the vets thought of me and my anti-war ilk. I'd never personally said ''baby killer,'' but I'd certainly thought it. Even more disturbing were the actual symptoms of PTSD. Depression, schizophrenia, and a lot of suicides. This went on for 436 pages.

I hated it. I didn't want to deal with it, and I didn't think the book-buying public would either. I wrote a memo stating my opinion, put it in my supervisor's box, and went home, mildly surprised to realize that the sun was long gone.

Jana was out. I had a Howard Johnson's macaroni-and-cheese for dinner and sat down for my nightly struggle with the muse.

I turned the radio on in the middle of a Crazy Eddie commercial. Then came a weather report with the possibility of rain, a piano introduction to a ballad, and *''Last night I waved good-bye, now it seems years. I'm back in the city where nothing is clear.''* It made me sad. *''But thoughts of me holding you, bringing us near.''* I could feel my mouth quivering unpleasantly. *''And tell me . . .''*

I couldn't tell him anything because, by that time, tears were spilling from the sides of my eyes. I cried through the rest of the song, feeling horribly confused and vulnerable and angry at the same time. The DJ said it was ''Weekend in New England'' by Barry Manilow. I knew that. I'd heard it before, but it had never done that to me. I had no strong opinions about Barry Manilow, one way or another. I knew I wasn't crying over the good old days in the Berkshires. I didn't know why I was crying. I hadn't cried since . . . I just didn't cry.

I got a Pepsi from the kitchen and went back to work, determined to put the whole thing out of my mind, which I did, until the next afternoon when I took a break from a sensationalistic, and no doubt spurious, exposé of a Satanic prostitution ring.

My new office had a smashing view of Central Park, including a playground. It was getting late, but I could see a bunch of kids playing. They looked so happy and carefree. Suddenly those damn tears were there again. Big tears. Gulping sobs that left me breathless. It lasted nearly ten minutes. I was mortified. At least no one heard me or came into the office. I waited until the coast was clear in the hallway before sprinting to the ladies' room to repair the destruction of my makeup.

After that, it happened at least once a day, sometimes twice. Always out of nowhere, caused by who-knew-what. Sunsets, bad books, good books, sad songs, and, sometimes, nothing I could even grasp on to as a clue.

One rare night Jana was home and we were watching television together. There was a camera commercial. "Do you remember the times of your life?" That did it. I was getting to know the drill, but it threw Jana for a loop. She stopped in the middle of nibbling a potato chip and stared at me in horror. She put a cautious arm out to try and hug me, which was embarrassing for both of us and didn't cut off the tears one minute sooner. While I was composing myself, Jana demanded an explanation. I told her what had been going on.

"Maybe you should see a doctor."

"Do they have an anti-crying vaccine that they shoot into you along with rubella?"

"A shrink."

"Oh, why didn't you say so."

I was being deliberately obtuse for the sheer fun of it, but when she said that, it reminded me of a certain psychiatrist who might know something about my dilemma.

"Now that I think about it, there is one son of a bitch I'd like a few words with. Now, what was that guy's name. Hammersomething, Hammersmith, Hammerschmidt. Karl Hammerschmidt. That's him."

"What are you doing, Marti?"

By that time, I was up and looking for the phone book. It was under a pile of fashion magazines. I started rifling through it.

"O.K., how many Karl Hammerschmidt shrinks can there be in this town?"

"How do you know he's in this town?"

"The case studies. He describes a guy in a wheelchair having a breakdown in the middle of Times Square and another one taking a header off of a skyscraper on Wall Street."

"I hope you are making sense to yourself, because you left me behind a long time ago. Are you crying because this city is full of crazy people."

"Cool it. The great detective is at work."

"Is this going to require beating people up or just being smarter than everybody?"

"I'm already smarter than everybody. If I do take a poke at anybody, it's definitely going to be this guy."

It turned out that there were five Karl Hammerschmidts in the Manhattan phone directory, and three were doctors. I immediately eliminated Dr. Karl Hammerschmidt, D.D.S. That left two. O.K., I thought, let's not have a loss of nerve now. Mike Hammer wouldn't freeze at having to dial a phone. Mrs. Marple's hand wouldn't shake in the process. *Ring. Ring. Ring.*

"Hello?" A high-pitched old woman's voice.

"Hello. Is Dr. Hammerschmidt there?"

"Hold on, I'll get him for you." I heard her calling out "Karl!" I could imagine her bony fingers imperfectly covering the mouthpiece so that I got to hear what followed.

"Karl, come in here."

"What is it?"

"It's someone on the phone."

"For me?"

"Yes for you."

"Who is it."

"I didn't ask. Maybe a patient."

"Then they should call at the office."

"Maybe it's an emergency. Will you take the phone already."

Then the deeply disgruntled and world-weary intonations came in clearly.

"So, what's the emergency?"

"I'm looking for Dr. Karl Hammerschmidt."

"You got him."

"Are you Dr. Karl Hammerschmidt, the psychologist?"

"Nah, I'm a proctologist. You got a problem?"

"No. Wrong number. Bye."

I hung up unceremoniously, revolted. I didn't even want to touch the phone again, but Jana was giving me fishy looks, and the great detective couldn't give up. One more number to try. *Ring. Ring. Ring.*

"Dr. Hammerschmidt's exchange."

A complete different breed. Cool, calm, and precise.

"Dr. Hammerschmidt, the psychologist?"

"Dr. Hammerschmidt, the psychiatrist," she corrected me pointedly.

"Right, where can I find him?"

"He has office hours during the day. Did you want to make an appointment?"

"I don't need an appointment, I just need to talk to him."

"Is this an emergency?" She was getting on my nerves and I'm sure vice versa.

"Yes, an emergency. Definitely an emergency."

"And what is the nature of the emergency?"

"Well, my father was in the war and he's been acting weird, and tonight he snapped. He's got a gun and he's holding it on my mom and two brothers and he says he's going to kill everybody. I know Dr. Hammerschmidt works with veterans, and I thought he might be able to help."

"Oh my god! Have you called the police?" Ah, the delightful sound of Miss Priss losing her cool.

"He said he'll kill us if we call the cops. You gotta tell me where I can find the doctor."

"Well . . ." The twit was still hesitating.

I gestured to Jana, who had gone from confusion to trying to stifle laughter.

She responded by playing the terrified wife.

"Oh, honey, please put the gun down. Please."

It wasn't exactly Jane Fonda, but I wasn't dealing with Pauline Kael either.

"O.K., O.K. He's teaching a class at NYU from seven until ten. Walsh Hall, room one-o-five-B."

I checked the time. It was 8:30. I signaled to Jana while silently pantomiming a scream. She produced the real thing and I gasped, "Oh no!" and hung up the phone.

I had Jana slap me five. Then I grabbed my leather jacket and was out the door.

It took longer than I thought it would. Sprinting two blocks and through Washington Square Park with my fringe flapping was no problem, but then I ran into trouble. I didn't know NYU that well, and there were no helpful neon signs saying THIS WAY TO WALSH HALL. I killed an hour asking people for directions. I went around in circles and nearly lost my patience before I found the grubby place, nearly hidden by the library. I ran up and down corridors until I realized that 105-B was in the basement.

Running down the stairs, past the yellow-and-black atomic symbol sign, I had to remind myself just why I wanted to see this guy. The hunt had almost become more important than the prey.

I opened the door of room 105-B. Nothing happened. Nobody turned around. There were no empty desks and nobody looked away from the professor. Maybe it was the dog.

I love dogs. This one was a beauty; a large German shepherd with soft brown eyes and alert ears, sitting at his master's feet. The master himself didn't particularly impress me. A man of about six feet with short, curly black hair, wearing a charcoal black suit. He seemed to be incredibly broad shouldered until I realized that the jacket was heavily padded. His eyes were hidden by dark glasses.

How could he hold the class's attention when he couldn't even make eye contact? Furthermore there was a noticeable stutter on certain words. I started listening to what he was saying and found myself as rapt as the rest of them. He was talking about a woman who was a nymphomaniac. This was good stuff and I didn't want to miss a word, especially when the woman was propositioning her own father and . . .

An alarm went off from a clock on the teacher's desk. The class let out a collective groan.

"Now, now, class. The f-f-first rule of professional psychiatry: when the session is over, it's over. Read chapter two for next time."

The voice was confident, almost arrogant despite the stutter. Some students stayed to talk with him, giving me the chance to get closer without immediately drawing attention to myself. I noticed a scar near the right side of his mouth that insinuated itself into his upper lip.

I tried to think of a witty opening line. "Dr. Hammerschmidt, I presume" wasn't going to cut it. I quashed an impulse toward "Why have I been a wreck since I read your stupid book?" Not knowing what to say, I crouched down near the German shepherd and presented my hand knuckles-up.

"Hi there. Good boy."

"It's a girl and she's on duty."

"Oh. I'm sorry."

I stood up.

"You're not one of my s-s-students."

"No. I'm sorry I crashed your class. I need to talk to you."

"I thought you might be an abnormal-psych groupie."

"Well, that was quite a lecture, if you wrote a book about that . . ."

"I've written a book."

"I know. I work for Heartman House."

"And you c-c-came all this way to tell me that you are going to publish my b-b-book and give me a phenomenal amount of m-m-money to continue my work and write another one?"

He was mocking me.

"No. I came all this way to find out why I've been crying every day since I read it."

Any reaction was difficult to discern behind the dark lenses, but he nodded his head slowly.

"Were you in Vietnam?"

"Do I look like I was in Vietnam?"

"I don't know. What do you look like?"

"What do you mean what do I . . . ? Oh."

So much for the great intellect. Dark glasses. German shepherd. Who would go to a blind, stuttering psychiatrist?

"I am five feet four inches tall. I've got brown curly hair down to my shoulders, which I will not cut short, no matter what my roommate or my hairdresser say. I've got brown eyes. I'm wearing my oldest, most comfortable bell-bottom jeans and a leather jacket with lots of fringe. I'm cute, working on pretty, but I'll never make beautiful. I was definitely not in the war unless you count seven years of protesting, including four years at Berkeley."

"Offering aid and c-c-comfort to the enemy."

"Not true pal," I exploded, ready to give him the whole "we're the real patriots" speech.

"I know, I know. You kids have no sense of humor."

"I have a great sense of humor. I'm a well-known laugh riot. Or I was until two weeks ago."

"Is that when the crying started?"

"The same day I read your book."

"Are you having your period?"

"What kind of male chauvinist–pig question is that?"

"Ignoring the hostility, it's a question designed to pin down some possible causes of your crying. There are some theories on an emotional syndrome revolving around the cycle."

"I'm on the pill. I get the thing on the fifteenth like clockwork. I have one bad-cramp day, but I usually smoke a joint and it eases up."

"Birth-control pills and habitual d-d-drug use both have links to emotional disorders."

"And they let people like you take care of crazy people? Come on. I've been on the pill a long time and everybody does drugs. Why the hell am I crying?"

I hated that whiny tone that was getting into my voice. I feared that an actual display was imminent.

"I really don't know. I suspect you've experienced some major trauma and possibly repressed it. The information about PTSD may have triggered a response, but your conscious mind isn't ready to deal with it. If you want to go into therapy, I can refer you to a colleague."

"Why wouldn't you do it?"

"I'm committed to my work with veterans. This," he gestured at the classroom, "is just to keep Effie on Alpo."

"Well, I don't need a shrink anyway."

"You're probably right."

He gathered his teaching materials into a canvas bag. Then he bent over to take Effie's leash.

"Come on, Effie."

She led him out of the empty classroom. He wasn't even going to say good-bye. At the door, he stopped.

"T-t-t-tell me. Is Heartman House going to publish the book?"

I shrugged and then remembered that he couldn't see me.

"I don't know. I hope not."

The door had barely closed behind him before I started crying.

The next day at work the phone rang in my office.

"Hello?"

"How's your f-f-father."

"O.K. as long as he follows his doctor's orders and swims in the pool at the condo every day."

"Not the madman on the rampage anymore?"

"Oh, that."

"You may consider it part of your allegedly side-splitting humor, but it wasn't very nice. The girl from the answering service was extremely upset."

"She was hassling me."

"She was doing her job."

"Whatever."

"You are a real hard case, aren't you?"

"I'm from Brooklyn."

"And how's the crying?"

"The crying is fine. Here's a hot stock tip. Invest in Kleenex. How did you find me anyway?"

"You told me where you worked and what you looked like. It didn't take Sam S-S-Spade to do the rest."

"Is that why the dog is named Effie?"

"Yes, as a matter of fact."

"I love mysteries."

"Do you just read or do you also write?"

"I write."

"How's your typing?"

"Excuse me?"

"I need some typing done."

"In case you hadn't noticed, I've got a job."

"That's good because I'm not offering you one. I'm asking for a f-f-favor. I'm between secretaries right now and my tapes are piling up."

I was ready to lay into him. Who did he think he was? But I still had the feeling that he held the key to controlling the sobbing spells that were wreaking havoc with my self-respect. So I told myself I was taking an early lunch and put down a manuscript about flora and fauna in the Swiss Alps.

Dr. Karl Hammerschmidt's office also turned out to be his apartment. He lived and worked in a brownstone on the

Upper West Side, not far from the Museum of Natural History.

Effie greeted me warmly: Dr. Hammerschmidt was merely cordial. The typing was easy enough, although the guys on the tapes were more hard-luck hurting vets. I wondered if Dr. Hammerschmidt wasn't a little obsessed himself.

I had ten pages ready to be messengered to the Braille service when he came in to make me nervous by standing there, as if he could see me. When I paused, he said:

"S-s-so, you're from Brooklyn?"

"Well, I wasn't born there, but you could say that's where I grew up."

In a way, I never went back to Heartman House, although it wasn't until January that I stopped showing up for work altogether.

Dr. Hammerschmidt had an unpaid girl Friday and I had a shrink without having to admit that I was getting therapy. I still broke into tears with monotonous regularity, but it didn't seem a cause for alarm as much as a mystery that would be solved in time.

By June of 1978, the spells were getting longer and I still had no idea what was causing them. On the other hand, I finally had a job I really liked.

5

That I got to sleep that night was a testament to the soporific effects of grueling anxiety with a little help from a *New Yorker* article about the Mud People of Papua New Guinea. It was running into its seventh stultifying page when my eyes finally gave up the ghost.

I got up the next morning and went to Karl's office as though it were a normal day. That was force of habit. Jana still hadn't called, and I had no place else to go.

It was not a productive work day. I couldn't concentrate on typing or marking papers or anything else besides David Price and who killed him. My gut feeling was that it had to be a jealous man or a scorned woman from his past. Karl smiled indulgently and wanted to talk about why it bothered me so much.

"Well, it is murder you know. And Jana is my best friend. I've got to talk to her. Maybe she knows something. It's a crime of passion, I just know it."

"You've got to start by separating the crime from *your* passion."

"Just when I start thinking you might be a real mensch, you say one of those shrink things."

"From Dr. Freud's little red b-b-book of witty epigrams."

"More like cheap clichés."

"Why don't you take Effie for a walk?"

"Why don't you go . . ."

The ringing phone interrupted me. I didn't know it was Jana as I barked her name into the receiver, but I wanted it to be her so badly that anyone else on the other end would have provoked certain hostility and possible damage to the phone.

"Jana!"

"Marti."

"Where are you?"

"Brooklyn."

"What the hell are you doing in . . ."

"Marti," she jumped in. "I need you to calm down."

She sounded pretty mellow herself. Maybe she didn't know.

"Doug called me yesterday. David . . ."

"I know. I found him."

"Oh my god! The cops think that you . . . they want to talk to you."

"I can't talk to them right now. Can you do me a favor?"

"I've been worried sick for twenty-four hours and you want a favor? You've got some nerve. What is going on? Who shot David? How come you're like a cucumber and I'm freaking out. He was your fiancé."

"But he was your idol." She sounded tired and sad. "As soon as I have the chance, I'll break into obsequious lament. And I promise if you do this one thing for me, I'll answer your questions and tell you as much as I know. Do the police have any ideas?"

"Aside from you, I don't think so. Oh yeah, Doug said something about a drug angle."

"Hell's bells and a barrel of monkeys."

I wanted to roll my eyes, but Karl, who was listening avidly, wasn't much of an audience for expressions.

"Marti, the favor?"

"What?"

"Meet a girl at school and get her home."

"Why?"

"Because her mother thinks it's dangerous for her to do it, and I would just as soon be inconspicuous for a while."

"So I'm supposed to play sitting duck? What's the kid doing in school anyway? It's June."

"She takes piano lessons."

There was no question of my not doing it. Tel Aviv all over again. Jana and Marti, the Dynamic Duo. When she told me where the school was, I actually considered refusing. I settled for a martyred sigh.

"The things I do for you. What's so special about this kid anyway?"

"She's David's daughter."

I didn't even try to top that. I just told Karl what was going on and that I was taking the rest of the day off. What was he going to do, fire me?

Then came the mental struggle. Part of me said I was being an establishment fink. The other part said I was actually looking out for my buddy by keeping tabs on the fuzz. I called the narcotics division of the New York Police Department and asked for Detective Kimberlin.

"Kimberlin here."

"Doug, it's me."

"Yeah."

"Jana just called. I'm going to see her."

"Tell her not to worry. The case is closed. Breaking and entering."

"Say that again slowly."

"Someone was robbing the apartment. Price was in the wrong place at the wrong time. That's it." There was a strained edge to his voice. "Come by the bar tonight."

The conversation was over. I was used to Doug's brusque attitude, but what he had said made no sense. I was so shaken by this development that I took the IND to Columbus Circle and made the connection without thinking about it.

How did we get from no sign of forced entry to breaking and entering? What happened to the famous drug angle? Since when did David have a daughter?

I looked out the window of the train and suddenly snapped to the fact that we had come out of the tunnel and I was on an El train. I was in Brooklyn.

On the first day of our collaboration, Dr. Hammerschmidt had wanted to hear about my childhood. I countered by telling him funny stories about Berkeley, about Israel, even about Quincy U. I thought I could distract him with the lesbian stuff. He kept asking about Brooklyn.

The *Reader's Digest* version went something like this:

While Jana's family was being uprooted at the whim of Uncle Sam, I was being reared along the trail of greasepaint and opening nights. I was not born in a trunk, but I did make my entrance in a hospital in New Haven.

Dad had come out of the army and gone to work for Mike Todd, the famous producer, master of ballyhoo, outsized personality, and hero of legendary proportions to my mom and dad. Along with the usual fairy tales, came showbiz lore of his exploits.

Mom was a chorus girl. Pictures indicate that she was quite a looker back then. She liked to imply that Dad stole her away from Mike Todd himself. For all I know, she still gets a laugh with that one from her condo cronies.

For the first couple of years, she didn't let me get in her way. She kept right on singing and dancing. I remember listening to Dad as he worked the phones and to Mom as she dished whatever unfortunate actress happened to be the leading lady, while mom was still in the chorus. It was like having two friends who happened to be grown-ups.

Things changed after Mike Todd died. Dad liked to say, always with a mournful shake of his head, "I told him not to get on the plane."

He tried to use his promotional skills to make my mother a star, a nonstarter of a mission if there ever was one. Instead she took up motherhood with a vengeance.

Dad became an agent, managing a few old-timers. He encouraged them to write books, which gave them something to promote, a reason to go on Joe Franklin, as it were.

Some of them actually made a little money. It kept us in middle-class comfort and allowed Dad to eat lunch every day at the Carnegie deli. When he had the heart attack in 1972, Mom said it was because he saw me on the news, giving Governor Reagan the finger. I blamed the pastrami.

I was eight years old when we moved to a four-room apartment in Williamsburg. I thought I was smarter and hipper than all the other kids, and I let them know it. You can imagine how popular this made me, coupled with the fact that I went into the third grade with children who had been together since kindergarten, where they had formed all their little cliques and alliances.

It might have been a typical unhappy childhood that one lives through and gets over, except for something that happened on the first day of high school.

All the students from PS 124 and Bridgeway Grammar School were being funneled together into Williamsburg High. This meant that fifty percent of the kids didn't know me. Mom and Dad's most fervent hope was that I'd manage to make friends with at least one. A wily odds maker would have taken bets on how quickly I could alienate the whole lot of them.

I had a new loose-leaf, sharpened pencils, and a Mickey Spillane book in my purse to read during lunch. I was looking for my homeroom when I passed a door near the auditorium and could have sworn I heard Dean Martin singing "Everybody Loves Somebody Sometime." I assumed someone had a radio on.

I poked my head into the room. At first I didn't notice the gawky kid playing piano, or the students in chairs who turned out to be the adoring claque from Bridgeway Grammar. All I saw was a thirteen-year-old boy with brown hair in a pompadour, brown eyes, your basic Jewish-boy nose, and more charisma than I had personally experienced since the time Dad snuck me in to see Sinatra at the Copa.

The boy did a big finish using an eraser for a microphone. Then he did an imitation of Ed Sullivan introducing Mort Sahl. The Sahl imitation wasn't that great, but I didn't care. I was in love. After years of feeling that I was trapped among mental midgets, there was someone who was as cool and hip and smart as I was.

The bell rang and the show was over. I got to homeroom with a song in my heart and a skip in my step. He wasn't in any of my classes, but some of his friends were. I found out that his name was Brian Bronstein. I couldn't stop writing it all over my brand-new notebooks. It was a great week, lived in the ecstasy of pure delusion.

I left a note on his locker telling him who I was, how great I thought he was, how smart and funny and handsome. I told anyone who would listen. Pretty soon the whole school knew. I went around humming songs like "He's So Fine" and "He's Sure the Boy I Love."

What soon became clear to one and all was that I wasn't the girl he loved. I wasn't the girl he liked or talked to or even acknowledged. By the second week, it was obviously hopeless. Giddiness gave way to nausea. "He's So Fine" was replaced by "Hurts So Bad."

Every day revolved around Brian. He was in the chorus, so I joined. He starred in every play, so I built sets just to be near him. I devised routes between classes so that I could see him. When we were in the same classes, I would wait for his funny lines and laugh too loudly so he'd know that I got it. Some days he would respond with a malevolent sneer, other times he simply ignored me.

I started hating him. The hate was as strong as the love had been, maybe stronger, but they had the same effect. I kept chasing and staring and plotting.

Karl eventually got me to admit that at sixteen, wild-eyed and frizzy-haired, I must have been an unattractive sight and that I could hardly blame a teenage boy for being put off. Back then, there was no such awareness and certainly no empathy. Brian Bronstein was my sworn enemy and my one desire.

How much did Brian affect my life?

He wrote an editorial in the school paper criticizing the war in Vietnam and I joined the next protest I could find.

The idea of running into him at a demonstration was irresistible. It never happened, but I kept going, eventually finding something in the cause itself that was as important as Brian.

I kept up my grades, although the time I spent paying attention in class was a distant second to the time I spent dreaming of Brian and writing stories about him in my notebook. I thought I was being surreptitious, but I sometimes got busted. Relations with my teachers were nearly as bad as those with my classmates.

Nineteen sixty-eight is generally considered the year America went crazy. By May, I was halfway there myself. Graduation was less than a month away. My parents were on my case to make a decision about college, but there were only two things on my mind.

Robert Kennedy was running for president, providing one of the few glimmers of hope that I felt for the world much less myself. On the other hand, Brian was still unattainable. There was one last opportunity and that was the senior dance.

David Price's daughter was named Lorraine, after "Sweet Lorraine," I guessed. I'd heard David play it enough times.

At least I didn't have to go anywhere near that damn high school to get her. Going to PS 124 was bad enough.

Williamsburg was deteriorating into the middle stages of squalor, and yet the kids using the playground seemed to be having fun. I'd never been one for hot fun in the summertime. My summers had been spent in my room avoiding the sun and my mom by reading.

It wasn't hard to find the music room. I let memories of off-key recorders and passionately banged bongo drums lead the way until they were interrupted by the worst cacophony passing for piano music I had ever heard.

I was barely able to make out "When the Saints Go Marching In." I walked into the room and sat my grown-up butt in a kiddie chair. I looked at the piano. The mayhem was being perpetrated by a girl of about eight with bouncy brunette pigtails, dimples, and big brown eyes. If you're fond of children, you'd probably say she was very cute. She finished with a flourish, oblivious to her own awfulness. I was impressed with the enthusiasm, if nothing else, so I made polite applause sounds.

She whispered something in her teacher's ear and ran out completely delighted with herself. I walked up to the piano teacher, who was playing some scales. Anything on key was a soothing pleasure. I smiled at him with gratitude. Even sitting down he looked tall and lanky. Fluffy light brown hair touched his shoulders. It was a pleasant face with a distinctly Semitic, although not gargantuan, nose. He was wearing a Brooklyn College sweatshirt, flared jeans, and blue Keds.

"Hi," I said. He stopped playing in the middle of a scale. He looked up and really saw me for the first time. I know because his eyes widened. I couldn't tell if they were more blue or more gray. Something seemed to be disturbing him. I decided he must have been expecting Lorraine's mother, so I tried to explain myself.

"Mrs. Price asked me to take Lorraine home. I'm . . ."

"You're Marti Hirsch."

"How do you know that?"

"You don't remember me?"

I thought about the places I usually know people from. Massachusetts, Berkeley, Israel, England. I drew a blank. I was going to make a joke about pot destroying my brain cells when I realized he had started playing a melody and I could name that tune in five notes.

He was playing "We'll Meet Again." As soon as I recognized it, I burst into tears faster and more furiously than at any time since the jags had started.

It all came back with a jolt. Senior Dance. 1968. Someone was playing that mushy song from World War II, our parents' war. The room was filled with sadness. Some of the boys in our class were going to Vietnam. None of them were my friends, but none of them deserved that.

That was how he knew me. It was the same guy who had been playing piano the first time I saw Brian. He was Brian's sidekick, accompanist, and stooge. Skinny, acne-ridden, hair dark with Brylcreem. Through my tears, I could see a lot of improvement.

I still couldn't remember his name until he put his arms around me and held me against his chest. It was the Senior Dance all over again.

The last night of my Brian Bronstein odyssey. I wanted to talk to him, but my mouth was dry with fear. I kept drinking punch. Some joker must have spiked it. I remember becoming dizzy and nauseated. I made it to the john just in time to avoid puking all over my black-and-red taffeta dress. When I returned from heaving, I was shaky on high heels and sweating bullets. I staggered out of the bathroom, looking for Brian. I had to confront him, to make him deal with me just once.

He was gone.

I assumed he'd gone off with Debbie, his girlfriend. They were probably steaming up his '67 El Dorado somewhere near the river.

If I had any dignity left, I lost it running out of the gym. My face was burning with tears and humiliation. I could swear I heard laughing behind me. Once I had gotten out, there was nothing to do but sit in front of the school, doubled over in my misery, feeling good and sorry for myself.

That's where Jerry found me. I was crying and shivering and afraid I was going to be sick again. Jerry Barlow, in his ill-fitting suit, put a comforting arm around me until I was all cried out.

The next day I came down with the flu and spent the rest of the summer in a feverish haze. I couldn't seem to get well. I even wound up in the hospital with pneumonia. On the bright side, I was too sick to go to Chicago for the Democratic Convention, which infuriated me at the time.

The only decisive action I took that summer was getting a late application to Quincy University. I wanted to escape, and Quincy was a secluded woman's college in the Berkshires. I'd heard from someone at a rally that the school had a reputation as a lesbian enclave. That sounded perfect to me. I was accepted and left Brooklyn in September of 1968.

I put Brian out of my mind, and for ten years, I didn't think about him, didn't talk about him, and as I told Karl so many times, never cried over him.

So there I was bawling and sniveling all over Jerry's purple Brooklyn College sweatshirt. It took the usual amount of time for the jag to stop. Once it did, and I had my breathing back to normal, I had no intention of talking about the past or what had just transpired.

I put some distance between us on the piano bench.

"So, is she as bad as I think?"

At first he had no idea what I was talking about, but he caught on. He smiled and then frowned. He didn't want to say bad things about an eight-year-old girl. His sigh seemed to come from somewhere very deep.

"I'll tell you, Marti, she's a sweet kid, but listening to her play, it's . . . its . . . She's awful."

"Any potential for improvement?"

"It can't get much worse."

"That's what you get for staying in Brooklyn."

"What . . . and leave showbiz?"

Lorraine came back to say good-bye to Jerry. Young ones are not my forte. I was a dismal failure with the nursery on the kibbutz.

"Hi, Lorraine. Your mom asked me to take you home, O.K.?"

It sounded pretty lame to me, but Lorraine just nodded. Maybe she was used to strangers escorting her home.

I looked at Jerry with a hapless gesture that I hoped would say "I'd love to talk, but I have to go," because I really did want to talk to him. I wanted to get information about David's kid, which might lead to information about David. There was also an urge to ask whatever became of a certain high-school wunderkind. Jerry smiled at me. Orthodontia had been very successful.

We waited at the bus stop across the street from the school. I kept thinking to myself that Jana was going to owe me big-time. The waiting wasn't uncomfortable, but not knowing what to say was. I didn't know if Lorraine knew that her father was dead, and I sure as hell wasn't going to be the one to tell her. I thought of trying to pump her for information about Mrs. Price, but I figured I'd meet that one soon enough.

When the bus arrived, we boarded and I looked around cautiously. The streets of Brooklyn didn't seem any more menacing than usual. Compared to Manhattan, it was tranquil. There were no snipers shooting from the elevated tracks, and the tough boys in the guinea T-shirts at the back of the bus didn't pay the slightest bit of attention to us. My greatest fear was that someone might think I was the girl's mother.

I didn't know what I was doing there. The kid seemed self-sufficient. She knew where she was going. The bus ride took us practically to Crown Heights. I wondered if David had been married to a member of the tribe.

One look at her and I threw that idea out the window. What answered the doorbell was a real tomato, complete with Lucy-red hair, who gave Lorraine a smothering hug and then whisked her off to her room. Clunky jewelry, higher heels than I'd ever be able to wear, and makeup applied with a glaring lack of subtlety. I figured she was collecting a lot of alimony. She and her daughter were living in a two-story house.

With all that space, the conversation ended up in the kitchen.

Jana was there, looking frazzled and jittery, but still beautiful. She formally introduced me to Carmen Price, whose habit of tapping her long nails repeatedly against the Formica tabletop soon started getting on my nerves.

There was a box of Oreo cookies on the table. Jana nibbled one from the side like a small rodent. Carmen took big bites, brushing crumbs aside as she went. Tension filled the air along with smoke from Carmen's Winstons.

"So," I said, nonchalantly, "which one of you killed David?"

They exchanged a look. I tried to keep my voice chipper without having it slide into manic.

"The cops don't care anymore. I just want to know. My shrink thinks it would be good for me. Closure and all that."

Still nothing.

"Jana, I got the kid home. Now you owe me. The last time I saw David was Saturday night. You guys were having the party at Fifty-four. My feet died on me around three and I went home."

"You didn't say good-bye."

"I didn't have the energy to get back to the private room. Besides, I didn't think it would be good-bye in the morbid sense of the word. Who knew David was going to get killed? Did you? I thought you were kind of bummed out, but you had so many reasons. You and David getting engaged, so you could stop lying to your father about the fact that you two were living in sin, and of course your show being a big success."

"Do you want to know what happened or do you just want to give me a hard time?"

"Sorry."

"I was a little upset. It was the news."

"What news? The city? The economy? Angola? And since when did you care about the news anyway."

"Since I saw the new ambassador to the UN from Qatar. They showed it on 'Live at Five' because there was a big protest."

"Good, those scum shouldn't even be in the UN."

"Marti."

"What?"

"It was Akhmad."

Our rabid nemesis had reappeared to haunt us. I shook it off. We were on our home turf now.

"Well, so what? What's he going to do to us?"

"I think he killed David."

"For what?"

"To get me back." She didn't actually call me silly, but her tone implied it. I controlled the urge to either laugh in her face or smack it.

"Let's pursue this idea just a little. What happened after I left the party? Omit nothing."

"Andy Warhol dropped by."

"Was he poisonous?"

"Well he had the fangs out, but he couldn't bite me and kiss up to Grace at the same time."

"Another fun night. Why did David leave without you?"

"He left pretty early. Maybe even before you did. He said he had things to take care of."

"At that hour?"

She shrugged. Well, it *is* the city that doesn't sleep.

"Why didn't you go with him?"

"I wasn't done with my drink."

"Does that mean you had a fight at your own engagement party?"

"It means that Grace wanted me to meet David Hockney, and Ricky wanted to tell me some new gossip—and I was worried about Akhmad being in New York and wanted to tell somebody."

"Why didn't you tell David?"

"I told David."

"The whole story?"

"Enough of it."

"What did he say?"

"He said not to worry."

"Which didn't stop you."

"Right."

"When did you leave?"

"Around four. Grace and Ricky took me home."

"In the limo?"

"Yeah. They wanted me to see if David was still up. Ricky had this idea to track down Natalie Wood and Robert

Wagner at the Waldorf. I was ready to hit the hay, but I thought David might be interested, so they waited while I went upstairs. I opened the door and there he was."

"Dead?"

"Uh-huh."

"Face up or down?"

She thought a moment. She must have had to relive the moment, but I didn't catch a hint of a shudder.

"Up."

"Lots of blood?"

"I don't think so. I mean, there was blood on the floor, but not on him."

Something about her composure aggravated me. I wanted to rattle her.

"You walk in, there's David . . . What did you do?"

"I got my tail out of there faster than you can say Jack Robinson. He might have been waiting for me."

"Akhmad?"

She nodded violently, with the widest, most sincere eyes imaginable. This elicited a scathing "Hah!" from Carmen Price, who could contain herself no longer. I turned my attention to the redhead, hoping that she would stop making that noise with her fingernails.

"O.K. What do you think?"

"I'll tell you one thing. Whoever whacked David, it wasn't no Arab guy in a robe."

She had the same accent as David, only worse, and spoke in staccato rhythms.

"Who then?"

"You ain't with the Feds or something?"

"Personally, I'd like to see the government of the United States overthrown, until it agrees to grant full rights to all its citizens. No, I'm not with the fucking Feds. This is personal."

"She had a thing for David," Jana interjected.

"Her and who else's army?" She turned back to me. "O.K., here's the deal. I tell you what I can, and after I tell you, you'll know enough to keep your mouth shut."

"Who would I tell? The cops don't want to know. The case is closed."

"Yeah? Well that don't surprise me neither."

"Why not?"

"I'm from Chicago."

"I never would have guessed."

"You want to know how I met David, don'tcha?"

"Let's say I do."

"David used to work in a club that was owned by my family."

"Yeah?"

"By the Parlocha family."

"Right." Obviously this was supposed to mean something to me. I wasn't getting it.

"You never heard of the Parlocha family?"

I was getting a big dose of the village idiot look. Jana hummed a few bars of *The Godfather* theme. I nearly choked on an Oreo.

"Now do you get the picture?"

"It's still fuzzy. Why don't you focus it for me."

"Jana here said you were smart. You ain't acting very smart."

"I'll try harder. What happened with David."

"So I fell for David as soon as I saw him."

"Did he fall back?"

"He said he did, so we got married."

"Wait a minute, David Price was the Waspiest Wasp I ever laid eyes on."

"You watch too many movies. It was no big deal. After Lorraine was born, we came to New York."

"What year was that?"

"Seventy, I guess."

"And when did you get divorced?"

She had the smile of someone savoring her next words so much that she was reluctant to actually deliver them.

"Who says we were divorced?"

I had a sudden feeling of kaleidoscopic disorientation usually associated with the first hit of really good hash. I tried to push back an onrush of confusion and think of a brilliant comeback.

"What?"

"David and I didn't want to be together anymore."

"Most people would get a divorce."

"Most people ain't the daughter of Angelo Parlocha."

"I thought I watched too many movies. I thought it wasn't like that."

"Sometimes it's exactly like that. Eight years, everything's fine. We're here, David's there. He comes to see Lorraine sometimes. He really loves the kid. What else he does, it's O.K. as long as I'm Mrs. David Price.

"Then last week, he shows up and tells me he wants a divorce. I said I'd ask Papa, but I wasn't sure what he'd say. David acted like he didn't care, like he didn't know what he'd signed up for."

Her cigarette was down to the filter. She stubbed it out in the full ashtray and immediately lit another one. Red nails stood out against the white paper.

"So I called Papa, like I do every weekend."

"And he said it's about time, have a nice day."

"And he went nuts. I knew he was gonna be mad, but this was scary. And you know when Angelo Parlocha gets angry . . ." She trailed off with a shudder that struck me as melodramatic.

"You think your father had David killed because he wanted a divorce?"

She nodded.

"That's a load of swill," said Jana.

I was inclined to agree. That didn't mean I was ready to swear out a warrant for Ahab the Arab either. Conceited bitches, I thought.

I needed a brilliant, Perry Mason question that would prompt a weeping confession from one of them, preferably Carmen.

The afternoon sun was shining in on her hair. She wasn't beautiful, but her hair was incredible. I thought about red and I thought about blond and I thought about a little girl with brunette pigtails.

I dropped the tough-broad act and put a sweeter, more feminine tone in my voice.

"I wish I had hair like yours. I didn't even know there were redheaded Italians."

"Oh yeah. My mother had hair like this."

She ran a hand through it. No sign of dark roots that I could see.

"So you're a natural?"

"Of course I am," she said smugly.

"So who's Lorraine's real father?"

"What are you talking about?"

She put on a superficial show of outrage, but she wasn't fooling anyone. I couldn't help smiling a little. Perry Mason would never have thought of that one. Della Street might have, though.

Carmen took a deep drag on her cigarette with a barely discernible shake in her hand. I wasn't sure how far I could push her. The words came out of my mouth before I could stop them.

"How could you?"

"How could I what?"

"You cheated on David Price. I would have given anything for one date, one night, one kiss from that man. You were married to him and you went with another man. How could you?"

I had lost control for a moment. Power shifted back to that side of the table. Jana and Carmen went from staring at me with a look somewhere between horror and pity to exchanging a look that made me feel like I was back in high school trying to chat up Brian's girlfriends. Carmen started that infernal tapping again and blew out smoke in a contemptuous stream.

"Maybe you had a case on David, but you obviously didn't know him. He could be a real jerk."

To me this was out-and-out blasphemy. I wanted to call the Inquisition to report her as a heretic. I wanted her to stop saying bad things about David. But I had pried open Pandora's box and the evil just kept spilling out.

"He'd stay up practicing all night, or go out on the road for weeks, or just get moody and not talk. It drove me crazy. Then I met Kenny. He paid attention to me. He made me laugh."

"He seduced you?"

"He didn't have to, not that it's any of your business. Look, if you think you can make a marriage out of just looking at someone, you better never get married."

I would have made it work, I thought to myself, forgetting that I didn't believe in marriage.

"What did David say?"

"About what?"

"About your putting the horns on him and getting knocked up to boot."

"He didn't know."

"Oh, come on. He'd have to have been color-blind not to figure it out."

"He never said anything to me."

"How did he act to Lorraine?"

"Like all fathers who ain't there enough."

"So what's with this Kenny? Kenny who? Kenny what?"

"Just a guy. A lawyer. I shouldn't even tell you that much. He's got nothing to do with this."

"Does he know about Lorraine?"

"Of course."

"Does he see her?"

"Sometimes."

"So he's around. He's in New York."

"You could say that." Her vowels were getting really ugly. I knew she was going to throw me out, but I had one more question.

"Does he still make you laugh?"

There was no answer, only a smile. There was more warmth and affection in that smile than in anything she had to say about David. Kenny must be one hell of a man. I'd have to meet him.

Lorraine came in asking for something to eat, effectively ending the interview. It was time to go.

I turned to Jana.

"You coming?"

She shook her head.

"I'm waiting until it gets dark, then I'm going to the Hamptons."

"Grace and Ricky's?"

"Friends of their friends."

"Safe from nomadic desert types."

"It's not funny. I'm scared."

"So why did you come here anyway?"

"Who would think of looking for me in Brooklyn?"

She had a point.

"What are you planning to do?" I asked Carmen.

"I'm taking my baby home to Chicago. We'll be safe there. And remember, I didn't tell you nothing about nothing."

I was starting to think that if David didn't talk to her, it was because he couldn't stand that atrocious grammar.

"By the way, could you give me Kenny's full name, address, and phone number?"

"Get out."

I got out. The air outside wasn't exactly fresh, but it was better than the smell of the musty kitchen and cigarettes. I looked up and down the street. There was no sign of Mafia hitmen or Arab abductors. Imaginary dangers aside, Brooklyn was still a place I wanted to get out of.

It was time to go back to Manhattan. It was time to talk to Doug.

6

It was good to be back in Washington Heights, but it wasn't good enough.

I couldn't be alone in my apartment with my confused jumble of thoughts and feelings. The closest thing I had to meditation was looking at dogs. Whenever the writing or the crying or life got to be too much, I would find playful pooches to concentrate on.

My apartment was just down the block from J. Hood Wright park. The selection that afternoon was especially frolicsome. They seemed much happier than I felt. I loved the sleek Dalmatians. Their legs looked fragile, but they moved so gracefully.

Dog-watching was good for my nerves but useless for helping me figure out who killed David. All I could think of was David's fair skin and blue eyes, his fingers on the keyboard as elegant as a Dalmatian's legs. I had to find out who killed him. There would be no life for me until I did.

Carmen, Jana, Akhmad, the Mob. It was a short list of suspects and I didn't know enough to make a case against any of them. I thought that Carmen was too cool a customer under the circumstances, but I could say the same thing about Jana, and I didn't want to say that.

I left the dogs and went home to take a bath. It took a lot of soaking and scrubbing to rid myself of Carmen's cigarette smoke and other traces of Brooklyn.

What I wanted was some sleep. No such luck. First, Karl called to check up on me and find out if I was working the next day. I gave him a definite maybe.

Next, Jana called to tell me that she was in the Hamptons and drawing some marvelous pictures. I wanted her to tell me that Carmen was a lying tramp, that David was a great guy, and that she, Jana, would never have cheated on him in a million, billion years. I didn't know how to make her volunteer that statement, so I said good night, and told her to keep in touch.

The kid next door made his presence known, with his hyperthyroid sound system and Bruce Springsteen fetish. When I heard the intro to "Rosalita," I figured I might as well give up on sleep and smoke some pot instead.

Once high, I had an urge to go out dancing. I knew I had to talk to Doug, but I really wanted to go to Studio 54.

Don't ask me what it's like to be one of the beautiful people, because I couldn't tell you. As an unpublished nobody, I remained mostly unknown to the hot shots, cognoscenti, and glitterati who made the scene and the columns. Liza Minnelli once burbled "Hi, how are you?" in my general direction. She probably thought I was someone else.

I was a second-generation hanger-on by association. My name was on the list at the sufferance of Jana and David, and theirs was due to Grace McCoy.

Yes, *the* Grace McCoy. The one who came to New York from Connecticut in 1970 with a million inherited dollars and by 1978 had vastly increased it with savvy real-estate investments, earning the sobriquet "Amazing Grace." She was expanding into restaurants, magazines, and record companies, specifically the one that David Price did a lot of his session work for.

David had introduced Jana to Grace on their first date, when he took her to the recording studio. It had been a long night of work, laying down tracks for an album by Jezebel, the disco diva du jour. Grace observed Jana doing sketches of the different musicians. With the impetuous genius that had built an empire, she asked Jana to do a picture of Jezebel for the album cover. It was just a matter of time before Grace was underwriting a show at the Cogan Gallery on Bleeker Street.

Grace had plans for Jana. They included making her part of the city's social set and that meant taking her to Studio 54. Jana asked me to tag along. I didn't want to go. I babbled about decadence, elitism, male chauvinism, and my aversion to that disco shit. Besides, David had been there before, he could take care of her.

She said that David would dance with me.

I went.

David did not dance with me.

In fact, no sooner were we in the door than they disappeared, leaving me blinking in wonder at the glittery massiveness of it all. I was standing alone amidst the lights and the music and crowds feeling abandoned and ready to walk out. Then a scruffy looking fellow appeared out of nowhere with a camera around his neck.

"Ricky Grant, pleased to meet you. Jana said you might need a bit of looking after."

Ricky, the house photographer, had an attractively dissipated, semi-shaggy, ripped jeans, shirttail-hanging-out look, as well as a jaunty British accent that was Cockney only when he wanted it to be. He was a coked-up dervish of talk and activity, bounding all over to get the shots, flirting with bartenders, introducing me to the doorman, slipping me drink chips, and compulsively dishing the best dirt, like which members of the Jackson 5 had more than three pubic hairs. He even showed me how to do the LA Bus Stop.

He was a charmer. I knew better than to get interested. He was Grace McCoy's husband for one thing, and homosexual for another. Before I knew it, it was four in the morning and I'd had the time of my life.

I went back the next night. I was allowed in, while some of the truly trendy, as well as the suburban pretenders, languished on the sidewalk.

I danced frantically to the same music that I had been deriding two days earlier. The first time I was part of a perfectly executed Hustle felt as good as the time I led the "Stop the War" chant outside the capital in Sacramento.

Jana couldn't even protest when I went shopping on my own and brought home A-line skirts and Qiana shirts. Good-bye office-tramp look, hello Dancing Queen. Platform shoes were a joy, compared to pumps. Two and a half solid extra inches were vastly preferable to a thin, shaky one-and-a-half.

Best of all, I never cried when I was at Studio 54.

One night I was dancing with a pretty boy whose name I hadn't caught. I thought he was getting very familiar with my hair. I also assumed he was a *fegele*, maybe one of Roy Cohn's friends. (When Ricky told me about that SOB, I nearly *plotzed.*) When the music stopped, he put his hands on my shoulders, getting real close. I was about to tell him off, when he whispered,

"I could do great things with your hair."

That was how I met Marc Rappaport, hairdresser extraordinaire. He did do great things, although I wouldn't let him take more than an inch off the length.

So much for dreams of strobe-lit romance, although in a funny way going to Studio 54 did lead me to Doug.

Funny, because Doug had never been inside the place. The man in the moon with a coke spoon would have given him an apoplexy all by itself.

I could spend hours dancing and still feel wired for sound. Maybe it was the music and the energy. Maybe it was just the contact high from the amount of the white stuff that was being used in that place.

I took long walks to calm down. It was a habit I'd acquired back at Quincy. I knew traipsing around New York after two in the morning was no kin to a late-night stroll through the Berkshire pines, but I did it anyway.

Between dancing and walking, I would relax enough to sleep for a while and face another day of Alpo, typing, and jousting with the good doctor. As ruts went, it wasn't a bad one.

One point of interest in my wanderings was the bar on the corner. It had a fabulous forties Art Deco neon sign in the shape of a martini. The sign, with its red outline, swirling interior, and jaunty swizzle stick had sold me on moving into the neighborhood. I was fascinated by the poetry of the words on the sign: 900 CLUB. OPEN 6:00 AM.

The first part was easily decodable. The street address was 900 South Pinehurst Avenue. I imagined that it had once been a swank nightclub, maybe a speakeasy during prohibition. Open 6:00 A.M. That kept me deliberating for hours on end. Even since the spiked punch episode, I had been a frantic teetotaler, but I'd met a few booze hounds in my time.

So let's assume you're an alcoholic, a real crawling around on the floor, holed up in the apartment for a week, calling old lovers on the phone with a bottle of warm vodka drunk. The kind who really needs that first drink at 6:00 A.M. Wouldn't you know it? Wouldn't you have something in the house? Might you not keep a hip flask about? What kind of person needs a drink at 6:00 A.M. and wants to be social about it? One day in February I had decided to find out.

It was cold enough that my glasses started to fog up as I walked in. I inhaled the unmistakable bar perfume of stale beer and cigarettes. There was a distinctly male aura. This was not McSorley's, however. No bell announced my arrival.

Those seated at the bar seemed engrossed in their respective libations. I was about to leave and write it off as a failed piece of sociology research, but I saw something sparkling in the corner. I wiped off my glasses. When I put them back on, a jukebox and a pinball machine came into focus. Something I could relate to. Between studying and demonstrating at Berkeley, I had devoted a considerable amount of time to pinball machines.

This one was a garish example of male chauvinism, the

"Charlie's Angels" model, vivid with hair and teeth and especially boobs. The jukebox was a sad specimen. Nothing had been added in years, except for a few disco tunes. I could see that the labels had been hastily hand-lettered.

I got change at the bar. The bartender was predictably grizzled. No one else gave me a glance, despite the fact that I was wearing a fringed jacket, metallic blue skirt, and platform heels. I took off the jacket to insure freedom of movement and put in one quarter for five balls. I also fed the jukebox and punched in a few songs.

Deep breath. Crouched position. Zen and the art of pinball. I pulled the plunger. Lights flashed, bells rang, numbers tallied up. I was rusty, but I still had the knack. I was one with the machine. I moved with the music. On my third ball I was 2000 points away from the free ball.

I barely registered someone placing a quarter on top of the machine to claim the next game. Then whoever it was started to crowd me. It threw me off and I drained the ball.

"Goddammit!" I cursed.

I tried to regain my composure. "Love to Love You" came on the jukebox. I took a long stretch. I cracked my knuckles. Another deep breath. No way would I give this creep the satisfaction of turning around. I got back in my stance and gave the plunger a hard pull. I gave the flippers a mighty whack to send the ball back to the top and bumped right into the son of a bitch who was tailgating me. That pissed me off, but I still had control of the ball until I realized that there was a high hard-one pressing against the small of my back, almost touching my butt.

I froze and the ball drained.

I pounded the machine in frustration, which pushed me closer to the body behind me. There were hands on my arms now. Was anybody watching this? If I screamed, would they come to my rescue?

I heard a voice in my ear. It had a New England accent, a pack a day huskiness, and a world of smug arrogance.

"My turn to play now."

"Then you're going to have to let me out, aren't you?"

"Is that what you want?"

"I'd like a peek at who's mauling me."

He gave me just enough room to turn.

I inched around ready to give him a piece of my mind and came face-to-face with the biggest teeth I had ever seen in my life. There were other features, of course. He had a shock of silvery hair, creases in his cheeks and forehead, and steely gray eyes, but I was mesmerized by those teeth. I practically expected to hear the theme from *Jaws* instead of "More More More," which was equally appropriate in its own sordid way.

He was wearing a suit that had seen better days and he needed a shave, but he had this smile, not a thing of beauty like David's, but a sardonic, knowing grin that said, "Bullshit need not apply." He looked tough and rugged, and I'd never gone for either of those things before. His smile gave me the shivers, and I don't mean shivers of fear either.

Later on, when I had plenty of time to think about it, I still couldn't come up with a rational explanation. When raw lust is involved, logic flies out the window.

I leaned against the pinball machine and met his gaze.

"Babe." He drew it out to nearly two syllables, giving me a full blast of cigarette and whiskey breath. I thought about the musings that had drawn me into that place.

"Do you always start the day with Jack Daniel's?"

"Jim Beam. Breakfast of champions. What about you, kid? Fruit Loops or Apple Jacks?"

"I sometimes get a piece of bread pudding from a Puerto Rican bakery around here."

"These spics got coffee?"

"The best."

"Then let's go."

"I thought you wanted to play?"

"I already won."

Arrogant, bigoted, and plain old obnoxious. I should have told him exactly where to get off. Instead I started to walk out with him. The cold morning air hit me at the door.

I ran back for my jacket. I spent the time it took to get to Chamorro's telling him about it.

The jacket had been left on the seat next to me at the Greek Theater after a Who concert.

"The really groovy thing," I said, watching my words turn to steam, "is that it looked just like the one Roger Daltrey was wearing. I waited till the place was practically empty and nobody came looking for it, so I figured it was meant to be my jacket. Cool, huh?"

I knew I was talking to a guy who had to be pushing fifty and wouldn't know The Who if they were playing "My Generation" in his living room. It was like trying to talk to Dad about the Beatles. Squaresville.

"Sounds like theft."

"Property is theft."

That one always went over big in the dorm. The good-old days, when sloganeering really meant something. We got to Chamorro's before I could start quoting Chairman Mao. Maria was behind the counter.

"Hi, honey."

"*Hola,* Maria. Two slices this morning and two coffees. How do you want yours?"

He was eyeing the floorboards suspiciously and acting as if he expected to see vermin under the glass cases.

"Black."

"Light and sweet for me."

"*Su amigo?*" she asked.

I shrugged.

Maria took another look.

"Not bad, honey," she said while handing me the bag.

I was going for the money in my pocket. He moved faster than I would have given him credit for and paid. I got a wink from Maria as we left. Were my dirty thoughts that obvious?

Sex had been on my mind from the moment I felt him pressing up against me. I'd been suffering a draught ever since leaving Israel. Before that I'd been feverishly doing my bit for the sexual revolution and vice versa.

Letters from the front would have gone something like this:

From Quincy U—

Dear Mom,

The scenery here is beautiful. I'm trying very hard to be a lesbian, but it's not as easy as it looks. Stephanie Diamond says I should stop sitting on the fence and start sitting on her face.
Any suggestions?

From Berkeley—

Dear Dad,

I love Berkeley. I study, and protest, play pinball and the town pervert is teaching me to read tarot cards. By the way, I finally lost my virginity. Thank god for pot, pizza, and dorm parties. He had long hair and a beard. It was either Jesus Christ or Charles Manson.

From Israel—

Shalom Aba and Ema,

If I ever see another fig, it's going to be too soon, but boy am I regular.
Kibbutzniks are even hornier than hippies. Nice Jewish boys from Long Island and Sabra women with big boobs. It's amazing that any farming gets done.

Things turned weird in England, where I suffered through a collection of crossed wires and mixed signals. One night I made eye contact with the boyishly handsome singer of a pub band in Birmingham. We went to his room. I wanted to get laid. He wanted to discuss the Bible and convert me to Christianity. Boy, was that a wasted night.

Wales was another close call. The guy looked fine in

clothes, but once they came off, I had to do an ethical no-no and claim a headache. Life was too short to deal with a gut that paunchy, a body that hairy, and a dick that small.

In Dublin I met the most charming, shining-eyed, drunken Irishman imaginable. He talked a blue streak but couldn't get it up to save his life.

Shortly thereafter, we said farewell to the British Isles and hello to the Island Manhattan. The whole city seemed to be in a sexual frenzy, but it stopped at my doorstep.

I had wanted David with an unholy passion. When that dream went up in smoke, I shut down the gates of desire. I had been right the first time. Men were scum. I put a picture of Gloria Steinem in my foyer as protection against encroachment.

Yet there I was on a frosty morning, walking inexorably toward my apartment with some guy whose name I didn't even know, on the pretext of eating bread pudding.

I tried to think rationally. This man was old enough to be my father. He wasn't even trying to hide his wedding ring. Nothing to compare to David Price's golden-boy looks, just that big lascivious grin and sheer physical presence. Fireworks were going off under my skin.

He passed the picture of Gloria Steinem without a glance. Some talisman.

The bag with the bread pudding and coffee lay untouched on the kitchen table while I held forth on how much I liked the apartment, its view of the George Washington Bridge, living in New York, etc. I was keyed up, tiger-tense with anticipation, not knowing what to do next, and on the verge of breaking into "I Love New York" when he interrupted me.

"Could you come here a minute?"

"Why?"

"Just come over here."

I took those steps with studied nonchalance, telling myself I was still in control of the situation. I stood in front of him with my hands on my hips, trying to look tough and self-assured.

He casually started unbuttoning my blouse. As the first button gave way to those big hands, I felt a spark go through my body. The illusion of control melted along with any desire for it. There was only one thing I desired.

The urge was so strong, it left me breathless. Two years of frustration were boiling inside me, and every touch of his hands on my skin added to the heat.

"What do you think you're doing?"

"Nothing."

"I beg to . . . uh . . . differ."

"Begging won't be necessary."

He kissed me and it came to me with an immediate, blinding clarity that this was a whole other world than the boys and girls I'd been playing games with. No fumbling. No doubts. Just impulse and action. No one had ever kissed me so fiercely. My arms circled his neck, and I hung on tightly as he carried me into the bedroom. Scarlett O'Hara, eat your heart out.

I started getting his clothes off. My shaking hands found two crescents of thick gray chest hair. I buried my face in them and inhaled his musky scent.

I closed my eyes and gave into a sense of his bigness. Big hands, big teeth, big body, and something else that was very big and very insistent.

Mr. Teeth had me on the bed, arms pinned, my mouth engulfed, and my legs spread. I felt him moving in and out of me with an intensity that bordered on fury. I heard him grunting. The hands grasped my arms tighter. And what happened inside of me shook me to my very core. It had never been that good in my life.

Either he was very good or it had been way too long for me.

I clung to him until I knew it was over.

As soon as I could move, I got out of bed. I had to use the bathroom. I had to get my well-worn flannel bathrobe on. Mostly I had to face myself in the mirror and ask a serious question.

How could I? I could practically hear Stephanie Diamond calling me a traitor. That smoky, boozy breath that I shouldn't have tolerated, much less swooned to. And let's talk about the body. I'd had emaciated hippies and muscular kibbutz types. The guy snoring in my bed had the vestiges of a good build that was now merely large, and largely going to seed.

I tried to feel suitably guilty, but I couldn't wipe the smile off my face.

I was most aware of three things. I was blissfully exhausted, my throat hurt, and I had a very angry man in my bed.

Getting into my leather recliner was as instinctive as wrapping my legs around the stranger had been a few minutes earlier. The chair was comfortable, while my bed had lumps in it older than I was. Besides, I didn't want to be in bed with him. Balling to beat the band was one thing, cuddling up was out of the question.

I dozed off, feeling wrapped up in the heat from the hissing radiator and the lingering warmth of my own orgasm, which kept unfolding in kaleidoscopic patterns in my dreams.

The music woke me up less than an hour later. It started with an earsplitting, amplified burst of harmonica. It was coming from the wall directly next to my bed. The guy woke up with a start. He looked momentarily disoriented and then just disgusted at the gravelly voice singing.

"The screen door slams. Mary's dress waves. Like a vision she dances across the porch as the radio plays."

He bared his teeth in a snarl reminiscent of a cranky basset hound. He wasn't an appealing sight at that moment. He yelled over the continuing din.

"What the hell is that?"

" 'Thunder Road,' " I replied calmly.

He pounded on the wall.

I shook my head wearily. I was used to it.

The apartment of my dreams with bridge view and martini glass on the corner had come at a ridiculously low rent. The first night that I slept there, I found out why.

Whoever resided on the other side of that wall took his or her chosen music way too seriously. You know the type. People who break into tears after two lines of "Where Have All the Flowers Gone?"; folks who pour over Bob Dylan lyrics as though they're the Dead Sea scrolls; and this idiot next door who kept playing those same three Bruce Springsteen albums over and over at all hours, always at full volume.

At first I didn't even know what I was listening to. One day I mentioned the situation to Karl. I described the style and quoted some of the lyrics to the best of my understanding.

"That's S-S-Springsteen."

"Who?"

"Bruce Springsteen. The Boss."

"The Boss?"

"That's what they call him. He was on the cover of *Time* and *Newsweek* in the same week."

"When was this?"

"In seventy-five."

"Well, I was in Israel then. Aren't you too old to know this stuff anyway. Besides, what does he mean by 'strap your hands cross my inches'? That's a fairly alarming word-picture, don't you think."

Dr. Hammerschmidt did a spit-take with his coffee.

"I think the word was 'engines.' 'Strap your hands cross my engines.' "

"Maybe this Boss guy should stop mumbling."

"Maybe we should get some work done."

Eventually I did start to understand the words. Even that ridiculous one about being "cut loose like a deuce, another runner in the night." I formed a mental image of my next-door neighbor as a pimply faced fifteen-year-old boy with overindulgent parents. The music wasn't that bad, but that New Jersey angst was really starting to get on my nerves.

I didn't have time or a voice to explain all that.

The guy hauled himself out of bed and retrieved the clothes that had been strewn on the floor. He dressed quickly and efficiently. He had somewhere to go but wasn't in a tearing hurry to get there. I heard him say "See you later, kid," and he was out the door.

Still blissed-out in my chair, I made a mental list of things to do. 1. Get the food off the kitchen table before the roaches show up. 2. Get a Sucrets. The Sucrets was necessary so I could 3. Call Jana and tell her I scored.

I didn't have the energy to do any of those things. Instead I composed an imaginary letter to Erica Jong.

Dear Ms. Jong,

Please be advised that I have just had a classic, textbook Zipless Fuck.

Yours Truly,
Marti Hirsch

Jana wound up calling me. She knew the minute I picked up the phone. She wanted to know if he was cute.

At the office, Dr. Hammerschmidt guessed fairly quickly that something sexual had occurred. Maybe the hoarseness gave it away. He wanted to know how I felt about it.

My feeling was that it didn't matter since I was never going to see him again. They call them one-night stands for a reason. See you later kid, my ass.

I spent that evening at home. So much to do. I watched "Barnaby Jones," got some writing done, had a crying jag, and went to sleep.

If God had wanted us to get a full-night's sleep, She would never have invented the telephone. Mine was screaming shrilly from the kitchen. It was either my mom calling with the word that my father's heart had given out, or Jana with some new adventure she couldn't wait to tell me about. I was betting on the latter. I grabbed the receiver and growled into the phone,

"This better be good."

"Babe. Where the hell are you?"

It was him. I was shocked but had no intention of letting him know that.

"Since you called me here, I'd say my apartment would be a pretty good guess."

"I told you I'd see you later."

"Yeah. So?"

"So get that cute butt of yours down to the bar. And wear something nice."

I stared at the phone in disbelief. What revolting male chauvinism. What complete egotistical arrogance. What was I going to wear?

Jeans and a T-shirt as an act of defiance? Something shiny and billowy? One of my skin tight, thigh-high leftovers from the Heartman House days?

I settled on a blue strapless sundress with a tight bodice. Never mind that it had to be ten below outside. I put on the leather jacket and hoped my platform shoes could get me down the block before hypothermia set in.

I was shivering up a storm by the time I got to the bar. I made an ungainly entrance. Four heads looked at me in unison. One of them was my friend, with his, by now, familiar grin.

He was flanked by a younger man with piercing blue eyes who looked me over and smirked knowingly. On the other side was an older gentleman. His bulldog features barely acknowledged me before returning to his drink.

It was the one at the end of the bar that really gave me the willies. Right there, equipped with a black mustache, beady little eyes, and a slack jaw, nursing a beer, was a uniformed policeman.

Cops? I hated cops, and there I was being introduced to three of them. In fact the young one with the macho stance was referred to as "my partner." The conclusion was obvious. I wanted to puke. I had fucked a cop. The president of the Young Republicans had been bad enough, but this was an all-time low.

While revolted recriminations ran through my head, I smiled and removed my jacket so that they could ogle my bare shoulders. The bastard with the smile preened himself in front of his associates before leading me out, no doubt with a lewd wink back at the assembly.

"You're a cop!" I tried to yell through chattering teeth as we were hotfooting (coldfooting, actually) back to my place.

"That's fuzz to you, isn't it, sister? Or do you use 'pig'?"

"I like 'Cossack.' Why didn't you tell me?"

"Like they say in the army . . . never volunteer."

After that I concentrated on speed. My nose was getting that sharp pain that means freezing. The jog wasn't working up much of a sweat. We got to my place. I couldn't get the key steady. He took the key and did it for me.

"Who said I was inviting you in?"

"I did."

"Why?"

"It ain't over yet."

I had a short elevator ride to come up with an answer to that. I couldn't think of one.

"So, just what kind of cop are you? Robbery? Homicide?"

I had an idea that the one mitigating factor to being involved with a cop was the possibility of hearing about cases. It appealed to my love of mystery.

"Narcotics Detective Douglas Kimberlin, at your service."

"Oh my god!"

"Yeah, but you can call me Doug."

"You should go."

"The hell you say."

He had me backed up against the door. One knee was pushing between my legs. Cold was being replaced by the heat emanating from his body. I looked up and down the hall. Nobody there. In two months I hadn't met a neighbor, and it was the middle of the night.

Maybe that was just as well. I realized that I was pressing

back against his leg and starting to generate my own heat, that I still wanted the son of a bitch.

"We gotta get inside," I said, so that he would let me get the door open.

It was another shaky key maneuver, but this time I managed.

We went tumbling in and landed in a heap on the floor. Later I'd find a bruise on my hip. In what seemed like no time, we were actually going at it, right there under my picture of Gloria Steinem.

All the hackneyed expressions of bad erotica that had passed my desk as a slush reader were actually occurring. Hot and wet. Legs wrapping. Powerful thrusting. Moaning and groaning. My tongue in his mouth, running over his teeth.

He broke away from kissing me to whisper in my ear.

"How do you like fucking a cop?"

"You bastard," I spat out, in between moans.

That sent him over the edge and I wasn't far behind. Yelling, screaming, heaving, shuddering, lights camera action, pinball machines, fireworks, the whole thing.

Doug rolled off and lay next to me, breathing heavily. He hadn't even taken his coat off.

I felt a mixture of giddiness and nausea setting in. How could I? Not just a cop, but a goddamned narc. A male chauvinist pig. Married. Big time *trayf*. I felt like I owed Gloria an apology.

On the other hand, the intensity, the passion, the orgasms! I started rationalizing that this could be a boon to my creativity.

"I wish I could write them this hot," I said.

"What."

"Sex scenes. I want them to snap, crackle, pop like Rice Krispies. Instead they just lie there like soggy oatmeal."

"Practice makes perfect."

"This must be the craziest thing I've ever done. If this keeps up, I'll be able to write that stuff they sell on Forty-second street.'' He was getting up. ''Where are you going, to call the vice squad?''

''I'm going home to get some rest. Now get up and kiss me good-bye.''

''Make me.''

''I just did. I'll see you in a few days.''

''A likely story. Can I ask you a question?''

''Make it quick.''

''What the hell are you so angry about?''

''I ain't angry about anything. So long, kid.''

Four months later, I knew more about Doug. I knew his roots were in Boston's South Side, that he'd fought in Korea, that he was proud of being a cop, and that his belief in drug laws was untroubled by a shred of doubt.

He lived somewhere in New Jersey, which is why his favorite watering hole was so close to the bridge.

I knew that he loved football and could wax elegiac about Joe Namath and the 1968 Jets. (My dad was the same way about the 1956 Giants.) He liked to hear the sleazy stories about the Oakland Raiders that I had picked up when I was at Berkeley.

Most of all I knew that I was right the first time. Detective Kimberlin was an angry man.

He was angry at drug dealers, pot-smoking hippies, lude-popping disco dollies, New York's privileged upper classes, department budget cuts, anyone who insisted that there was still corruption in the NYPD, and probably a lot of other things I never heard about.

What I didn't know was my place in the scheme of things.

Was I the current ''babe'' in a sequential string or one of a simultaneous harem? And what about Mrs. Kimberlin? Did she know? Did she care? Was I committing an even more unfeminist act by betraying my fellow woman?

I wrote a story about her. I named her Laura and put her in Teaneck, New Jersey. I gave her two kids and a Chevy station wagon. The idea of the story was that Laura's husband cheats on her, and all the people in her world know about it and gossip amongst themselves, but no one knows how she feels.

I showed the story to Jana and I read it to Karl. They both said the story was good, but that I should break up with the guy immediately. I immediately had doubts about the story, which joined the pile in the drawer. As for breaking up . . . well, I just couldn't.

Sure, I hated everything he stood for. I assumed he felt the same way about me. I liked to taunt him. I deliberately used hippie slang. I took to leaving roaches in the same ashtray that he used to put out his Camels. He represented danger and excitement. I hated myself every time we were together, but I liked being with him. At least I never cried when he was around.

Dr. Hammerschmidt told me I was conflicted. I told him it was a good thing I wasn't paying him.

Now I was going back to the 900 Club on a mission. I was going to pump Doug for information. I put on the blue dress. It was much more appropriate on a murky night in June. I wore it with a white linen jacket.

It was déjà vu all over again when I got there. Three of the original cast were there. I knew them now. I knew enough cops to populate a season's worth of "Kojak" episodes.

Doug was contemplatively nursing his Jim Beam. On his left was his partner, Johnny Rostelli, a compact toughie from Belmont Avenue. He was always polite to me, but even as he raised a glass in greeting, I got the impression that he thought I was a slut and he'd get a free shot when Doug dumped me.

On the right was Captain Tom Morrison from Homicide. As usual he acknowledged me with the least amount of motion possible. Tommy was a throwback to the gaslit days of Irish cops. He reminded me of a puffed-out bullfrog with thinning reddish hair.

Pervasive disgruntlement was the order of the night. No smiles at the 900 Club. I sat down on a bar stool and took off my jacket. It wasn't for show. I was just warm.

"Why so gloomy?" I asked Doug.

"This goddamned case."

"David Price?"

"Yeah."

"But you said it was closed. Breaking and entering."

"That's what I said."

"I think that's crazy, though not any crazier than some other theories I've heard today."

"Such as?"

"Never mind, it's too ridiculous. So, did the forces of law and order actually find the perpetrator of the B-and-E? I'm getting good with the lingo, huh? Someday I'll use it all in a book."

Captain Morrison focused on me with a pained glare.

"Doug, if you can't keep her quiet, will you at least take her home."

"Aw, come on, captain. I think she kind of brightens up the place." That was Johnny, not even bothering to pretend he wasn't trying to look down my dress.

"Keep your eyes where they belong, partner."

Men. They show you off like a piece of meat, then get mad at the other dogs when they start slobbering.

"Could I please get a straight answer from one of you guys? David Price was my friend. Did they get the creep who killed him?"

Doug scowled into his Bourbon.

"Queens says B-and-E."

"Brooklyn says A&P has creamed corn on sale. What do you mean, Queens says B-and-E?"

Johnny and Captain Morrison were fidgeting, firing sidelong glances like warning shots across the bow.

"Are you saying the fix is in?"

Doug gave me a real mean look. I had just hit his sorest spot. He was clean, therefore the department was clean. Fix was a fighting word.

"Come on, let's get out of here."

At my apartment he showed no interest in our usual activity. He just paced like a pissed-off panther in a cage and chain-smoked. I sat in my recliner, trying to get as much information as I could without provoking violence. He had never hit me, but I didn't doubt he was capable of it.

"Doug, will you please calm down. I don't care if the case is closed. I just want to know what happened. Like what kind of a gun was it?"

"Thirty-five caliber handgun. Saturday-night special."

"Easy to get, impossible to trace?"

"Something like that."

"How about the apartment. I've been there and it's like getting in to see the crown jewels. Security guard on duty?"

"Security guard in the can."

"The killer was lucky."

"Maybe just patient."

"Anything stolen? Was the place trashed?"

"Not a serious turnover. We won't know what's missing until Miss Crowley shows up and makes an insurance claim."

"Can I see the police report?"

"Are you nuts? I shouldn't even be telling you this much."

"Cool it man. What's the harm? I'm just some broad living on welfare, right?"

"I should turn in you and the shrink."

"The same day I buzz your wife."

"Don't push it, babe."

The teeth were clenched. I could picture him putting a fist through the wall.

"Tell me about the drugs. I didn't know David did anything. He looked so pure."

"My mother used to say, "Every shut eye ain't sleeping, every sickness ain't death, and every good-bye ain't gone.' "

"Which means what?"

"Which means Mr. Pure had cocaine and marijuana on his person when we found him."

"How much?"

"Single servings. If I busted him, I'd say possession, but not intent to distribute."

"Was any of it in his person? What did the autopsy say?"

"It said death by shooting. Get it through your skull. Price died cause he walked in on some two-bit scumbag with a piece."

"According to Queens," I said pointedly. Instantly I knew I had stepped on a mine.

He stopped in the middle of pacing, turned to me with flashing eyes and flared nostrils. It might have been a good time to shut up, run away, maybe call a cop. (Maybe not.)

I kept going.

"Be a real detective, Doug. The David Prices of this world do not become the victims of anonymous creeps. Something very strange is going on here. Maybe the drugs were planted as a red herring, but whoever planted them didn't realize that Queens was going to put the kibosh on the case for whatever reason they have. There's two threads to unravel right there, but the place to start is Queens. As if Brooklyn wasn't bad enough. So the big question is, Who in Queens has this kind of clout, and is it outside the department or inside?"

"Will you just shut up about it!" he bellowed.

That was when I looked up and realized that he was looming over me. I'd never seen him quite that angry. The hand was up, ready to go. I tried to brace myself against a hit. He held himself back with resigned disgust.

The mood definitely needed to be changed, and I couldn't think of any good jokes.

I pushed the recliner all the way back. Then I cautiously ran a foot up his leg and used it to gently massage his crotch until I felt return pressure against my foot. He was still angry but no longer violent. Now it was the kind of anger I was used to. I did an exaggerated lip lick that Jana had taught me. I pushed down the top of my dress.

The grimace gave way to the wolfish grin. Soon he was on top of me in the recliner.

My body responded but my mind wouldn't follow. If I came, I didn't notice, which was too bad, because Doug really knocked himself out. He was moaning and spazzing and biting my neck. All I could think about was Queens and who wouldn't want David's murderer found, and why not.

Doug collapsed on top of me. I still had a fondness for the roughness of his jacket against my skin, the composite aroma of Camels and Jim Beam and Brut, and even more than I wanted to admit, the feeling of his silvery hair under my fingers.

What I didn't like was feeling like a whore.

It was bad enough to be having an affair with a man who stood for everything I despised, just because the sex was great; but letting him fuck me so I could get information was just plain ugly. All of a sudden I didn't want his hulkingness so close to me.

I gave him a nip on the ear. His whole body twitched. I assumed I had his attention.

"Doug," I whispered.

He made some kind of noise that I translated as "what."

"How did the cops know?"

"Know what?"

"To go look in David's apartment. Did someone hear a shot? Who reported the murder?"

I could feel his facial muscles sagging. His body shrank away from me. There was an air of disgust between us as thick as the stench of urine in the 42nd Street subway station.

I had rubbed his face in the fact that I was using him. Well, what had we been doing with each other from the beginning?

He wouldn't look at me. He zipped his pants, knotted his tie, and pulled a comb through his hair. I felt I had shattered whatever sick bond existed between us.

He would walk away and it would be over. Just let it go, I told myself. Myself didn't listen.

"So, Dougie, does this mean we're not going to the policeman's ball together?"

He seemed to relax a little and managed to look at me with a hint of the old shark smile.

"It means you talk too much. We got an anonymous tip to go to the Price place."

"From a residence or a pay phone?"

"Untraced."

"Male or female?"

"Can it, babe. Breaking and entering. Case closed. I'm going home. I'll see you in a few days. Maybe."

7

"Would you like to t-t-talk about it?"
"It's a long story."
"Where are we now, Seventy-second Street?"
"Uh-huh."
"That gives us thirty blocks. What happened yesterday?"

Karl, Effie, and I were headed downtown on Broadway. Perfect New York summer weather and the whole world seemed to be outside to enjoy it. Traffic flowed smoothly, pigeons cooed, construction workers were well behaved. Everyone seemed so goddamned happy.

I wanted to jump off the George Washington Bridge, and not to go swimming either.

The dog had sensed it the minute I walked in. If Karl couldn't figure it out from Effie's sympathetic whines, he probably guessed that something was up when I started ragging him about the size of the shoulder pads in his jacket. That morning they struck me as being offensively large. When I stooped to my mom's favorite line—"Who do you think you are, Clark Gable?"—the doctor suggested we leave early and walk instead of taking the subway.

I could never figure out Dr. Hammerschmidt's method. Sometimes he would wait so long to say something that I would wonder if he was deaf too. Other times he'd pepper me with questions until I felt he might as well shine a light in my eyes and work me over with a rubber hose.

He stayed quiet while Effie led us down the street and I led him through the events of the previous day. It took me till 55th Street to get through it. Then he said one of those shrink things that used to leave me breathless with disbelief.

"So what's bothering you?"

"I should turn you in for malpractice. What's bothering me? David is bothering me. I still don't know who killed him."

"Who cares?" He said blandly. "He stays d-d-dead regardless. The official word is breaking and entering."

"But Doug as much as told me that there's some kind of cover-up going on."

"Even if that's true, David seems to have been a creep. I thought s-s-so when you first told me about him, and his wife doesn't appear to have a much higher opinion. He made you unhappy."

"David didn't make me unhappy. I made myself unhappy."

"Very good."

"What is this? A test of the emergency psycho-babble system?"

"Are you still annoyed about my shoulder pads?"

"Your Doug, I mean your dog dresses you funny."

"Your Freudian slip is showing."

"That's black silk nightgown to you."

"The one he bought you?"

"Well, it's not like I actually wear it. He hates my robe. I hate his guts."

"Sounds like love to me."

"Never."

"Were you c-c-crying last night?"

"After he left."

"And this morning?"

"A little."

"Why?"

"I don't know. Maybe it's just gotten to be a habit.

They'll have to send me to Synanon and cut my hair off. My hairdresser will love that."

"Doug said *maybe* he'd see you in a few days."

"Which has what to do with what?"

"Has he ever said *maybe* before."

I was starting to tear up, right there on the street.

"Does it feel more like David or more like Brian?"

"Like none of the above, pal. Why bring up Brian? Brian is not relevant to this."

"You went to Brooklyn."

"Well, it wasn't my bright idea. It was David's bimbo wife and the kid and everything. I wasn't interested in a trip down memory lane."

"But you g-g-got one. What did you s-s-say that man's name was?"

"Jerry. Jerry Barlow."

"I don't remember you mentioning that name before."

"I was playing for sympathy. I didn't want to tell you that one of those bastards acted like a human being once."

"He'd be an interesting person to talk to."

"Why?"

"He was a friend of Brian's."

"Probably still is."

"So he was an insider during your t-t-time of trials. Maybe he could help you see yourself."

"I'm trying to solve a murder, Doc."

"There's more than one mystery in your life, Marti. You should think about priorities. And a word of c-c-caution. Don't try to sneak up on anyone in those shoes. They'll hear you coming a mile away. Where are we now? Forty-third?"

"Forty-fourth."

"Good. First stop, Port Authority."

I spent the rest of the morning being watchful and inconspicuous. Karl's work in the field took us to the doughnut shop at the Port Authority bus station, where he had a session with a security guard on his break. Nedicks was a drop-in site for two construction workers and a cheery fellow in a wheelchair who was canvassing for some charity. Those were the lucky ones. They functioned.

All I had to do was observe their body language from a suitable distance and be ready if tissues or policemen were necessary. I'd dispensed plenty of Kleenex, but so far no boys in blue. The crying was not pretty to watch and made me even more self-conscious about my own outbursts.

Karl said I was missing the point. The ones who cried were the ones who could work. They were psychologically wounded. Tears were a way to wash the wounds so they didn't become infected. I pretended to understand.

When I pointed out that I wanted to stop crying, he said that my case was different because my trauma wasn't battle-related. As soon as we pinpointed the source, we'd be halfway there.

The real basket cases rarely cried. Those were the really awful ones. The PTSD had laid them so low they couldn't work. They could barely get out of bed. I thought I knew about depression until I saw those guys.

Even as I was keeping an eye on Karl's patients, my mind was on the David Price case. I was still inclined to the woman-scorned theory. Someone as hurt as I was, but with bigger *cojones*. It had to be someone in the circle. Jana? Carmen? Grace?

Grace was a well-known dyke. How about Ricky? He definitely had *cojones*. I didn't much like it as a theory, but it was a place to start.

Besides, it gave me an excuse to go to Studio 54 and do some detective work. If I was going dancing, I needed a manicure—so I could go see Marc. Perfect. As soon as our last visit was done, I asked Dr. Hammerschmidt if I could be excused for the day. He wanted me in the office the next morning to type transcripts. I said I'd be there.

"Marti, honey, when are you going to let me do something with that mop?"

He brandished his shears at me playfully.

Marc sported the postmodern greaser look, complete with

sideburns, a curly pompadour, and extremely tight blue jeans.

"You stay away from me with those things, sweetie pie. I don't have an appointment for at least two weeks. I'd come over and hug you, but I think Lavonne here would kill me."

"You're damn right. You keep your fingers right next to that fan until I say you can move them."

"O.K., O.K. Can you talk a minute, Marc?"

"Few minutes," he said, lighting up a Kool. "You'll never guess which local-news prima donna is in the back room for her weekly touch-up."

"Who?"

"Sorry." He put a finger over his lips. Marc was a tease, but he wasn't indiscreet. Ricky Grant, on the other hand, would tell you the name, sexual proclivity, and last five partners at the drop of a hat.

"Speaking of dying, did you hear about David Price?"

"Who?"

I pantomimed playing piano, drawing a warning glare from Lavonne.

"Oh, that pretty boy. I thought he was a natural. Well, it just goes to show you."

"Not hair dyeing, dead dying."

"From what, terminal cuteness?"

"Terminal gunshot."

"Are you serious? Is this one of those sicko, try it out on your friends, writer jokes?"

"Dead serious."

"I don't know what to say. I'm sorry, I guess. I saw him at that party and a few times at Studio Fifty-four. I know he had you in a tizzy."

"Did you ever talk to him?"

"Not much. He wasn't my type. Not butch enough."

"It wouldn't matter. David was straight."

"Well, I know he was an item with Jana Crowley, but the way he was dropping beads at the party, I thought he might be a switch hitter."

"Dropping what?"

"Oh, you've only taken Fag-Hag One-o-one. You still need the immersion course. 'Dropping beads' is deliberately using a bit of lingo to find out if you're among friends. You should take notes."

"She ain't doing no such thing." Lavonne had a client at her other station, but she was still monitoring me.

"Well, anyway, Mr. Price started coming on like the ghost of Tallulah. It was almost like he was practicing a foreign language, so I thought maybe he was a closet case getting ready to come out."

"Coming on to you personally?"

"Don't act so shocked, sweetie. Although now that I think about it, he was more interested in getting a rundown on all the local talent. Sort of a who's who, or at least a who is, if you catch my drift."

"Did you tell him anything?"

"That's not my gig. Then he just went off and started talking to someone else. I saw him at Studio Fifty-four once after that, but then he was doing that 'Hi there, I'm Mr. Hetero God Almighty.' So who offed him?"

"When I find out, I'll let you know. Are you going out tonight?"

"You mean will I be at Studio Fifty-four, so you don't stand there like Little Bo Peep looking for a sheep to dance with? I don't know, hon. Why don't you get yourself a date for a change? How about that nice little narc of yours? He could park his holster in my alcove anytime."

"Oh, Marc. I have to, but you? I don't know what's worse, that sugar daddy you're always looking for or the rough trade you can't stay away from."

"*Mee-ow.* Don't start clawing my balls just because you've got your name on the list and no one to walk in the door with. I gotta go, hon. Don't want Chuck to end up looking like Jean Harlow, and you didn't hear me say that."

"Hey, Lavonne, are these nails ready to move yet?"

"Yeah, I guess they'll be O.K., if you don't get them all chipped up again."

"All right, I'll try. Hey, could you get me a phone book?"

"Do I look like your damn slave?"

"Never mind. It was a dumb idea. You probably don't have Brooklyn anyway."

"What are you looking for there?"

"I'm not sure. I think the chemicals in here are messing with my head."

Outside I breathed what passed for fresh air in New York. It didn't completely wipe out the really dumb idea. Neither did a subway ride back to 169th Street or a sit-down with the dogs in the park. I didn't see any Dalmatians, but there was this one frisky, sad-eyed cocker spaniel with floppy ears that seemed to be looking right at me. Without even realizing it, I started singing softly.

"Won't you please say hello to the friends that I know, tell them I won't be long."

I caught myself and hurried out of the park, trying to outrun tears and memories.

I needed a distraction. Nothing on TV. Did people actually watch the "Mike Douglas Show"? I turned on the radio and there was that stupid "Grease Is the Word" song. Trying to write was futile.

"Keep smiling through, just like you always do . . ."

The phone rang.

"Hello?"

"Marti, it's Jana. Where have you been?"

"Some people still work for a living."

"But you're not one of them."

"What do you want?"

"Is that any way to talk to a grieving widow?"

"Grieving bigamous fiancée."

"Why are you being a bitch? Rough session with Dr. Weinerschnitzel?"

"Rough everything. Come back to the city. We'll get another place together. It'll be like old times."

"Not any time soon. I'm going to Chicago for David's funeral, and then I'm going to visit Daddy."

"Still running from Akhmad?"

"I don't care if you don't believe me."

"Gee, did I say anything like that? Your show is doing business. You should be in town milking the situation for all the publicity you can get."

"Well, I'm not. I'm flying out tomorrow morning under a fake name."

"I think you're overreacting."

"Whatever I'm doing, I'll need some stuff from the apartment."

"Good. The cops want you to go over there and let them know if anything was stolen."

"Nothing was stolen, and I'm not going near that place."

"You want me to get the goodies?"

"Yeah. You don't mind, do you?"

"Well, it's a chance to see the scene of the crime. How am I supposed to get in?"

"You've got the keys."

"Since when?"

"I gave them to you."

"Hold on a minute."

I found my peace-symbol key ring in my pocketbook. Key to my front door, apartment, mailbox, key to Karl's apartment, Karl's front door, and two unidentified keys.

A sudden memory: David and Jana's housewarming party. David's musician friends, some of the waitresses from Swenson's, the new next-door neighbors, and me.

David and Jana held court in the living room, their dual star-power making everything sparkle. I couldn't take it. I wound up in the kitchen, sharing a joint with the drummer. I gave a guilty start when Jana walked in. She always said she didn't mind my smoking weed, but I suspected that deep in her heart was the Okie-from-Muskogee morality of a Major's daughter.

At that moment she looked high herself. Well, why

shouldn't she? She was moving into the magic town house with Prince Charming. She handed me the keys. I looked at them and then at her. I was in one of those primo weed moments when everything seems to make sense. I nodded sagely and pocketed them. At some point I must have transferred them to my key chain.

I returned to the phone.

"Why did you give me these?"

"Just in case."

"Just in case someone got murdered?"

"Just in case I lost mine and David wasn't around."

I let it go, but mentally filed it under *B* for Bullshit.

"So what do you need?"

"Black things."

"Could you be more specific?"

"Like for a funeral. Black dress, shoes, lingerie. My flight is United Ten-eleven out of JFK. It leaves at nine, so you have to meet me at the gate before that."

"What about the drugs?"

"You might want to grab some aspirin, and I think there's some Dramamine in the medicine chest."

"I mean the drugs that the cops found on David."

"Oh, fiddlesticks!"

"Jana, every time I bring this up you go into your little hick routine. Now, we both know that Major Crowley didn't raise any children that stupid. Don't jerk me around."

"Well, it's just plain silly. He was holding it for a friend."

"I've heard that one before. Hell, I've used that one before."

"Are you going to get my stuff?"

"Yeah."

"Thank you, Marti. You're the only one I can count on."

"Please don't leave."

"I have to. I'll see you at the airport. Bye."

I was left muttering "bitch" to a dead line. Jana was the

closest friend I'd ever had, and now she was abandoning me.

"They'll be happy to know that as you saw me go . . ."

I wasn't going to let myself sink into the self-pity that beckoned so invitingly. I grabbed the phone and dialed 411.

"How may I help you?"

"In Williamsburg, PS one-twenty-four."

"One moment please. That number is five-five-five six-one-two-three. Have a nice day."

I could tell she didn't mean it.

I dialed half hoping, half dreading, that no one would be there.

"PS one-twenty-four, Mrs. Dolan speaking."

"Is Jerry Barlow there?"

"He's giving a lesson right now. Is this an emergency?"

"No, I wouldn't say it's an emergency."

"Would you like to leave a message?"

"Could you ask him to call Ms. Hirsch at 555-1222 as soon as possible?"

"I'll tell him."

"Gee, thanks."

I tried the television again. Did people really watch Dinah Shore? I flipped around. "Speed Racer." "Spider-Man." Local news bimbos with dyed hair.

"We'll meet again, don't know where, don't know when."

Come on, Kid Next Door. Crank up the Springsteen, you little worm. Even that song about Sandy. The one where he's all upset because the waitress lost her desire for him. (Who could blame her?)

I was out of marijuana and it was too early to pick up on St. Nicholas Avenue. I could have made a makeshift joint out of the roaches in the ashtray, but I told myself I wasn't that desperate.

I turned on the Toodleloop. "This week's number one song . . . 'Too Much, Too Little, Too Late.' " I started to eye those roaches speculatively. The phone rang and I nearly knocked over the ashtray getting to it.

"Hello."

"Is this Ms. Hirsch?" He sounded puzzled.

"Uh-huh."

"This is Jerry Barlow. Marti, is that you?"

"Yeah. Thanks for calling back." Words started tumbling out of my mouth without benefit of coherent thought or editing. "It was really good to see you the other day and I was wondering if . . . it's like this . . . I'm working on this murder thing, and I'm going to Studio Fifty-four tonight. . . . Have you ever been there?"

"No. Have you?"

"Oh yeah."

"I'm impressed. You must be a famous writer with a pen name."

"Don't be silly. How do you know I write?"

"Twelfth-grade English. I sat in back of you and nearly went blind trying to spy on that story you were writing in your notebook when Mr. Katz wasn't looking."

"Oh my god. That was some poor excuse for a romance, wasn't it?"

"But it kept threatening to get hot."

"And you were peeping?"

"Forgive me?"

"Sure, fans are always appreciated. So, am I coming off like a pinhead?"

"I don't think so. What do you mean you're working on a murder? Are you cop?"

There was a tone of suspicion. Even a nice Jewish boy from Brooklyn distrusted the police. It was downright heartwarming.

"Just a concerned citizen trying to clean up a mess. And I need to talk to you about it."

"Why me?"

"It's David Price"

"What's David Price?"

"The deceased"

"You mean Lorraine's father?"

"Putatively."

"You still use those big words that nobody else knows."

Another brutal blast from the past. All the abuse I'd taken for having a large vocabulary. It was enough to drive a girl to William F. Buckley fantasies.

"I thought it was cool. I just couldn't understand you."

"What about Brian? Oh god, I wasn't going to say that. Strike the question."

"Brian always understood the words."

"You're wasting your time teaching piano. You should be a diplomat. The State Department could use someone like you."

"Please. Dealing with avid mommies is all the diplomacy I want to deal with."

"How about proud papas?"

"You mean like Mr. Price?"

"For example."

"None of this makes any sense."

"If I promise to explain it, will you go out dancing with me?"

"Even if you don't."

"What an unusual thing to say. And if I buy you din-din will you answer some questions for me?"

"I don't know anything."

"Be a mensch. Indulge me."

"O.K."

"I've got a craving for deli. Can you meet me at the Second Avenue Deli at tenish? You know where that is?"

"Yeah, I know where it is. Isn't tenish a little late for din-din?"

"Early for Studio Fifty-four, and we'll need sustenance. We may be out late. I hope you don't have any lessons planned for tomorrow morning."

"Nothing important."

"Jerry, I really appreciate this. I promise I'll have my head screwed on straight by the time I see you."

"I'll be there at tenish."

"Bye."

Well, at least I had a date. I could settle down and watch some television. Dinah Shore seemed to be a very nice lady. No wonder people liked her.

8

It was a good thing that the school year was virtually over before the senior dance, because I never went back. Not for my final report card, not for the graduation ceremony (naturally Brian was the valedictorian), and certainly not for that ridiculously maudlin ritual carried out as far as I know at high schools all across America every June: yearbook distribution.

You know the drill. Everybody reads the yearbook. The yearbook committee blushes modestly, as well they should. Then everyone runs around the school in a lemminglike frenzy, asking their friends to inscribe some touching message in the book so that they can be remembered forever.

I had no friends. There was no one I wanted to remember. The only feelings I had were for Brian, and his image was etched in my mind with the acid of unrequited love.

Without a yearbook, I tried to dredge Jerry out of memory. Back in high school he was a geek. Maybe Brian's shadow had stunted his personality growth. I couldn't even conjure him in any non-Brian situations. He said he had sat in back of me in Senior English. I'd have to take his word for it.

From our brief encounter the previous day, I knew there had been improvement, but I was not prepared for the man who met me at the Second Avenue Deli at tenish. He was leaning against a white Mercury Cougar.

"Hey, Marti. Over here."

I tried not to do a double take and failed.

"Jerry. Looking good!" I blurted.

"Hard to believe?" He said with a self-deprecating smile.

"No, nothing like that."

He was attired in black pants, tailored to hang at that perfect point before loose becomes baggy, and flared enough to be stylish without being last-year's style. He wore a boxy jacket in deep blue. Once we were seated, I noticed that he had nice eyes. Of course there was still that nose, but he was almost handsome. What a difference ten years makes.

Rationally I wanted to ask questions about little Lorraine Price and her daddy. Emotionally I couldn't look at Jerry without thinking of his kindness on the worst night of my life and wanting to talk about Brian Bronstein. Sure it would hurt, but what good are wounds if you can't rub salt into them?

I stalled by nibbling on pickles. Jerry looked at me with a warm smile. I assumed it was masking thoughts along the line of "sure you've got your head screwed on straight." Maybe this date had been an impulsive mistake. Where was the waiter with my bagel?

"I'm sorry," he said.

"Huh. What did you say?"

"I said, I was sorry about yesterday."

"What about it?"

"You know, playing that song. I didn't realize you would get so upset, but I should have known."

"Well, you know, it's just Brian."

"Of course."

"But that's a long time ago. I don't feel it anymore."

The catch in my throat made the lie pretty obvious. Luckily the food came so I was able to focus on my bagel-and-lox plate while Jerry started in on his corned beef on rye. He wouldn't let the topic go.

"It's been hard on all of us."

Maybe being Brian's buddy wasn't all it appeared from the outside looking in.

"So what's old Brian up to these days?"

Jerry froze in the middle of a bite and gave me a look that should have stopped me short. It was beyond Martian and way past village idiot. Like I'd announced my intention to commit infanticide on national television.

"I keep expecting to see him on Johnny Carson or winning an Oscar or something. Jerry what's the matter? Is there a problem with the corned beef?"

The blue-gray eyes started to go watery. He put down the sandwich with a deliberation that spoke of a struggle for control. He must have won because the water never went anywhere and his voice was steady. I'd have to ask him how he did that.

"I thought you knew about Brian."

"Knew what?"

"When you started crying . . ."

"I was thinking about the dance. I never did get a chance to thank you."

He shook his head as if to brush off my gratitude. He took my hands in his. I looked down at the hands and then up at him.

"Jerry, what the hell . . . ?"

"I have to tell you something, Marti, and I don't want you to freak out."

"Look, it really was a long time ago. I'm very happy now. I'm seeing this wonderful guy. So if Brian got married, it won't blow me out of the water."

All lies.

"Marti, Brian is dead."

"What did he do, trip on his ego and break his neck?"

"I'm not joking. He was killed."

"Holy Moly! There must be an epidemic. If it wasn't too implausible, I'd think it was the same person who killed David. You know, someone who has it out for every throb who ever broke my heart. Hey, Jer, could you let go of my hands. You're hurting me."

"You didn't let me finish. Brian was killed nine years ago in Vietnam."

"What was he doing in Vietnam?"

"There was a war Marti, it was in all the papers."

"Ooh. Mr. Sarcasm. Why wasn't he safe in college with a deferment or even in Canada. A smart guy like Brian shouldn't have been drafted."

"He didn't get drafted. He enlisted."

"Alan Funt's coming through that door any minute, right? Brian Bronstein, who wrote the anti-war article in the school paper that changed my life, enlisted? That is the craziest thing I have ever heard in my life."

"That's what I told him. So, are you O.K.?"

"Why wouldn't I be. It's not like I was his girlfriend. Or a friend of any kind for that matter. I'm sitting here envisioning Brian being blown to smithereens and it's not affecting me in the slightest. On the other hand, Brian deliberately hugged everybody but me at the cast party for 'Good News,' and that I can never forgive or forget. That will make me cry here and now, completely humiliating both of us and messing up my carefully applied makeup if you do not let go of my hands so I can eat my bagel and lox. What are you smiling about?"

"You used to do that in English class."

"What?'

"Answer a question with a monologue. You'd go on and on until I thought you were going to pass out from lack of oxygen."

I couldn't eat. The bagel stuck in my throat.

"Jerry," I said, hearing a scared child talking.

"Yeah."

"Why didn't Brian like me?"

He closed his eyes and opened them slowly. He took a sip of coffee. Then he took off his jacket and placed it over the back of his chair. He had on a light blue Lurex shirt. It was open to the chest, and I could see some hair along with a modest Jewish star. He didn't want to answer. I wouldn't let him off the hook. I just kept staring into his eyes. (What kind of Jewish boy has blue eyes anyway?)

"I was hoping you wouldn't ask that kind of thing," he said finally. "Because I don't have a nice answer. Brian was my best friend since we were six. I still miss him. But he could be a jerk. Maybe nothing could have made him feel like you did, and you really did piss him off, but he could have been a little nicer."

"Did you ever tell him that?"

He shook his head.

"Maybe I should have. Then again, I told him not to enlist and look what happened."

"Why did he do such a stupid thing?"

"Debbie."

"Debbie wanted him in the army?"

"Debbie wanted him to leave her alone. He proposed before the dance and she turned him down. He was at the recruiting office the day after graduation."

"I didn't think he was the grand romantic–gesture type."

"You never got to see his good side."

"I'm really sorry. I mean, I've got my own feelings about Brian, but I am sorry you lost a friend. I wish I'd known. After the dance, all I wanted was to get away and forget Brian and the rest of you ever existed. If it wasn't for this murder, I wouldn't even have been in Brooklyn. Can I ask you something having nothing to do with Brian or our beloved alma mater?"

"Can I finish my corned beef first?"

I found myself admiring how neatly he ate. I was staring and he caught me at it. I was on *shpilkes* until he took the paper napkin off his lap and put it on the plate. Leaning forward, he fixed me with his own gaze.

"Go ahead. What can I tell you?"

"Did you ever meet Lorraine's father?"

"Do you mean Mr. Price or the other guy?"

I had to smile. He smiled back. It was sweet and a little goofy, but nice. For the umpteenth time, I thought to myself how much his looks had improved since high school.

"You were one of the smart ones, weren't you?"

"Would you believe me if I told you I got Brian through algebra?"

"I don't know, let me think about it. In the meantime, David Price, official father of Lorraine. What can you tell me?"

"Like I said before, nothing. I only met him twice. The first time was at a PTA meeting."

"Any impressions?"

"I know the mothers couldn't take their eyes off him, even when they were sitting next to their husbands."

"Good old David."

"And at the recital . . ."

"Wait a minute. You let her play in a recital?"

"Scales, arpeggios. Something she couldn't mess up, I thought. I was wrong."

"How'd he take it."

"That's what I was going to tell you. I've known kids who just had no talent, but never one who was untalented with such enthusiasm. I was standing there watching them, Mr. and Mrs. Price. I was waiting for his reaction."

"You knew he was a professional, right?"

"That's why Lorraine wanted to learn. She talked about her daddy so much that I didn't even realize the parents were divorced. I had a major foot-in-mouth moment the first time Mrs. Price came to a parent-teacher conference. She brought the other guy, and I called him Mr. Price. I got some pretty icy looks. It was a natural mistake. He looked like he could be Lorraine's father."

"What did he look like?"

"Kind of average, I guess. Dark hair, dark eyes. Hair with a little curl. He had a gap between his front teeth. Oh yeah, he smoked a pipe."

I tried to make the words coalesce into an image.

"Kenny smokes a pipe," I muttered.

"You already know about Kenny?"

"I don't know his last name."

"Neither do I. Mrs. Price said he was a friend of the family. He just sat there quietly while I told Mrs. Price that her daughter was a bright girl who needed to concentrate on her schoolwork more and her Barbie dolls less."

"What did you think?"

"I thought something was fishy and that it was none of my business."

"What happened at the recital?"

"Lorraine was awful. I thought Mr. Price was going to give me a hard time. Lots of parents, when the kid can't play, they blame the teacher. But nothing happened. He sat there nodding to himself as if he'd just figured something out."

"Like why the daughter of such a talented musician seemed to be devoid of any natural ability?"

"I wouldn't have phrased it that way exactly."

"I know. I'm a bitch. Did David talk to you?"

"After the recital. We talked technique. He asked if I was doing anything professional. I said I was happy teaching fourth grade and doing a few lessons on the side. Right then I could see him discount me. I could see why Lorraine liked those Barbie dolls."

"Why?"

"Because Mr. Price looked like a Ken doll if I ever saw one, and I can't say he had much more personality."

"Wow. For a straight guy, you can be quite a bitch yourself."

"I've been married to a few."

"Poor baby. I think it's cool that you became a teacher, but why didn't you go into show business? You had talent."

"But not star power or ambition. That was all Brian. I always wanted to teach. I like being around kids."

"I wanted to be a teacher."

"Not a writer?"

"Well, that too, but in college I was majoring in American Lit with a teaching minor."

"You'd be a great teacher. I'll never forget that time in English class when you called 'Gunga Din' imperialist swill."

"In the middle of the night, I used to make up courses I wanted to teach. Instead of counting sheep, I invented syllabuses. Literature of Mystery—From Oedipus to Mike Hammer."

"I'd sign up for that."

"But there'd be no teacher."

"What happened?"

"I was doing great. Acing all my classes, taking courses in Developmental Psych so I could understand the learning process. I was one credit from my B.A. Little problem. I actually had to student teach. Piece of cake, right? I was all ready. Notes. Lesson plan. I knew it backwards and forwards. And when I got up in front of the class, I just froze. Almost passed out."

"What was the lesson on?"

Tender Is the Night.

"I bet you could have done that with your eyes closed."

"I should have, because I saw all those eyes looking at me and I couldn't talk. I couldn't breath. I got flop sweat. They practically had to take me out of there on a stretcher. That was the end of my teaching career. Five days later, I was on a plane to Israel. I spent six months on a kibbutz."

"I thought of doing that."

"Not recommended. I didn't mean to go rambling on about myself. Have you got your dancing shoes on?"

"You bet."

"Then, let's go. Studio Fifty-four, here we come."

9

I knew in my heart that it was nothing but a gussied-up old warehouse, but I loved going to Studio 54. It made me feel like I was at the center of the universe.

Naturally I hated feeling that way. I spent a lot of 1978 wondering where my ideals had gone. The feminist zeal collapsed in the gleam of Doug Kimberlin's teeth and my sense of outraged social justice couldn't withstand the glitter of the mirrored ball inside the hottest spot New York had ever known.

Coming out of the subway that night, I had a few moments of smugness. Jerry was certainly a presentable escort to walk in the door with. I hoped Marc was there. Eat your heart out, sweetie.

The spectacle started over a block away: the lights sending beams into the night sky, high enough to greet arriving space travelers; the traffic jam that seemed to be composed entirely of limousines and of course the crowds. Mind you, this was just a Wednesday night.

Most of the crowd would never get in the door. They were supplicants. They were pathetic.

My smugness gave way to panic. I'd gotten in by myself on Saturday night. Now David was dead and Jana was elsewhere. Had my status changed? Could I get in without a fairy godmother? Was I still on the list?

I nearly stumbled on my platforms. Jerry got a firm hand

on my back. I walked toward the door, trying to look confident. Jerry was bigger and taller, but I was the one leading the way, shoulder first, through the crowd. The velvet ropes led to the gates of heaven. St. Peter was an easy sell compared to Jimmy Shapiro.

The life and death decision of who got in and who didn't was made by Jimmy with the merest tilt of his head or the flick of an ash from his cigarette. I'd seen him standing up and knew for a fact that he was only five foot six, but seated on the stool by the door, wearing a maroon leisure suit with wide lapels, he looked much taller.

He was blessed with full lips, smooth brown hair, and long-lashed brown eyes exuding a moist sensuality. He always looked as though he had just shaved in a hot, steamy shower. I knew more than a few men and women who wanted a piece of Jimmy.

What Jimmy wanted was a mystery. I thought of him as the man who knew the secrets. He alone knew the criteria beyond wealth and fame that got you past the beefy guards. He knew what went on behind closed doors. He knew whether or not he used any substance stronger than those Winstons. Most of all, he knew his own side of the sexual spectrum and he wasn't telling anybody.

If I walked right up to him and said, "Who killed David Price?" I'd get the same condescending smile that had broken so many hearts set on breaching the fortress.

I planned on getting that answer on the inside, so I called out, "Hey, Jimmy," and kept my fingers crossed.

He looked at me impassively, possibly taking a minute to size up my date. There was a cigarette puff and we were in. My bonafides must have been good. I left grumbling masses in my wake and accepted an admiring eyebrow raise from Jerry.

The night's ritual continued outside. Jerry and I proceeded to the heart of darkness.

It was amazingly crowded, when you consider how many people were kept out.

The first stop was the bar. Of course Studio 54 was full

of bars, but the first-floor bar next to the coat room was the last, best hope for human conversation. I ordered a club soda from the shorts-clad muscle boy behind the bar. Decorative, but not my cup of tea.

Jerry looked surprised. It might have been the specimen dispensing his beer or the fact that I waved off his efforts to pay and handed in one of those drink chips that Ricky Grant was always giving me. It could have been disbelief that two kids from Brooklyn were actually in there. At the time, I thought he was curious about my club soda. I felt compelled to explain.

"I'm allergic. Whoever spiked the punch at the senior dance nearly killed me. I got sick as a dog. By the time I finished puking, Brian was gone."

Suddenly there was an expression on his face between perplexed and stricken. I figured Brian was a touchy subject. Whatever Jerry was going to say was lost, because I heard the opening notes of "Native New Yorker" and I had to dance to it.

I pulled him out on to the main dance floor. Flashing strobes, twirling balls, glittering crowds all around us. I hoped that if Ricky was up in the rafters, seeking famous folk with his high-powered zoom lens, he would take at least one picture of us, nobodies though we were.

Such an adrenaline rush. I felt so much a part of it all, so alive, and excuse me for saying it, beautiful. That left one question. Could Jerry Barlow dance?

He danced with me as if we'd been dancing together for years. Four bars into "Native New Yorker," he had his arms around me and we were keeping time like Fred and Ginger.

Beginners luck, I thought. Then came "Love to Love You," "Miss You" (which meant that Bianca wasn't there), "Emotion," "Got to Give It Up," and others that I didn't even know the names of. I'd never danced that well with anyone. For once I didn't feel like I had two left platforms. I lost myself in the blood-shaking volume of the music and the way my skirt flared out on the turns. The lights made Jerry's hair look almost blond as he led me through the whole disco-dance playbook, even steps that I had never seen before.

There was a break in the music. I tried to catch my breath and think of a witty reaction to our terpsichorean compatibility. ("Let's put on a show and save the city.") The man in the moon tooted some coke, the lights all changed colors, and I could have sworn I saw Ricky Grant waving at me from one of the upper-level railings. My glasses were tucked in my purse for safekeeping, so it was hard to tell.

The DJ decided the time had come for The Hustle. At the first few notes, folks came away from the bars and out of the VIP room. Line dances were always the best opportunity to rub elbows with the stars. Brenda Vaccaro once stepped on my foot.

The requisite pattern assembled. As always I found it ridiculously exhilarating. The perfection of the first pivot turn made me feel like I was in a group orgasm.

The whole night was taking on the same kind of giddy unreality as that first night with Doug, but it wasn't about sex. I had no interest in Jerry that way, even when we danced to "More Love" and he ended up supporting me in a back-bending dip.

I heard the beginning of "Never Can Say Good-bye," but I really needed a rest. I couldn't breath. My makeup had long since floated away in a sea of sweat. Jerry followed me off the floor. I took him in the direction where I thought I had seen Ricky. I put on my glasses so that I could get up the stairs without colliding into anybody. I was so busy trying to watch my feet that I bumped right into someone.

"Look, dearie, if you can't watch where you're going, then stay home in Scarsdale."

"Hi, Ricky."

"Oh, it's you. So sorry. I thought you were still down there trying to give all and sundry a look at your knickers."

Ricky always looked like such a mess. I wasn't sure how much was image and how much was real dissipation. I had to talk to him, if he would let me get a word in edgewise.

"You'll never guess who's here tonight. Pippa Weintraub of the Bel-Air Weintraubs with that half-wit she calls a fiancé and their Great Dane, and if you ask me who's getting the quim in that menage, I'd put my money on the bow-wow. Who's your friend here? He was cutting quite a rug with you out there."

"An old . . . uh, friend. Ricky, Jerry. Jerry, Ricky." Jerry put out a hand to shake, while Ricky, operating on his own weird system of etiquette, put a hand on Jerry's shoulder and gave him the once over twice.

"That's quite a beak you got there, old man."

I thought I was going to die. I hoped Jerry wasn't going to hit him or something. I saw him take a beat to assess the situation and respond calmly,

"Well, you know what they say about men with big noses."

He just let it hang there completely innocent and completely provocative, silencing my motormouthed friend so that I had a chance to talk.

"Ricky, is Grace here tonight?"

"Not yet. The dear girl has to do some work to keep me in this luxurious lifestyle." He gestured at his patched jeans. He had removed the hand from Jerry's shoulder and now had it perched on his own hip. He was scanning the room. I didn't know how much longer I'd have his attention.

"I need to talk to both of you. It's really important. It's . . ."

"David," he finished for me. "Jana told me you were asking questions. I don't quite see you as Sherlock, dear, and if this boy is your idea of a Watson, I don't know what the world is coming to."

"World ends, film at eleven. Come on Ricky, I'm sure you knew that I was crazy about David."

"Bums in the Bowery knew that."

"Gee, and I thought I had it so well hidden."

"Not from anybody with a brain."

"So you can see why I'd be upset that it's not getting any attention."

"Why should it? David Price was very good at what he did, which was being faceless, playing pretty riffs on forgettable records, and looking smashing at all times. He was quite the charmer, but he could also be a giant prick."

"There's an alarming image."

"Rather delightful, actually."

"You and Grace were with Jana just before she found him in the apartment, right?"

"So what?"

"So I just want to get you guys to sit down and talk to me somewhere where I don't have to scream to be heard. I may want to write a book. Something that will make me rich and famous enough to get in here on my own. *In Cold Blood* for the '70s. I want you and Grace to give me input, impressions."

"Information, you mean. I really am a nice guy, Marti, but I don't appreciate being conned by a rank, if sincere, amateur, so please stop trying. Come by the room around two and I'll see what I can do for you." I saw his focus shift and I knew I'd lost him. "Oh look, there's Andy. Let's go see whose literal dick he's metaphorically sucking."

He went careening down the stairs, leaving me with more drink chips. He acted like his alcohol capacity level was the model for the world.

I took Jerry to one of the upstairs bars. He had a screwdriver. I had another club soda. Talk below the screaming level was impossible, so I couldn't make excuses for Ricky's rudeness, but Jerry seemed to have taken it in stride.

Aside from a momentary speculation regarding what they said about men with big noses, I just couldn't imagine Jerry Barlow as anything but the nebbishy kid from high school. He did have nice hair. Back in high school he'd kept it slicked down with Brylcreem, now it was blow-dried and hanging against his face.

We sat at the bar, indulging in a little celebrity gawking. Richard Dreyfus walked by. Ricky had once told me that

Dreyfus was a perfect asshole. Was that like a massive prick, I wondered? Had Ricky ever perused David Price with the same sleazy interest he'd shown to Jerry? Had it come to anything? Had the recital been a revelatory trauma or merely a confirmation of something already suspected? Why was Jerry holding my hand?

He wanted to dance some more. The questions would have to wait. We went whirling off into the music. "Disco Lady." "More More More." "Don't Leave Me This Way." "Nights on Broadway." "You Make Me Feel (Mighty Real)." "Heaven Knows."

One question wouldn't leave my mind. At the same horrible cast party, I'd taken my eyes off Brian long enough to see Jerry dance the Twist. It was not a pretty sight.

"Where the hell did you learn to dance like this." I could hardly hear myself over the throbbing speakers. I wasn't even sure he'd heard me as we executed the slide, where his hands had to go from the end of my right arm to the end of my left. When we faced each other again, he shouted back at me.

"Ever hear of Odyssey Two Thousand?"

When that registered, it caused me to blurt out, "Holy shit!" trip over my own feet, and nearly barrel into the couple dancing next to us. Jerry was able to prevent that, but not my embarrassment that my eighteen-year-old, gawky self had made an appearance. To keep me upright, he had to hold me very closely. I smelled a mixture of sweat and hair spray.

He steered me off the floor. I was still reeling from what he'd told me. Studio 54 was the apex, but Odyssey 2000 was the original. That was the disco in Brooklyn where Nick Cohn had discovered the culture and written the *New York Magazine* article that became *Saturday Night Fever*—and put disco on the map of national consciousness. Hanging out at Studio 54 was like being in Miami when Jim Morrison exposed himself. Hanging out at Odyssey 2000 was like seeing the Doors when they played at the Whiskey A Go-Go.

Jerry Barlow had come a long way in ten years. I wondered how I looked to him. Then I wondered why I cared. I had other fish to fry. It was time to meet Ricky in the VIP room. Jerry had knocked me for a loop. Maybe I could return the favor.

I'd only been in the room a few times, and I couldn't get in alone. Ricky Grant was my letter of transit. He was practically bouncing with excitement and stimulants. He guided us past the usual suspects. Old and new money, Eurotrash nobility and superstars. I couldn't see Jerry's face, so I didn't know who did or didn't impress him. His jaw definitely dropped, however, when he found himself face to face with Grace McCoy.

Well, why not? Amazing Grace had practically been mythologized in the *Post* and the *News*. Her money was being invested in New York City after Washington had told her to drop dead. What's more, her investments paid off. The buildings, the stores, the record company, the gallery. Moneymakers all. So who wouldn't be impressed when seeing her in the flesh. Those eyes dominated the otherwise small-featured face, with both their emerald green centers and the dark circles that attested either to her work ethic or her excessive social life.

She was five feet five inches of pure intensity conveyed through stillness. Her sandy hair and fair, freckled skin could have been the banner colors of Wasp Connecticut. It was odd to be so close to her at all, but the moment went completely surreal when in response to my politely offered hand, she reached around and enveloped me in a hug. I'd never even been introduced to the woman before, and here she was embracing me like I was her long-lost sister.

"You poor dear. It's so awful, isn't it?"

The voice was Katherine Hepburn with a dose of Locust Valley lockjaw.

"You mean about David?"

Grace nodded her head morosely. I remembered Jana telling me that Grace treated David like a son. Ms. McCoy seemed more distressed by David's demise than anyone I had talked to thus far.

"So much talent, so much promise, such a decent man."

I was glad somebody thought so.

"And it's so sad for you," she continued.

"I was just a friend."

"But such a good friend to David and Jana both. I saw her before she went away. She was utterly distraught. I'm so worried about her."

"What about her show?"

"Well the show goes on, of course, and the next one will be even bigger."

"I'm trying to find out a few things about the murder."

"But that's all been cleared up, hasn't it?"

"Ms. McCoy . . ."

"You must call me Grace."

"Grace . . . Jana is scared to death of Akhmad el Hassan. Carmen Price believes there may be an organized-crime connection. The police have declared a B&E without apprehending anybody. I think something extremely fishy is going on. Because I care about Jana so much, I want to find out what it is. I think the place to start is the night of the shooting, so I want to ask you and Ricky some questions about what happened when Jana found the body. Can you help me, please?"

I ran out of words and breath at the same time.

Grace bit her lower lip, revealing reluctance along with perfect, tiny teeth.

"Well, we certainly can't talk here. Why don't you come by the house for some late dinner. Then we can discuss this whole dreadful matter. Your friend is welcome too, of course."

Dinner at the Second Avenue Deli had been forever ago. The house, in this case, referred to a Park Avenue townhouse that made Jana and David's accommodations seem like a Hell's Kitchen tenement by comparison. I'd never been there, but I knew that Jana and David had.

"Grace, this is Jerry Barlow."

Grace put out a hand. For a second I thought Jerry was going to kiss it, but he managed to compose himself in time to just shake it tentatively. She told us to meet her in twenty minutes by the side entrance.

I made a quick trip to the VIP bathroom. I wanted to unload a few club sodas and collect my thoughts. Unfortunately I was distracted by the ubiquitous sniffing sound and the sight of Pippa Weintraub emerging from a stall with her Great Dane

It was also impossible to think clearly once we were inside the limousine, a Cadillac Brougham with a creamy leather interior, for which a herd of cattle had given their lives. Ricky was snorting out of a small bottle, Grace was talking on the car phone—in German, no less. No wonder she had been featured in *Ms.* magazine the month before.

When the conversation ended, she allowed herself to slump wearily against her husband. He placed a protective arm around her.

I cleared my throat to get her attention.

"Uh, Grace . . . maybe this isn't the best time, but . . ."

"No dear, it's fine. We can talk now, but why not wait until we're at the house. We are almost there."

"We are?"

A glance though a briefly lowered window proved that we had glided to posh environs, where trouble seemed far away. I reminded myself that Jana and David's neighborhood had looked safe and David was dead.

The thought should have given me pause, since I was in a car with my number-one suspect, but I was quickly losing confidence in that theory. Ricky Grant was a gossip and a coke head, but the affection and concern between Ricky and Grace prejudiced me in his favor.

Grace McCoy was in almost every respect the woman I wanted to be. She had a successful career, self-confidence, and someone who loved her. All of which was more than I could say for myself.

10

Our foursome eased out of the Cadillac and my bout of self-pity was blown away by the same 2:00 A.M. breeze that rippled through Jerry's hair and created a Marilyn Monroe airlift with my dress.

The building was old and so was the doorman who doffed his hat and then went back to his vacant stare. His twin was operating the ancient, creaky elevator. The five bodies made a tight squeeze. Jerry and I were pushed together. The ominous shudder of the elevator made me wish for the reassuring strength of his hand, or maybe it was that weird vibe that I just couldn't shake.

The doors opened and we all trooped out, not bothering to bid adieu to our silent sentinel.

Grace, all efficiency, was ready with the key. As soon as we entered, I knew I was in over my head. The apartment seemed to stretch on forever. Beautiful furnishings were everywhere. The best, no doubt, that money could buy. They were all testaments to the wealth she had added to the already-considerable McCoy fortune.

What made her truly formidable was power. The power had its roots in the money, but had become a separate entity. The walls of the foyer were covered with pictures. One side was mostly devoted to Ricky's star-studded work, including a picture of Jana and David where they both looked so happy and glowing and perfect that I couldn't stand it.

There was also a framed sketch of David in three-quarter profile that I knew was Jana's work.

The other wall had pictures of a more official variety. They featured Grace with every public figure imaginable, from the governor to the presidents of all five boroughs. Power. Grace McCoy could engineer a cover-up with impunity, if she so desired. The question was, did she?

She would do it for Ricky's sake. I could feel it. Was I mad for even suggesting such a thing in her presence? Probably, but there was no choice.

No servants were in evidence, but someone had made preparations. A late dinner, as Grace described it, was a buffet of breads, cold cuts, and salads. The beverage list was restricted to beer and soda.

Another benefit of money is being able to take it for granted. Ricky grabbed a Lowenbrau and settled back on a couch that would have been covered in plastic should something so beautiful have found its way into our old apartment in Brooklyn. He put his feet, still in boots, up on a coffee table made of highly polished mahogany. Grace sat in a large chair that was undoubtedly the seat of power.

I think she ate a bologna sandwich on white bread with mayonnaise. She was definitely sipping a Fresca. A picnic at home with Grace McCoy and Ricky Grant. *New York Magazine* would have paid big bucks for that tableau.

Jerry and I were left with the other couch, directly opposite the one that Ricky was now lying on. Jerry was eating a ham-and-cheese sandwich on rye bread. Not very kosher. I noshed on the best potato salad I had ever tasted, and washed it down with a Coke. It was all very cozy.

Jerry looked relatively calm. Maybe his awe circuits had been blown and it was time to just lie back and enjoy.

Unfortunately I couldn't do that. Sure I was overwhelmed. Sure this was social climbing beyond my wildest dreams. David was still dead.

"Grace, I'd really like to talk about . . ."

"David. Yes, I know."

Again there was a sense of burdensome sadness.

"I suppose I've been trying to avoid the subject. Well there's nothing for it but to come out and face the music, as it were."

I wasn't sure if that was a confession, a Freudian slip, or her idea of a joke. I didn't react, so she continued.

"I thought David was incredibly talented. I told him that he was invaluable for studio work, but he wanted to put together a jazz combo."

"Jazz is dead."

"So I told him, not that he needed to hear it from me. He would go on about how he was interested in music, not money, but that he wanted money to take care of Jana. Of course if anyone could have made it, it would have been David. With his talent and his charm and his looks . . ." She had her eyes closed as if picturing him. Maybe those rumors of her lesbianism were less than accurate. She took a deep breath and continued more calmly.

"We went back and forth. As a matter of fact we talked about it that night. Maybe that's what gave him the headache."

"Must be your fault he's dead then, Gracie."

That was Ricky, actually appearing to wind down and fire off a bon mot from the depths of the sofa.

"It's hardly amusing, dear."

"How about Jana?" I went on, not wanting to lose control of the conversation.

"She was in a bit of a state. I do remember thinking that for an engagement party, the whole thing seemed rather bleak."

"Do you know what was bothering her?"

"The Arab."

"She told you about that?"

"Not until after she came down from the apartment. We'd been thinking how marvelous it would be if we all went to the Waldorf for breakfast, and then Ricky got the idea of playing pranks on Natalie and R.J., so we sent Jana up to see if David was game. The poor girl came out looking like she'd seen something horrible, and of course she had. She was completely distraught. Then it all came out. I wish she had confided in me sooner. I might have been able to do something."

"Like what, having Akhmad thrown out of the country."

It was the elfin face that made her chilling smile so effective.

"So you believe that Akhmad Mohammed, or those acting on his orders, murdered David Price with the intent of then abducting Jana Crowley?"

I tried to keep the incredulity out of my voice.

"Well, Jana seemed quite convinced, and she was so upset I couldn't just call her a liar."

"Load of rubbish," interjected Ricky.

"It was preposterous of course," Grace admitted.

"Which leaves David Price the victim of an aborted robbery attempt?"

"Not necessarily."

"You do know something."

"I know some things. I suspect others."

"Do the police know anything?"

"The police know what they want to know."

"Before this gets too Kafka-esque, who killed David?"

"Think Orwellian. I didn't say I know for a fact. I do think perhaps the answer lies closer to home than the Middle East."

"I read in *Ms.* how you never like to beat around the bush. Well, right now we're going around that bush so fast, I'm getting dizzy."

"I am sorry. This is quite difficult. I don't like to be indiscreet."

She seemed to be gripping her Fresca very tightly.

"David is long past worrying about secrets now."

"I suppose you're right, dear. David was married once before . . ."

"Yeah, yeah, Carmen the Mafia princess. How did you get that scoop? David wasn't exactly advertising it."

"I like to know about my employees. I like to know who they know and why. I wasn't happy about David's situation, but he was so talented that I thought an ex-wife of dubious associations could be overlooked."

"This is going to come as a bit of a shock, Grace, but there was never an official closeout on that merger."

I didn't think her eyes could get wider, but they did.

"Are you certain of that?"

"Oh yeah."

"How do you know?"

"Heard it straight from the cow's mouth."

"Good one, luv."

"Thanks, Ricky."

"Stop that both of you. We needn't be cruel, but we must be sure. I know these people. They have the most Neanderthal mentality. I've managed to steer clear of them mostly because none would deign to do business with a woman. It's an insult and a lifesaver at the same time. I know this much, if there was no sanctioned divorce or annulment, then David may have signed his own death warrant by having an engagement party."

I couldn't believe it. I considered the mob theory only one step less ludicrous than the idea of Akhmad swooping in to claim Jana. Yet there was Amazing Grace accepting it completely.

I looked around the rooms for signs of sanity and found none. If anyone disagreed with Grace, they weren't picking that moment to say so. I felt the mental ice getting thin. I decided to try and skate in Grace's groove.

"If it is organized crime, does that mean that the Mob is also orchestrating the cover-up out of Queens?"

Thin shoulders shrugged eloquently under a cashmere sweater.

I turned my attention toward Ricky. He had gotten a second wind and was revved up and ready to go.

"Richard dear," I said archly. "Do tell me what was really going on between you and David."

Suddenly Richard was on his feet, smoking a Dunhill and pacing. Dynamic energy kept his puffy, baggy-eyed features from collapsing and anger propelled him around the room.

"You think you've got it all figured out, don't you sweetheart?"

"Spare me the vapors, Ricky."

"You're good, Marti, but I'm a damn sight better. I show you the ropes and you try to use them to strangle me?"

"You wouldn't?"

"Well, of course I would, but that's hardly the point."

He sat down and resumed his frenetic puffing.

"What is the point?"

"The point is, rather sadly, that there was nothing of any sort going on."

"Did that bother you?"

"Not for more than a minute. Nothing that moves is out of bounds, but nothing that uptight about his own hetero credentials is worth the trouble, no matter how pretty."

"I heard he was dropping beads."

"Well, it's a good thing he never dropped any around me, or I would have shoved them right up his bloody arse without a lubricant."

"I thought you liked David."

"David Price was scum but . . ."

"Don't tell me, some of your best friends are scum."

"You should give up the amateur detective stuff and work on your writing."

"Yes, dear," Grace chimed back into the conversation. "When you finish your next project, you should let me know. Maybe I can help you place it."

"Even if it's crummy?"

"Jana and David both told me how much they admired your work. David was especially concerned about your insecurity. He thought you should be published."

"David? David Price said I had talent?"

"Yes."

I didn't even know he had read my stuff. Jana must have shown it to him. I felt the beginnings of a crying jag, deep in my chest. The room turned blurry. I turned to Jerry in a panic. He saved my bacon one more time.

"Look at the time. I think we have to be running along."

It sounded like an escape line from a boring barbecue, but it did the trick. In a flurry of hugs and kissy-kisses and pleases and thank-yous, we were ushered out. I caught a last glimpse of the pictures on the wall, especially that sketch of David that Jana had done.

David. What a guy. I felt warmer toward him than I had since the day I introduced him to Jana. The tears had been short-circuited, but the glow remained.

We exited the building. I noted a slow-moving squad car keeping Park Avenue safe for the filthy rich.

I hummed "More Love" and tried to dance toward Broadway. I heard a distant throat clearing.

"Earth to Martha Hirsch, come in please."

I opened my eyes. Jerry was under a streetlight.

"Marti Hirsch, reporting. No one calls me Martha except my mother."

"Marti, did you learn anything?"

"David thought I had talent."

"About the murder?"

"I'll find out who did it, if I have to take on the whole Mafia."

"I don't think it's going to come to that."

"Why not?"

"Because I didn't believe them. With all the money and glamour and all that stuff, I still think they were scared."

"Of little old me?"

"They talked like they were in a movie."

"The rich are very different than you and I."

"Thank you, Mr. Fitzgerald. What time is it anyway?"

"You're a grown-up now, Jerry. You can stay out past curfew and leave every light in the house on and sit up close to the TV set. And we're not done yet."

"Oh yeah?"

If that was a hopeful note of lust in his voice, I had to quash it immediately.

"Down boy, we've got another stop to make."

"At this hour?"

"Gotta check out the scene of the crime."

"Are you serious?"

"Yeah. I have to pick up some stuff for Jana, and if I happen to snoop around while I'm there . . . well, you get the idea. We need to get to Broadway to get a cab."

"I must be going crazy because this is starting to make sense."

"I've got a blind, stuttering shrink I can recommend."

"Perfect. Are you sure we can get a cab?"

"Of course we can get a cab. This is Manhattan, not Brooklyn."

"Are you sure it's safe."

"To get a cab?"

"To be out on the street."

"You'll protect me, right?"

"I'll try."

"That makes me feel much better. Come on."

I started singing again. Jerry joined me with ragged but enthusiastic harmony. Soon we were singing and dancing along Broadway.

A cab did pick us up, despite our shenanigans, and we continued singing and giggling, ignoring fishy looks from our driver, until we arrived at the designated address in the East 30s.

We were at The Scene of the Crime.

11

Ricky and Grace lived in a building that exuded eccentric wealth. Jana had abandoned the character of the Village for a cookie-cutter co-op with crew-cut security clods who managed to be missing in action when it really mattered.

The one heading toward me looked enough like a real policeman to activate my loathing of all things constabulary. I had a key, but he knew I wasn't a tenant. Mr. Security opened the door, blocking the entrance with his massive frame. He was big and beefy, reminding me not just of a policeman but of a soldier.

Jerry was standing behind me, his shoulders hitched in a primitive, masculine pose of aggressiveness. He was prepared to fight for me. Touching, but unnecessary.

"Hello. I'm Marti Hirsch."

I put out a businesslike hand. He wasn't prepared for that.

"Derek Boonton. Nice to meet you ma'am."

He had a southern accent.

"This is Mr. Barlow. We're from downtown."

"Downtown?"

"Yes. We have a few questions about the Price B&E. Didn't they tell you I was coming?"

"Uh, no ma'am. No one said anything to me. Isn't it awfully late . . . ?"

"Well, it's certainly too late to keep us standing out here."

"Oh yeah. Sure."

He stood aside. I entered and started looking around critically.

Jerry got into the spirit of the game. While I stared Derek down, he started flipping through the pages of the sign-in book.

"Were you the one on duty that night?"

"Yes, ma'am," he replied miserably. "I already told the police everything."

"Well, now you're going to tell me," I said sharply, jangling the keys for emphasis.

"There ain't much to tell. I saw Mr. Price come in after midnight. Then I saw Miss Crowley come in around one. She was in a big hurry. She barely said hi. She barely looked at me."

"Why should she look at you?"

"Because I said hello."

I stared at him coldly.

"I try to be nice to everybody."

Another one of Jana's admirers. No mercy for this idiot.

"Then what happened?"

"Well, it was maybe five minutes later, she came down in the elevator and ran right past me. She looked scared. I didn't know what was going on. Another twenty minutes went by and the police came in, and the shit really hit the fan."

I flared my nostrils in a show of displeasure.

"Sorry, ma'am."

"The official word from the NYPD is that David Price was the victim of a burglar who came in through the front door."

Derek had been acting like such a whipped dog that I was surprised to see him straighten his spine and meet my gaze with a pair of soulful brown eyes.

"Yes, ma'am."

"And they conclude further that the intruder got through

the front door while you were away from this area."

"I took a break at 12:35 A.M. and was back here at 12:45."

"Can anyone prove that?"

"It don't matter. It was long enough. It was the same break I take every night per instructions. I expect you'd know that if you work downtown."

He had soul and guts, but I had nothing to lose, so I called his bluff.

"You can call and check, Derek, but just remember, Jerry and I are on your side. It's the cops who are thrilled to be able to point at you, and it's everybody else downtown who's got to bow and scrape to them. They're getting ready to can you."

He wasn't reaching for a phone, but he wasn't spilling his guts either. I knew my first story wouldn't hold up much longer. Time for a quick rewrite.

"Look, I'll be honest with you. We are from downtown, but we're not important. I'm a secretary and Jerry's in accounting. We know what's going on and we don't want to see you get a bum rap. So I figured if I came down here and talked to you, maybe I could get something to prove it wasn't your fault."

"Why would you stick your neck out and come here in the middle of the night for that?"

I thought fast and put a dramatic catch in my voice. It was a jump, but sometimes you have to go with your instincts.

"My father was in the service like you, and he . . . well you know . . . he wouldn't want me to let a good guy get the shaft."

I shook my head. Jerry put a reassuring hand on my shoulder.

Poor Derek. His good heart and strong will were up against industrial-strength bullshit. The conflict was playing out all over his face with misguided loyalties clouding the issue.

I wasn't sure which way it was going to go.

I heard Jerry say, "Come on, man, if it means anything to you, this is the time to be honest."

Bravo, I thought.

Derek had a pack of Marlboros on the security station. He took his time lighting one and taking a deep puff. Then he did something that really pissed me off. He started talking to Jerry as though I weren't there. I had to listen through my internal rage to concentrate on what he was saying.

"Well, it sure ain't about this job. I've just been doing this a year. It's the best job I've had since I got back from 'Nam, but this city is for the dogs. If they're fixing to fire me, they better hurry up. I'm going home. Maybe not back to Georgia, but somewhere better than this."

I held my breath. Jerry had the ball and if he didn't run with it, we were up the creek.

"So what really happened on Saturday night?"

"Mostly what I said. People were coming and going like every Saturday. When I saw Mr. Price come in, he said he was expecting someone."

I couldn't control myself.

"Did he say who?"

"Nope, just that whoever came looking for him, I should let up."

"And did you let anyone up?"

"Nope. I swear it. I didn't see anybody till Jana, I mean Miss Crowley came in."

"How could someone get in?"

"They could've had a key or just picked the lock."

"Picked the lock?" said Jerry.

"It ain't that hard."

There was a defensive tone. Like a kid making up a story as he went along. Well, why not? I was doing it. It was time to find out who was better. I shook my keys to get his attention.

"What do you think happened?"

"Telling you may not be real smart."

"Telling me may be the smartest thing you've done in awhile."

He ran a hand over a head that was wearing a fuzzy crew cut as if he were still government issue. He decided to spill it, but not to me. He looked past me to Jerry again.

"I went up there with the cops. I saw Mr. Price lying there with blood all over. He was shot up close. Even if someone got in through the front door, it was Mr. Price who opened the door up there and got blown away."

"Are you sure about that?" I asked.

"The last time I saw a scene like that was when my buddy let the wrong whore get too close in Saigon. It may have been a robbery, but there wasn't a struggle."

"So you think he was killed by whomever he was expecting?"

"Maybe."

"You're a cagey guy, Derek."

"Thank you, ma'am."

"We're going upstairs to take a look at the apartment. Don't take a break until we get back."

"They still got that place sealed up."

"That's nice."

The light on the elevator said it was on the fifth floor. Come on already, I thought.

"Hey, you," Derek called out.

Jerry and I both turned around, but Derek was still talking man-to-man.

"Do I know her from somewhere?"

Jerry gave me a quick glance. I shrugged. He looked back at Derek.

"I don't know. Maybe you should ask her."

The elevator arrived and we stepped in, leaving Derek paralyzed with his own stupidity.

"That was perfect Jer, where have you been all my life?"

"Where have *you* been?"

I could have given him the whole itinerary, but it didn't take that long to get to the fourth floor, and I got the impression that wasn't what he was really asking.

The yellow-and-black striped tape across the door of Jana and David's apartment gave way to tearing. Before using the key, I tried to pick up the psychic vibrations of the killer. Nothing came through. Straight telepathy was never my forte.

David's ghost was not hovering in the apartment, but there was a spectral quality to the chalk outline that showed where the body had been. It was soft and rounded. David's outline should have been sharp and crisp and scented with that fabulous aftershave he always wore. In the center of the outline was the bloodstain, or what remained of it. I tried to reconcile that faint rust-colored blotch of about a square foot with either the gorefest that Derek had described or the "not much" that Jana had come up with when I asked her if there was a lot of blood.

I wished that I knew real ballistics, instead of what I had picked up from my mystery habit. I craved a look at the police file. Well, that wasn't going to happen, and Jana needed some clothes.

I glanced around the living room, not knowing what I was looking for and certainly not finding it. I love reading Mickey Spillane (and don't think I didn't get some serious lectures from Stephanie Diamond for that), but the scene in *I, The Jury* where he finds his friend's notebook after the cops have searched the place, always struck me as less than believable.

Next stop was the bedroom, the largest room in the pad. The room was dominated by an unmade king-sized bed. I tried, but failed, to suppress the inevitable image. As far as I was concerned, ecstasy with David would have consisted of being wrapped in his arms, looking at his perfect face, kissing his lips, and melting into bliss with no unseemly flesh or fluid to mar the moment.

I looked in the closet. It was like something out of *The Great Gatsby*. All those beautiful suits in nubbly tweeds and creamy grays. That stuff had to be costing a pretty penny. Not to mention the apartment and the goodies in it.

Did sessions pay that well? Even with Jana's payment for the album cover and whatever she was selling through the gallery show? It wasn't like Jana was shopping at Village thrift stores either.

I grabbed a suitcase from the bottom of the closet and threw anything of hers that was black into it. A few dresses, skirts, some shoes. In the chest of drawers, I found sweaters, blouses, and lingerie. Maybe she'd meet someone at the funeral. I stashed some of her jewelry into the zippered pocket on the side.

I was getting ready to shut the whole thing when I saw Jana's sketch pad lying near her side of the bed. I didn't have much time, but I decided to spend some of it finding out what Jana had been drawing lately.

Mostly disco scenes. There was a dead-on picture of Andy Warhol. Some park scenes from around the corner, and then the torn edge of where a page had been ripped away.

I needed to go to the bathroom. There was a big facility down the hall from the kitchen, but the little one attached to the bedroom would do just fine. Aside from a place to empty my bladder and stare at the impression that the waistband of my Leggs pantyhose had made in my stomach, there was the opportunity to get some of Jana's cosmetics and sneak the tiniest peek at the medicine chest.

I packed two shadows, one mascara, a liner, and a compact. The medicine chest yielded nothing of interest. (What did I expect, syringes and glassine envelopes?) Feeling disappointed, I decided to treat myself to a glimpse at the underwear of the deceased.

Before I could look for the Skivvies, I spotted a piece of paper on top of the bureau. It was about half the size of a sheet of typing paper. From the creases, it appeared to have been folded many times into a much smaller square. Before I could investigate further, Jerry called out from the front room.

"Marti, I think we've got a problem here."

I thought of saying, "What you mean 'we,' paleface,"

but a certain urgency in his voice caused me to eschew wisecracks, stash the paper in my purse, and get out there with Jana's suitcase.

Jerry was sitting behind David's upright piano, playing what sounded like the baseline to "Tragedy." Our friend Derek Boonton was glowering at him fiercely. That was definitely trouble, especially when he fixed that gaze on me and caught me red-handed, so to speak.

"You ain't from downtown. You're one of Miss Crowley's friends. You were here when they had that big party."

"I am not one of Jana's friends, you dumb hick. I'm her best friend," I enunciated with great umbrage. I could almost hear Jerry's fingers cringe at the keyboard.

"And now you're trying to remove evidence from the scene of the crime."

Jerry played a few notes of the *Dragnet* theme.

Derek wasn't carrying a gun that I could see, but he was certainly big enough to hurt me and he could definitely get me in a lot of trouble. I'd been flying all night on a feeling of glamour and omnipotence, but the ugly New York dawn could be seen through the window. I had the sinking feeling that the jig was up. A sniggering voice inside my head said, "O.K., smart-ass, write your way out of this one."

I was so scared that I started stuttering, like Dr. Hammerschmidt.

"W-w-w-what are you going to do?"

"I'm gonna call the police and tell them that someone is snooping around here and trying to enter a crime scene under false pretenses and maybe even stealing stuff. That's what I'm gonna do."

If he had threatened me with violence, I might have continued sniveling. Maybe even the specter of his fellow security goons would have kept the fear of God in me. Derek Boonton was about to learn a very important lesson: never threaten me with pigs. It really annoys me, especially from male chauvinist, establishment finks.

"You want to call the cops, go right ahead, but if you want to reach Captain Morrison, the head of the Homicide department, you have to call the 900 Club up in Washington Heights, where he's probably downing a few with his good friend Detective Kimberlin from Narcotics. Maybe you met him already? Anyway, after you get through telling Tommy, I mean Captain Morrison, that I've been a bad girl, I'll tell Doug, I mean Detective Kimberlin, about how you're going around saying that David Price was shot by someone he knew and was not the victim of a random breaking-and-entering, which is the official finding of the New York City Police Department."

"And why would he believe you?"

"Because I'm his lover."

"You're full of shit."

"You don't believe me? Well it's the truth, pal. I'm fucking him. We do the dirty deed. Get it on, bang-a-gong. That silver-haired upholder of law and order is getting his *schvantz* copped by yours truly at least once a week. That just might give me some credibility about blowing the whistle on you, if you try to blow the whistle on me. What do you say to that?"

"I'd say it wouldn't be the first blackmail that's gone on around here."

He moved toward a phone. I shot a look at Jerry. All I got was a helpless head-shake.

"The number is five-five-five, nine-o-one-two. The bartender's name is Sid."

"She'll do it," said Jerry. "I've seen her do worse."

Derek looked at Jerry and then at me. He lowered his head in submission.

"You're really something, lady."

"Since you're standing there, why don't you make yourself useful and call a taxi for us."

Getting a cab would have been simple enough, but asserting my dominance was more fun.

I watched Derek dial. I heard him give the address. He put the phone down.

"Your cab will be here in five minutes."

He was talking to me. I couldn't take the time to savor victory. I had a new piece of the puzzle to worry about.

Derek had said there was blackmail going on. Blackmail? What did blackmail have to do with this?

12

The city had passed from the end of the night to the beginning of the day.

I thought the cab was especially smelly until I realized it was me. I needed a shower and a change of clothes. I wanted to get out of my brassiere. I had to get home and take my birth-control pill. I felt like I needed to sleep for two days.

"Marti."

"What?"

"You need to tell the driver where we're going."

"Oh yeah. Right."

I'd been starting in on that sleep prematurely.

"JFK," I said yawning. "You don't have to schlepp out there with me Jerry. I'll drop you off by a subway station. You should probably go home and get some sleep."

"Not as much as you should."

"I'm a big girl. I can dance, dance, dance all night."

"You may think you're Julie Andrews, but right now you look like Sleeping Beauty. I'll take you to the airport."

"In what?"

"In my car."

"What car?"

"The one I was leaning on in front of the deli. Remember?"

"Vaguely."

I opened the window of the taxi. It was going to be another warm one. I heard Jerry give the driver directions back to 2nd Avenue. I could have used some of Ricky's coke. I'd never bought the stuff. I didn't know if they sold it in plastic bags or papers like the one I'd gotten that time in Times Square.

I started smiling to myself. It wasn't my second or even third wind, but whatever it was, it blew me awake and was going strong by the time we got to Jerry's car. He tried to give me money for the cab. I wouldn't take it. It was still my treat, at least until I got in the front seat of Jerry's roomy Mercury Cougar.

I watched him start the engine and pull out, as though he were doing a magic trick. I thought of true New Yorkers as masters of the bus and rail, not cars. Jerry was a smooth driver and a smooth talker. Not in a seductive way, but just to keep the conversation going so we would both stay awake.

"How can you afford all those cabs? You must have a great job."

"I'm officially unemployed."

"Then maybe you shouldn't be throwing the *dinero* around."

"Not so, señor. You have no idea just how much money you can get from unemployment, welfare, the city, the state, and the Feds when a psychiatrist says that you are emotionally disabled and cannot work."

"That's some racket."

"They love it at Zabar's when I show up with my food stamps."

"All I've got is the teacher's union."

"A racket unto itself from what I hear."

"Touché. Can I ask you something else?"

"Be my guest."

"Is it true about the cop?"

Ouch. I wasn't expecting that. I'd been so caught up in my head game with Derek that I played my trump card with Jerry in the room. It wasn't the kind of thing I usually went around shouting at the top of my lungs.

"Yeah," I said defensively. "We all sleep with the wrong people sometimes, right?"

"Some of us just marry them."

That ended the conversation, but started wheels spinning in my head.

I wanted to ask him who, what, when, where, why, and how, but it wouldn't have been nice. Instead I concentrated on what I still wanted to ask Jana.

We arrived at the airport and Jerry steered the car toward the American Airlines terminal. He tried to park, but a sky cap waved him away menacingly.

"Jerry, thanks for everything. You've been a gem and a joy. Go home and get some sleep."

"I'll take you back to the city."

"You don't have to do that. I'll get a cab."

"I'll go into a holding pattern. Just look for me when you come out."

"You are interfering with my autonomy."

"Do you want to argue with me or do you want to go give your friend her stuff."

I let it go. There wasn't that much time.

In fact, when I found Jana, she was pacing and looking at her watch. Grieving, mortal fear, running for her life. It all seemed to agree with her. I believed that someday there would be equality between the sexes, if we fought for it long enough. There would never be equality between the beauties of the world and the rest of us.

"Marti, what have you been up to and with who?"

"That's 'whom' and why do you ask?"

"Well you look awful, but happy in some weird way."

"I feel like heaven and I've been through hell. By the way, did you know that the night security guard at your building had a crush on you?"

"Derek?"

"Uh-huh."

"I assumed it."

"Any idea why he would use the word 'blackmail'?"

I caught her reacting to that. A millisecond of shock followed by the image of perfect calm.

"How come you never told me that David liked my writing?"

"Who said that?"

"Grace."

"Grace? I don't know what to say, Marti. You know I love your stuff. You gotta start sending it around, but David read sheet music and *Downbeat* and the *New York Post*. He wasn't much for books. I'm sorry. Oh, for pete's sake, don't cry."

Was I crying? I sure was. All goopy and snively. Well, what the hell? It was an airport. People cried there all the time.

"When will I see you again?"

"I don't know. I'll keep in touch."

"You know I'm going to miss you."

"Me too. I've never had a friend like you."

"Now you're crying."

"Oh, good lord. My mascara!"

The muffled voice on the loudspeaker was announcing boarding for her flight to Chicago.

"Who was blackmailing David?"

"Why would anyone want to blackmail David?"

"The usual reasons."

"I have to go. I don't know what you're trying to say, but it sounds dangerous."

"Is that a threat?"

"I'll call you soon."

I watched her go through the gate. I watched men watching her walk through the gate.

The ominous parts of our conversation clung to me as well as the obvious truth that David had never read my stories, much less liked them. I felt heavier walking through the terminal than I had when I was encumbered with Jana's suitcase.

Morning was irrevocable. I blinked into the sunlight. I was dressed for a night that had passed. Planes roared overhead. People were going far away. The only place I had to go was to work.

I was supposed to be there at 8:30. There was no time to go home and shower. Besides, access to my bed could prove dangerously attractive. I starting waving for a cab when I heard a honking horn trying to assert itself in the din. There was Jerry, three lanes away from me and waving frantically as he tried to hold his spot. A hotel bus was threatening his rear bumper.

I walked into the flow of traffic to get to him. A few drivers expressed their anger, but I was past caring. I slid into the car. Two thoughts ran through my mind. One was that I was too old to stay up all night. The other was that Jerry was either a hell of a guy or a real idiot. I wouldn't have done something like that.

It was hard to think ill of someone with a moving car and a sweet smile at that moment. Big band music was playing on the car radio. WNEW AM.

"Squaresville," I muttered.

"Where are you living these days?" he asked.

"Who wants to know?"

"I want to get you home, and I don't think Studio Fifty-four is open yet."

"I've got a great place in Washington Heights, but we're going to West Seventy-ninth and Columbus."

"Why?"

"Some of us have work during the summer."

"I thought you were riding the gravy train."

"Even the gravy train has a fare these days."

I didn't want to get into the whole thing, but I had to keep talking or I would fall asleep and never wake up. Sarah Vaughan singing "Make Yourself Comfortable" wasn't going to keep my eyes open.

"Hey, Jerry?"

"Yeah."

"Which lucky girl did you marry?"

"Girls."

"More than one?"

"That's right."

"Were they all the wrong person?"

"Both of them."

"Who was the first?"

We made an abrupt lane change and I had to hold on to my door handle to avoid being thrown against him.

There was silence in the car except for some inane babbling from Jim Lowe.

I cleared my throat.

"Whoever killed David Price is going to be pretty sorry," said Jerry shaking his head.

"Why do you say that?"

"You never stop."

"I'm not interrogating you. You don't have to tell me."

"I don't mind talking about it. I'm just afraid you'll laugh at me."

"Why would I laugh?"

"I married Debbie."

"Debbie Rubin?"

I wasn't sure what was about to come out of my mouth. Maybe laughter, maybe a yelp of disbelief. Debbie and Jerry? Jerry, the nerdy sidekick and Debbie, the chosen princess? No way.

"When? How?"

"After Brian got killed. Debbie felt responsible. She really did love him. She just wasn't ready to marry him then. I guess she needed a shoulder to cry on and a friend to talk to, and I was the natural one because I was his friend."

"Sort of an Eddie Fisher and Elizabeth Taylor thing."

"I didn't think of it that way."

"You didn't have my parents. Why was Debbie the wrong person?"

"For all the reasons that you're probably thinking. She couldn't get over Brian. She'd look at me and think of Brian. She told me she was going crazy. Finally she went to a psychiatrist."

"What happened?"

"She found out what she needed was to get away from

me and go to Big Sur so she could take seminars at the Esalen Institute. She says she's happy there."

"I'm sorry."

"Don't be sorry. We had some good years together. We went to the theater practically every week. She helped me get through college. I held her together as long as I could. We just couldn't go on with only Broadway and sympathy. I guess I knew it was over when she ran out crying during the finale of 'Follies.' "

"So, who was Mrs. Barlow the Second?"

"Anita Hernandez."

"Hernandez, like the Spanish teacher at our high school?"

"Daughter of a third cousin."

"That must have given your mom a heart attack."

I thought I was being funny, but I got a wounded look as we came into the city.

"Stroke," he said.

Well, how was I supposed to know?

"Anita needed an American husband to get a green card."

"You'll excuse me if I'm totally out of line, but have you ever considered marrying someone because you were passionately in love with them?"

"I thought I did. That was my big mistake. I loved Anita so much that I put up with everything. The lies, the tears, the games. I kept forgiving her. I only reached the end of my rope a few months ago. She was flaunting herself with José or Julio or whoever it was right there at Odyssey in front of all our . . . well I guess they were all her friends. At least she taught me how to dance."

We were making good time up 8th Avenue.

"Are you seeing anyone now?"

Why was I asking? What did I care?

"The next woman I go out with is going to regret it. I'm ready to hurt somebody for a change."

White knuckles gripped the steering wheel. He was more

intense at that moment than at any time in the nearly twelve hours we had been together.

"It kind of scares me," he said softly.

I started feeling the full weight of fatigue. I didn't want to fall asleep. We were close to 79th Street.

"Jerry, can I call you at home?"

"Sure, but if you're planning on any more nights like this, you have to give me time to recover."

"I am a night owl, but this was extreme. I hope you had a little fun."

"More than I have in a long time. So where do I drop you off?"

I gave him the address and he gave me his phone number.

It wasn't really a date, so I didn't think a kiss was called for, but a handshake would have been ridiculous after all that soul-baring. I ended up giving him a forehead kiss, which was still pretty silly. I was left with a fleeting, tactile impression of extremely soft hair. I waved good-bye as he drove out of sight.

I tried to steel myself for a day of tape transcriptions, grading essays, and maybe a quick probe of my own psyche.

The doorman gave me an odd look. It wasn't till I was in the elevator that I looked at the distorted, round mirror in the upper corner and got a full picture of the damage. I looked like a refugee from the law firm of rumpled, crumpled, and tangled.

At least Dr. Hammerschmidt wouldn't notice. There was the smell, but maybe that wasn't really so bad. O.K., I thought. Here we go. Big smile, big energy.

"Good morning."

"Hello, Marti, how are you?"

"Fine, thank you."

"You've been out all night, haven't you?"

Did I hear a sniff?

"How did you know?"

"You sound tired."

"No, no. Bright-eyed and bushy-tailed. Ready to work."

"Were you working on your m-m-murder case?"

"Yes, I was."

"Did you learn anything?"

"Lies, lies, lies. Everybody's got something to hide except for me and my monkey. Shall I make some coffee? Should I feed Effie? Do you want me to type anything?"

"What about the boy from high school?"

"All grown up. He's very sweet." A yawn came out. "Very sweet. Great dancer. He could probably use your help. He's got some problems."

"Did you talk about high school?"

"A little."

"Would you like to sit down in my office and tell me about it?"

"Why don't I sit at the typewriter and get some work done?"

"C-c-come into my office."

He meant business.

It was all over as soon as I felt my tush hit the big, soft, comfortable couch with my legs and feet following closely behind.

I don't even remember falling asleep.

13

I sure as hell remember waking up.

It wasn't just the dull ache that throbbed all over my body, or the paws of a large German shepherd pressing on my legs, that made it memorable. I was woken up by the sound of my own crying. That was a new one.

My eyes were caked shut with congealed tears. When I managed to get them open, I caught Dr. Hammerschmidt with his glasses off. I'd never seen his unfocused eyes. It was a disturbing sight, made more so by the expression of concern that was knitting his bushy eyebrows.

My blurry vision and bleary eyes made it seem like I was still dreaming.

"Oh my god, the dream!" I blurted, suddenly remembering the whole thing.

I sat up so abruptly that Effie bolted to her master for safety.

One side of my dress had gotten wedged up past my pantyhose. Most of my left leg was visible to anyone who wanted to look. This wasn't a problem, since the only man in the room couldn't see. I wasn't doing so well myself. I looked for my glasses and tried to pick the remaining sandman dust out of my eyelashes.

"Tell me about the d-d-dream."

"Hold on a second. I'm looking for my glasses. Oh, here

they are. The damn things fell off the couch. How long was I out?"

"Less than ninety minutes. You've probably been in deep REM sleep for half an hour. The crying s-s-started about f-f-five minutes ago. What caused it?"

"It must have been the snakes. Oh my god!"

"Start at the beginning."

"I was down in the subway, standing on the platform. It was afternoon and it was hot. A bunch of trains went by. The A and the E, I think, but I didn't get on any of them."

"Why not?"

"I don't know. I don't think I wanted to go anywhere. I was looking for something. I tried talking to people, but it was like they couldn't understand me and they kept pointing toward the tunnel. So I went in."

"In the t-t-tunnel?"

"Yeah. I climbed right down. I wasn't scared of getting run over by a train. I just kept walking, and the further I went, the more I felt like I was going to find it. It was a really great feeling. Like being high. Really good and clear and strong."

"What went wrong?"

"Snakes. Big yellow snakes. Coming at me out of the darkness."

"Are you s-s-scared of snakes?"

"Not usually. But these were big yellow snakes with big teeth and they were biting me and, yes, I was scared!"

I was hyperventilating. I clutched for a wad of Kleenex, as much to stifle the panic as to wipe away a new flood of tears.

Karl nodded slowly, seemingly oblivious to the whole display. I should have been used to his cold professionalism, but when I felt so raw and hurt and vulnerable, I wanted something more human. I felt rejected by my own therapist.

"So come on, Doc. Interpret for me. What the hell does it mean?"

"What do you think it means?"

"I don't know what it means. I don't know what's going on. I think I'm going crazy. We've been plugging away at this over six months and it's getting worse."

"I think we're making p-p-progress."

"I'm a candidate for a private room at Bellevue and you think we're making progress?"

"We're getting c-c-closer to the root cause, the traumatic event. S-s-so now the trauma is expressing itself in the coded language of dreams. All we have to do is break the code."

He had a crooked smile, twisted by the scar. He looked pleased with himself in a Dr. Frankenstein way.

"So get out your Dick Tracy decoder ring. What's the scoop?"

"Well," he said slowly, "I'd say that the s-s-snakes and the tunnel suggest a sexual component."

"Oh no, not again. Look, for the umpteenth time, I've never been raped, molested, coerced, fondled, or caressed against my will."

"That you remember or acknowledge."

"What the hell is that supposed to mean?"

"I'm still concerned about your relationship with Stephanie."

"Typical male reaction to feel threatened by a perfectly natural lesbian connection, which I sought out, let me remind you."

"M-m-marti, I'm trying to help you, not debate sexual politics. What about Doug?"

"I'm not crazy about who or what he is, but I assure you, I am nobody's sexual victim."

"Let's talk about your father."

"My father? You've got a sick mind, you know that, Doctor? Forget Freud and his phallocentric, psychosexual obsession. I was down there looking for something. It's about finding the answer to who killed David and the fact that it's getting dangerous. Jana threatened me. Grace and Ricky practically tried to buy me off. It's like when someone beats up Philip Marlowe and tells him to get off the case. I must be getting close. I'm going to solve this thing, I swear to God."

I started to get up, only to discover that I was still dizzy from fatigue. I settled down with a thud.

"You should go home and get some s-s-sleep."

"What about work?"

"I'll manage. Come back when you're able to work or when you need to talk. You'll probably c-c-continue to have vivid dreams. Write them down. The answers are there."

I got up carefully. Effie rubbed her head against my leg. Karl rose to walk me to the door.

"I feel guilty. I'm sorry, but I just can't do anything until I find out who killed David."

"Then find out. Just remember that life is not a novel, no matter how much it feels like you're writing it. At the risk of sounding condescending or pat-t-ternalistic, please be careful."

"I'll try."

I was too shaky to brave the steps down to the subway station, so I took one more taxi cab home. A quick look at my mail provided the heartening news that my unemployment check had arrived. The minute I was inside my apartment, I started shedding clothes.

Sleep and cleaning were equally pressing needs. I settled in for a long, hot bath, where I could go into a semi-coma. Then, feeling deliciously clean and sleepy, I wrapped my body in a robe and my hair in a towel and staggered into bed, clutching the comforting smoothness of the Toodle-loop and hoping that I wouldn't have any dreams.

I must have been on the wrong line when they were handing out luck.

This time the tunnel led to a giant ballroom full of faceless people in formal dress. There were staircases, but no matter how many staircases I ran up and down, I never got anywhere. What was worse, I knew I didn't belong there. I wanted to belong and get away at the same time. Finally

I came to a well-lit landing with some pretty flowers.

That's when the bees showed up. They were surrounding me. I pushed them away with my hands and woke up crying again. I was all sweaty and the towel had come partially undone. I unwrapped the rest of it and used it to wipe sweat and tears off my face.

I picked up the radio, which had fallen on the floor, and put it back on my night table. Then I fell asleep again.

It wasn't dreams that woke me up. It was the thumping bass riff of "Spirit in the Night," from the other side of the wall. The lyric was particularly sophomoric. Who'd want to go to a place called Greasy Lake? Not my idea of a good time. That riff always disturbed me, though. Especially at that volume, easily drowning out my poor little doughnut-shaped A.M.

I got up and tried to stretch my muscles.

A foray to my refrigerator was fruitless, vegetableless, and meatless. I needed to do some shopping. There would be some cash in my sequined disco purse, which was lying on the floor.

Along with thirty dollars in cash, I found the folded up piece of paper from Jana and David's house. Now I had a chance to examine it.

About half the size of a letter, printed on coarse white paper. A crudely drawn figure representing a curvaceous woman and the words PLEASURE PALACE EROTIC MASSAGE. An address on 7th Avenue off 42nd Street. The funny part was that I already had one just like it.

I knew what my next step in the investigation would be, but it was too early. More sleep seemed unlikely with the kid next door at home. Couldn't his parents ship him off to camp or something?

I settled into my chair and watched "Hollywood Squares" and "Match Game." I turned off the set before the news came on.

I brushed my hair out and tried to decide what to wear. My first choice would have been a Bogie-esque trench coat, but all I had was a yellow rain slicker, and there wasn't a cloud in the sky. I settled for jeans and a peasant blouse that I had borrowed from Jana, because it looked so comfortable and it was too big on her anyway.

Jana would soon be at the funeral, knocking them dead in the black dress I had packed for her. I couldn't wait to hear about it, not to mention getting some real answers about David.

I thought of David all the way to the glorious filth of Times Square. What brought you down here, I wanted to ask him. It wasn't the food, of course, although a street corner shish kebab and a Nedicks orange drink tasted ambrosial, topped off with a Hostess cupcake for dessert.

I was ready to take on the world, or at least my next potential informants.

Out of thirty movie theaters, only two of them were legitimate. Wedged between marquees offering the usual XXX swill, the Monarch was showing *The Swarm* and at the end of the block, there was a hefty line for *Star Wars*, which looked like it would be playing forever. Well, why not? It was a damn good movie. I'd seen it there with Doug.

One morning back in March, I had been half listening to "Tenth Avenue Freezeout" through the wall while I watched Doug dressing to go home, when he said, "Meet me downtown tonight."

"What?"

"Tonight. I'll be in the car on the corner of Forty-third and Seventh. Be there. We're going to the movies."

"You mean like a date?"

There was a pause while he zipped his fly.

"Yeah, like a date."

I couldn't wait to get to work that day. For one thing I was helping Karl formulate his grades for the midterm papers, which was an interesting intellectual exercise. Mostly I wanted to drop this little nugget into the stew of my own talking cure.

"Since when do clandestine, extramarital affairs involve

dates, especially when there seems to be no point to the relationship, except sex?''

''Maybe he wants it to be something more than that,'' Karl suggested reasonably.

''I hope not.''

''And how exactly is the affair c-c-clandestine? He flaunts you in front of his colleagues, doesn't he?''

''He uses me as an object and I let him. Andrea Dworkin would never forgive me.''

''Or Stephanie Diamond, for that matter.''

''Go ahead, remind me. Why couldn't I just be a sensitive lesbian and live in Woodstock and bake bread?''

''T-t-too much kneading?''

''I've heard of pets looking like owners, but never shrinks talking like patients. Do you think it's possible that the whole thing is getting too sordid for him and he wants to give it some kind of legitimacy? He is a pillar of conventional society, after all.''

''What do you think?''

''I don't know. Up to now the only emotions I've been able to discern are lust and rage. Sometimes I can't even tell them apart.''

''Maybe spring is in the air.''

''He's no young man, and I doubt he knows what a fancy is. I should be finding someone who shares my intellectual, political, and moral view of the world, not shacking up with a Republican-voting cop.''

''Are you going on your date?''

''Of course I am.''

March wasn't particularly springlike. I was shivering when the battered Plymouth that Doug and Johnny used as an unmarked car came up to the corner. I got in the backseat, which made me feel like a prisoner.

I was confused. Were we dropping Johnny off, or was he going to join us on our date? Weren't they both supposed to be on duty? Then I realized that Doug was looking for a parking space. Gee, I thought, why not just double-park, like everybody else? What was he afraid of, a parking ticket?

He paralleled into a spot across the street from one of the smaller book stores. There was a disturbance in the doorway, and suddenly Doug and Johnny were bursting out of the car, weapons drawn. They were joined by two uniformed officers who appeared from nowhere.

I sat in the car, wondering who he was trying to impress. Was I supposed to be overwhelmed with his macho prowess in busting the two-bit worm who was now eating concrete and hearing his Miranda rights? Maybe this was a way to show some more of his fellow officers who he was boffing.

I watched for a while, but when you've seen one act of police brutality, you've seen them all. My glance floated over to the side of the street that we were parked on.

Two young men were watching the scene unfold. They were also hard at work, although it took me awhile to realize the actual nature of their business. What they were obviously doing was shilling for a whorehouse. They were handing out fliers and making a pitch that I couldn't hear through the closed window.

Then I noticed that with one or two people out of the bunches walking by, there was some kind of financial transaction taking place, involving a small package and a quick hand-off. They were dealing drugs across the street from a narcotics bust.

I admired that kind of chutzpah. I decided to match it. Doug was going to be occupied for a while. The opportunity was irresistible.

I rolled down the window and made the universally recognized pantomime for smoking a joint. This caught the eye of the one working the north corner.

He seemed amiable enough, with slightly glassy eyes. Long hair fell into his face. He wore a black T-shirt and torn jeans with a denim jacket. He couldn't have been more than nineteen. He was attempting to grow a beard, but the results were unimpressive.

I put up five fingers to let him know I wanted a nickel bag. He took an appraising look at the action across the street, which seemed to be reaching a climax.

"You a cop?"

"Just along for the ride."

"Which one you with?"

"None of your beeswax, junior."

"Everything on this corner is my business."

"How come he's getting busted and you ain't?"

"'Cause this is our territory and he tried to move in, so we complained."

"You complained to whom?"

"The Better Business Bureau." He cracked up as if he were the funniest cat since Lenny Bruce. Someone was definitely partaking of the merchandise.

I looked across the street. I could see Doug dispatching Johnny to take the poor schmuck to headquarters in a black-and-white. That took care of three being a crowd.

"He's a cop, you know."

Did he think he was telling me something I was unaware of, or was this an attempt at humor?

"You know him?"

"And he knows us."

"And he's never busted your ass?"

"That wouldn't be friendly."

Then I got it. Perfect spot. Perfect setup.

"You're a snitch?" There was the goofy smirk. "And you set that guy up?"

He stopped chuckling when he sensed my disgust and outrage.

"Well, you're going out with a cop," he shot back in an accusatory voice.

By this time, his partner, a mean-faced redhead with a full beard, had come over.

"Hey, what's going on here?"

"Yeah," the other said, suddenly nervous, "are you gonna buy, or what?"

"Is this good stuff?"

"Best price, best quality."

"Yeah, right."

I handed over the five and he handed me the folded up piece of paper. I tucked it into my bag just before Doug came back. The two guys made an audacious show of nothing going on. Doug opened the car door and helped me out of the backseat. He offered me his arm and we walked down the street like a real couple.

"Sorry about that, babe. This job . . . at least that slime is going away."

"How'd you get him?"

"We've had an eye on him for months, but we finally got him on a big hand-to-hand buy with witnesses. It's a good bust."

"Do you want to go back to my place?"

"I said I was taking you to the movies."

"What are we seeing?"

"*Star Wars*. My oldest kid keeps saying how great it is."

How old was his oldest, I wondered. Older or younger than me?

As first dates go, it wasn't bad. Doug bought me popcorn, held my hand in the darkened theater, and gave me a chaste good-night kiss at my door at about 10:00 P.M.

Five hours later he showed up and buzzed my apartment with a heavy paw. He came upstairs in his usual smoking, boozy fury and proceeded to fuck me silly.

Of course, I'd already beaten him to the silly part. The new dope had been liberally sampled while my analytical mind dissected *Star Wars*.

I was attracted to Han Solo, who embodied the true anti-establishment, rebel spirit. Luke was the militaristic idealist, the kind of young fool who actually enlisted in Vietnam. The part that really irked my psyche was the Princess. I liked her strength and spunk, but it drove me crazy that she had to be rescued. How could men respect women as equals when they had to be rescued? Plus the fact that she was played by Carrie Fisher, which brought up Liz and Eddie and Debbie and it was such a *shandeh* and Mike Todd would be spinning in his grave and suddenly I was thinking about my parents instead of the movie. That's the problem with pot. It never lets you think linearly.

Usually I managed to cover up being stoned when Doug was around. When he showed up to do his King Kong/John Wayne/Superman act, I was too far gone to care. In between my usual screaming and moaning, I found myself panting, "Use the Force," and breaking into giggles.

If he noticed, he didn't say anything.

After that night, I kept looking for a way to up the social ante. I came up with the idea of inviting him to a party. It turned out to be a memorable event, but I didn't have time to dwell on it just then.

I was back in Times Square. Marti Hirsch was on the case.

The piece of paper from David's apartment was identical to the one that had cloaked my nickel bag. I wanted to know why. The most likely people to ask were the two hoods who seemed to own that part of the street.

I had a sudden vision of them being plugged into the whole city, or at least its sleazy underbelly. They could be as omniscient and powerful as Jimmy Shapiro. I could probably walk up to the guy with the long black hair and ask him who killed David Price. He might just know.

At 8:00 P.M. there was lingering sunlight and plenty of heat. The Times Square night shift hadn't completely kicked in yet.

On the corner, the redhead was nowhere in view. That was just as well. The other one was more talkative. He looked happy to see me. Maybe it was just the glazed smile of the perpetually stoned.

"Hi," I said.

"Hey."

"Remember me?"

"I dunno."

"I was in the cop car. You sold me some stuff."

"Oh yeah. You go with Dougie."

"Dougie? You call him Dougie?"

"Well, not to his face. You know, he's too old for you."

"Yeah, well you're too young for me, pal, so don't even think it."

"Don't flatter yourself, lady. And just for your information, I've had plenty of older women."

"Hey, Chuckles, the sordid and, no doubt, imaginary details of your sex life are not what I came down here for."

"You want to do some more business?"

"You could say that."

"What do you want?"

"What do you got?"

"We got weed, we got hash."

"How about information?"

"Hey, man, I don't know nothing about nothing."

"Then what do you tell Detective Kimberlin, excuse me, Dougie?"

"Oh, man, that's just a sideline, a little, you know, status quo."

"You mean quid pro quo."

"Yeah, whatever."

"I don't want you to narc on anyone. I'm just trying to find out how a friend of mine got one of your fliers."

"We give out tons of those things. Most guys just stick it in their pockets. Some guys sneak back later."

"And you wrap them around the bags."

"We don't want to be too obvious. What makes this friend of yours so special?"

"He's dead."

"So why don't you talk to your cop friend about it."

"'Cause right now, I'd rather talk to you."

I showed him a twenty-dollar bill. He shrugged as if he didn't care. I proceeded as if he had agreed to tell me everything I wanted to know.

"So this guy, my friend, he had blond hair, not too long or anything, blue eyes, kind of delicate features."

"Sounds like some kind of queer bait."

''Nah. Real nice clothes, though. Good suits. Not the kind of guy you'd usually see down here.''

''That could be a lot of guys.''

''Yeah, I guess you're right. I don't have a picture to show you. Let's see, he had an accent.''

''Like what?''

''Well he was from Chicago, and he talked like that.''

I did my best impression of that hideous vowel sound.

He got it. I could see the light breaking through those befuddled features.

''Hey, what's going on here?''

It was the other kid. He was an intimidating presence with a shaggy beard and unkempt hair. He had glowering eyes that had been inflamed by something a whole lot stronger than marijuana.

''She wants to know about Blondie. You know, Pretty Boy.''

''So what?''

''He's dead.''

''What is she, a fucking cop?''

''No, man, she's just checking it out. Right?'' he said to me, over his shoulder.

''Yeah, that's all. Just checking it out.''

''Well, fuck that shit. We don't know nothing and I wouldn't tell her if we did.''

He was breathing fire. I had the feeling that this partnership was not long for survival. My scruffy, but relatively sane, friend was still trying to help. I sensed him becoming increasingly wary.

''Come on, Gary, she's got money. She just wants to buy some info, like you-know-who.''

''You never fucking shut up, do you?''

He pulled back like he was going to punch. Instead he laughed maniacally at the flinch. Then he careened off, jabbing the air like a punch-drunk boxer and muttering to himself. I raised my eyebrows and got a shrug in return.

''You should pardon the expression, but what is his fucking problem?''

"He's messed up. He's been doing a lot of angel dust. He thinks he's Al Capone's nephew or something."

"Remind me to stick with weed. What's your name anyway?"

"It's Matt."

"O.K., Matt, before young Mr. Capone comes back on another tear, are you going to tell me about David, or am I getting out of here, taking my money with me, and going someplace that feels safe."

"Well, he didn't buy from us that much."

"But he did buy?"

"Just once or twice. He thought we were scum. You should talk to Hannah. He usually saw her."

"Is she one of the . . . uh, girls?"

"Hoowas."

I had to smile. His Bronx accent was worse than that Brooklyn monstrosity I'd once had.

"I can't believe David would need to see a prostitute. I mean he was . . ."

I stopped myself before I could say the word "perfect."

"He was buying stuff from her."

"Oh? I thought the pharmaceuticals were your department."

"We don't deal nothing heavy. It ain't worth it. If you want something hard, you gotta talk to Hannah. PCP, smack, ludes, all that stuff."

"Do you know which one David was buying?"

"Nope."

"Would Hannah talk to me?"

"I dunno. Maybe. For money. And by the way. . . ." he trailed off.

I gave him the bill that had become crumpled and sweaty in my hand.

"Matt, you've been really helpful. I know this is kind of a long shot, but could you talk to Hannah. Tell her I just need fifteen minutes and I'll pay her twenty. Does that cover her time?"

"Better make it thirty, a hooker won't even look at you for twenty."

"Fine. I'm going to the coffee shop across the street. If she's interested, she should come over there. . . . Oh, hell."

Gary was stumbling in our direction again.

"You want to fuck her, don't you. You got the hots for that slag," he yelled out.

"Slag?" I asked pointedly.

"He's messed up."

It was getting dark with finality. The streetlight's glare made him look even worse.

"Hey, Matt. Let's go down to the Village tonight and pick up some real girls."

"You should get out of here," Matt advised me in a protective manner that pushed my buttons.

"I can take care of myself."

I couldn't resist the opportunity to get indignant, no matter how scared I was.

"Look lady, just go over there. I'll try to get Hannah to come out and talk to you, O.K.?"

"Thanks. You should be careful. When he finally blows, I wouldn't want to be around."

I lost track of time at the coffee shop.

Questions were pounding at my brain like a Keith Moon drum solo.

Why was David buying drugs? Why was he consorting with hookers? Why not get drugs from his fellow musicians, if he was so inclined? Was he being blackmailed about drugs, hookers, or none of the above? Did the blackmailer kill him? Who goes down to the Village to pick up girls?

I drank a couple of ginger ales very slowly and ignored looks from the waitress. I tried not to think of Hannah refusing to talk to me. I also tried not to think about her usual business. I approved of drug dealing, but the particulars of prostitution left me a bit queasy.

As time passed I started thinking that she wasn't going

to show up. Thirty probably wasn't enough. What are hookers worth these days anyway, I wondered. More than writers? The hell with her. I'd been waiting over an hour and I was going to leave as soon as I could work up the energy. Maybe I'd have another ginger ale first.

"Are you the nosy lady?"

I looked up. She was tall with tawny skin and high cheekbones. Her hot pants looked barely legal, and the legs went on forever.

"Yeah, that's me. I wanted to talk to you."

"I know. About David. Where's the money."

I gave it to her. She sat down next to me at the counter.

"You got fifteen minutes and you better not be no cop."

"No cop. No Fed. No nothing. How long were you selling drugs to David."

"A long time. I knew him before he met her."

"Her?"

I didn't appreciate her lighting a cigarette while the meter was running.

"Jana. His girl."

"He told you about Jana?"

"They was gonna get married."

"Was he using?"

"Never around me."

"Selling?"

"Oh lord, no. You think he'd be caught doing something like that?"

She had a lilting accent; Jamaican, as far as I could tell.

"So what was he buying for?"

"He called them party favors."

"Why not buy from the other musicians?"

"That's who the favors were for."

"This is making less than no sense."

"That's your problem."

"Was he buying anything but drugs from you?" I asked suggestively.

"He could really hurt you that way."

"What?" I exclaimed, having a sudden image of David as a violent sexual beast. Yuck.

"I offered him for free once. He said he only wanted the best. That hurt, you know. All he wanted with me was the dope and the talk."

"What kind of talk?"

"Mostly gossip, like a old woman. He wanted to know who's buying, who's selling, if any body's got any kinks that I know about."

"I don't get it."

"He was always asking if I was turning any tricks with famous people."

"Were you?"

She shrugged. Thirty bucks didn't buy the answer to that one.

"So you and David never . . ."

"I bet you didn't either, girl."

"Who killed him?"

She shrugged.

"Any ideas?"

"I don't know. Maybe one of those dope fiends. Maybe someone wanted some goodies and he didn't have none. Those boys can go crazy. Your time's up."

She didn't look at any watch.

I had a sudden compulsion to go home and take a shower.

Some time early the next morning, the phone rang and woke me up. I had been dreaming about a taxi cab and I didn't want to find out where it was going or what kind of vermin awaited me there.

"Hello?"

"Hello, dear. This is Grace."

I was still out of it.

"Grace?"

"Grace McCoy."

That woke me up in a hurry. Grace McCoy was calling me.

"Hello, Grace. Yes. What is it?"

"I thought you might be interested in some news."

"Yeah."

"Well, I've been talking to some friends at the State Department and Akhmad Mohammed will be leaving the country this afternoon."

"Really?"

"Yes."

"How did you make that happen?"

"The diplomats were working on it, but they were meeting resistance from intelligence."

"Ratface, I bet."

"No one was identified as such. However, it was purported that Mr. Mohammed had been helpful in the past."

"Holy Moly. That's what was going on. They weren't planning an attack, but Akhmad was feeding some kind of information to the CIA."

"Perhaps. I made it clear that a U.S. citizen would be willing to make the connection public. It seemed to expedite the procedure."

There was a rich note of self-amusement in her voice. It must be fun to be that powerful, I thought.

"Are they deporting the slimy, wog bastard?"

"Now, now, dear. A suitable face-saving arrangement has been worked out."

"You didn't use Jana's name, did you?"

"Of course not. You must give me credit for a modicum of discretion."

"That's good. She would freak out. She never even told her father she was shacking up with David, and she certainly wouldn't want him to find out about Akhmad. So now she can come home instead of hiding out with her folks."

"If you speak to her before I do, please let her know. I'd like to arrange some publicity for the show. There might be a book."

"Do you think she should be doing that so soon after . . ."

Maybe I was overstepping my bounds, but Grace was treating me like an intimate, so I acted like one.

"I think it will be just the thing."

I could hear the savvy businesswoman contemplating the publicity possibilities. She was the backer of Jana's show, after all.

"Grace, can I ask you something?"

"I thought you had asked all your questions. I have a board meeting today."

Not so intimate anymore.

"Well, it's just one thing. It came up last night after we left you. I think someone might have been blackmailing David."

"What?" She sounded genuinely shocked.

"Blackmail."

"Well, he never mentioned anything to me. What could anyone have to blackmail David with?"

"I'm not sure, but I'm going to find out."

"Well, do be careful, dear."

She hung up, leaving me with the impression that she was more disturbed by the idea of David being blackmailed than by the reality of his being shot to death.

Let's think about this a minute. If David was being blackmailed and the blackmailer killed him and someone in Queens was using their clout to get it hushed up, then maybe . . .

I found myself staring into a mental chasm as empty as my refrigerator and stomach.

Time to go shopping. Time to get some information. Not at the same place. Asking the checkout clerk at the A&P who killed David Price would be silly. On the other hand, I felt like I had asked everyone else in town.

Detectives in books always have plenty of sources. Cops, snitches, reporters. I'd tried Doug. I'd talked to Matt and Gary. I'd even paid Hannah thirty bucks. I didn't know any reporters, unless you counted the few columnists who were still working that Dad had once fed items to.

I didn't know any real reporters, but I did know Les

Hutchins. Back in Berkeley he turned out pamphlets for the Black Panthers and wore his beret perched precariously atop a Billy Preston-sized afro. Even then, however, he always seemed to be more interested in hanging out at the University Theater, watching old movies. In 1978 he sported a sleeker head of hair and did political organizing in Harlem. He also wrote inflammatory movie reviews for the *Amsterdam News*. Sometimes he got me into revival houses on his press pass.

One of the reasons I survived election night '72 (the year we didn't have that McGovern victory party) was that Les showed up at my dorm and got me involved in a lengthy discussion of the merits of Dick Powell as Philip Marlowe as opposed to Humphrey Bogart. It was the most irrelevant conversation imaginable, but it kept me from acting on the nearly suicidal despair I felt that night.

Maybe Les knew something about Queens. Maybe he knew somebody who knew something. Maybe I just wanted to talk to someone who had nothing to do with David Price. Luckily I had Les's direct line at the *Amsterdam News*.

"Hey, Les, it's Marti Hirsch. How ya doing?"

"Yo, babe. Long time, no see."

I had to smile. Les's "babe" was so different from Doug's verbal leer as to be a whole different language.

"Been to any good protests lately?"

"That ain't the way no more, Marti. Why don't you come here and help me get this dude into the state senate?"

"No way. I'm too old, I'm too tired, and I never want to feel that pain again."

"What you got to be so cynical about? We got a decent fellow in Washington."

"For how long, Les?"

"Look, if you just gonna waste my time with a downer attitude, I'm gonna hang up this phone and get some work done."

"No, don't. I need some information."

"About what?"

"Queens."

"You mean the ones in the Village or that place that's almost Brooklyn?"

"The latter. Who's got real push there? Who could make something happen or not happen?"

"Why are you asking?"

"Just research for something I'm writing."

"Bullshit. Try again."

"It's a long story."

"I got time."

"It's not about politics."

"Everything's about politics."

"Les, I just need to know."

"I know who you're talking about. I just want to know why you're asking."

"I'm trying to find out who shot a piano player named David Price."

"Ask the cops."

"The cops are writing it off as a B-and-E, when all the evidence appears to the contrary. From what I've gleaned thus far, the word not to pursue the investigation came from Queens."

"That's some heavy shit."

"Tell me about it. So who's the main man?"

"This don't sound like the kind of thing Superman would be messed up in."

"Superman? Like Clark Kent?"

"Assistant D.A. Kenneth Cooperman. That man has been cleaning up Queens like a white tornado. He won't cut no slack for nobody. That's why they call him Superman. People are saying he's got a big future. Mayor, governor, who knows?"

Why did that name sound familiar?

"Wait a minute. Is he the one who's cool about dope?"

"That's the one."

A few months before, I'd been watching "Firing Line." Buckley was inveighing against lawless youth or some such malarkey, and this tweedy type had sat there, puffing a pipe with a barely concealed smirk. He'd then stated unequivocally that he saw no point in wasting taxpayer money in the harassment and prosecution of recreational drug users if there was no other criminal activity involved. Buckley appeared to be on the verge of an apoplexy. I thought that if that guy ever ran for anything, he'd definitely get my vote.

I tried to remember the face, but all I could really see was the pipe and the grin. Dark hair. Kenneth Cooperman, Queens Assistant D.A. Kenny, last name unknown, father of Lorraine. Coincidence?

"You still there, girl?"

"Still here."

"I don't think Superman's the one you're looking for. The guy is clean."

"What's his story?"

"I don't know too much. He worked for Allard Lowenstein and for Bobby Kennedy before that."

"Doing what?"

"Campaign organizing, I think."

"Do you know which state?"

"Not off the top of my head. Queens really ain't something I think about too much, but I hear good stuff about this guy. His rep is tough, but fair."

"I appreciate what you're saying, Les, but right now I'm walking on so many red herrings, my feet are starting to smell. This is the only lead I've got and I'm going to follow it."

"Who do you think you are anyway, Christie Love?"

"I should look that good."

"Why don't you and me go to the Regency this afternoon and check out the MGM Musical Summer series. They've got *Show Boat* today."

"You're not going to write one of those '*Show Boat* is racist' diatribes, are you?"

"Course I am, but mostly I want to see Ava Gardner."

"There's no way I can sit through *Show Boat*. I'd be a mess at the end. Remember what happened at *Camille*?"

"You still got that waterworks problem?"

"Yeah."

"What does your shrink say?"

"Either I'm getting better or you'll be visiting me in the loony bin."

"Or the morgue."

"That's a nice thing to say."

"You might be messing with some bad dudes. You don't know what you're getting into."

"I'm going to find out. And, Les, if any of this comes out in that rag you write for, you will rue the day."

"You're gonna have to work on that tough-guy thing a little harder, if you're planning to intimidate anyone older than four."

"Bye, Les."

My mind was racing. If Kenneth Cooperman had been organizing in 1968, he might just have been doing so in Chicago, either in preparation for the convention or the campaign that everyone thought there was going to be after the convention. That might have put him in Chicago at an optimal time to become acquainted with Carmen and eventually father her child.

It was a flimsy, circumstantial case. The more I believed it, the more I thought I was crazy for doing so. There was only one way to find out.

I was going to Queens.

14

Thursday was hot with a touch of humidity in the air. The train felt close and musty. It was one of the old ones, with seats in rows, covered with ribbed plastic that was held together by large strips of fraying tape. Starched suits were wilting all around me. I was cool in cotton but feeling uncomfortable.

Something was wrong. Something didn't fit. I was on the right track, but I didn't know where the train was going. I tried to push the feeling away or at least distance myself from it. I told myself to remember the feeling for when I wrote the book. It was only a feeling. I was in complete control of the situation.

Except I wasn't. Assistant District Attorney Cooperman wasn't waiting for me in his office. I hadn't called to make an appointment naturally, but I was still miffed. His secretary said he was in court and did I want to leave a message. I did not. I wanted to see this guy and no wheels of justice were going to stop me.

I hadn't been in a courtroom since my last arraignment for disorderly conduct. The Queens County Courthouse was newer than the one in Berkeley, but the air of desperation was identical. No one was happy to be there, except for the court groupies who projected a sad insanity of their own.

The ones in the back row of room 201 were especially avid as they watched Kenneth Cooperman make mincemeat of a defense attorney and the psychiatrist he had put on the stand to bolster an insanity plea.

I'd half expected to find him wearing a red cap and blue tights, but this Superman did his crime fighting in brown tweed and worked the courtroom with the lope of a western gunslinger. I spent the rest of the morning watching him elegantly demolish every witness the defense came up with. It was quite a show. When the judge called a recess for lunch, I nearly booed.

Cooperman was surrounded as he left the courtroom. I attached myself to the fringes of his group. I wouldn't be dislodged, even when I had to be extremely rude and elbow my way into the elevator. That got his attention.

I grinned at him. He smiled back with a puzzled look, revealing a small gap between his two front teeth.

"I have to talk to you," I called out.

He nodded absently, but continued talking to the woman next to him who carried a clipboard and wore a bun in her hair that was probably wrapped as tight as her ass.

The elevator stopped in front of a cafeteria that wasn't even as charming as your average high-school lunchroom. Miss Bun was replaced by suits and some tinsel-toothed gopher who brought the assistant D.A. his lunch on a tray.

Most of the crowd had dispersed to various Formica outposts. I planted myself across the table from him and tried to catch his eyes with a gaze that would let Kenneth Cooperman know that he had to deal with me.

The approach didn't work. A bowl of Jell-O interested him more than I did. I found myself shifting uncomfortably and finally walked away. I was embarrassed and frustrated. I grabbed a napkin from the tarnished metal dispenser on an adjacent table. I wrote the words "David Price" on it and marched back to his table. My platforms clicked aggressively. To make sure I got his attention, I cleared my throat loudly.

He looked up and I thrust the napkin into his hand. He took it and gave me another look of bewilderment. I kept my eyes on him. I wanted to gauge any reactions as he read it. There wasn't much. He didn't faint or break out in a sweat. He just cocked his head in a way that reminded me of the RCA dog. He did say something to his minions that made them disburse, but even that was done casually.

You are one cool customer, Kenneth Cooperman, I thought to myself. My stomach churned in fear that I was wrong. If I were mistaken, I was about to have a giant omelette on my face.

He took a pipe out of his jacket pocket and went through the whole lighting procedure. The movements were unhurried. He made an almost offhand gesture with the pipe stem, telling me to sit down. Face-to-face, I could see the tension in his jaw. He'd break his pipe if he kept biting on it like that. I'd gotten to him.

I tried to steady my own nerves. Come on, Marti, this is important. Don't blow it. Too bad I don't have a hidden tape recorder. I've got to remember everything he says. Wait a minute, he just said something.

"What did you say?"

"You're very bold, aren't you?"

"Why shouldn't I be?"

"This is a public place."

"I'm not hiding anything."

"Everyone's hiding something, Miss . . . ?"

"Hirsch, Ms. Marti Hirsch."

He wasn't relaxed anymore. He knew who I was. Carmen must have told him about my attempt at the third degree. She'd been coy about his last name, but there I was anyway. I must have been his worst nightmare come true.

"I know about David and Lorraine and Carmen and the Parlocha family. The only thing you're hiding from me is where you come from. I can't place your accent."

"Where I'm from? I'm from nowhere."

"Like what? Iowa?"

"Worse. Upstate."

There was a self-deprecating charm about him. Carmen had said that he made her laugh.

"So what brought you to Chicago?"

"Bobby."

Hearing that name gave me both a moment of pain and frisson of victory.

"Nice Jewish Boy meets married Mafia tootsie. It makes perfect sense."

Poor Kenny. He was in his early forties, his career was heading for the heights, and I had his reputation in the palm of my hand and was being a bitch to boot. He seemed like a nice guy and wasn't bad-looking, in a way that was both rugged and intellectual.

"One night I went to this bar with some campaign workers. A bunch of the girls were nuts for the piano player. I thought I was talking to one of ours when I said that I didn't think the guy was so hot. Then I heard this woman say that the guy was her husband. I turned around to apologize, but when I saw her, I couldn't think of anything to say. Then she said that she didn't think he was so hot either. That was how I met Carmen. I have to get back to court. I don't know why I even told you that. Who are you working for?"

"What did Carmen tell you?"

"Not enough, obviously."

"I'm less than nobody. I'm on psychiatric disability. If I even try to tell anybody, you can tell them I'm crazy."

"That's very comforting."

He was getting up. I wasn't done yet.

"Who killed David?"

"I don't know."

For no good reason, I believed him. I had to scoot to keep up as he walked away.

"Then why the cover-up?"

There was a pause and an impatient foot tapping while he waited for the elevator. Then he said in a deeply felt whisper, "I want to protect my kid."

"What about the blackmail?"

He turned and stared at me in genuine shock. The returning lunch crowd pushed us into the elevator.

"What are you talking about?"

"You want me to say it right here?"

The charm had been replaced by clammy desperation.

"Go ahead."

"Someone was blackmailing David Price and I think it was the same person who killed him. Right now all roads seem to be leading to Queens, Mr. Assistant District Attorney."

I said it in a conversational tone of voice. I counted a total of eight in the elevator. I could only hope that was enough potential witnesses to dissuade Superman from trying to throttle me.

From the look on his face I wasn't so sure. It was a mixture of anguish, outrage, and who-knew-what-else.

"You think I was blackmailing David fucking Price?"

That got everyone's attention. The secretaries stared with big mascaraed eyes.

I nodded my head in the affirmative.

Kenny threw his head backward and looked up at the ceiling. Maybe he was going to try and escape up the elevator shaft. Maybe he was going to pass out. Then I realized he was laughing. A deep chuckle with just a touch of hysteria. He managed to compose himself enough to look right at me and snap, "You're a fool, Ms. Hirsch, and you don't know anything," before striding out of the elevator.

I was left behind in the empty elevator feeling poleaxed. I rode up and down three times, trying to make sense out of what had happened. I felt disoriented, as if I were riding the Cyclone at Coney Island. I stumbled back to court to watch the day's victor in action again.

Something was wrong. He was still making all the right moves but the rhythm was off. The magic was gone. It was a disheartening sight. I left the courthouse and made a beeline for a local park. I needed to see some dogs.

I found myself in a playground full of children. So low was my affection for young ones that I managed to go through two colleges, three continents, and months of celibacy without missing a birth-control pill.

The presence of screaming moppets added to the feeling

of oppressive humidity. Sweat was dotting the front of my dress in random patterns. The only salvation was the clarion call of the Mister Softee truck. A large chocolate-and-vanilla twist. Sweet bliss.

O.K. Marti, concentrate. I kept coming back to the moment when my house of cards collapsed. "You think I was blackmailing David fucking Price?" My first thought was, If you weren't blackmailing him, then who the hell was? The more I thought about it, the more I kept hearing the emphasis: "You think *I* was blackmailing David fucking Price?" He wasn't stressing blackmail with any degree of shock. He just couldn't believe that I thought he was the blackmailer because . . .

And Grace had sounded equally shocked when I indicated that David was being blackmailed.

For a second I thought I was going to throw up the ice cream. My hand started shaking so badly that I dropped the rest of the cone to the ground. It landed on the grass to become a feast for ants. They'd have to be fast. The ice cream immediately started to dissolve in a deluge that I thought was my tears, but turned out to be a shower of painfully heavy raindrops.

The kids scattered. I was left alone to cry in the rain. I finally had a good reason. David Price, the most gorgeous man I had ever laid eyes on, who I would have done or given anything for, if he had only bothered to ask, was a blackmailer.

He was blackmailing Kenny about Lorraine. He was blackmailing the recipients of his party favors. He was blackmailing anyone whose guilty little secrets he could pick up from Hannah. For all I knew he was blackmailing Akhmad, Grace, and the entire Chicago Mob. People from coast to coast and all around the world had reasons to knock him off.

It was the most awful thing I could imagine. It made me think that his piano playing wasn't so good after all. It made me want to die, and I wasn't even being blackmailed.

What if I were being blackmailed? What if I thought it

was finally over and then some smart-ass broad got in my face, announced that she was nuts and that she thought I was the blackmailer? The fact that she's crazy and wrong doesn't mean she won't eventually figure it out or that somebody else won't. Whoever else does might turn out to be sane and mercenary.

I had to tell Kenny that I wasn't like that. I didn't care that he was Lorraine's father or Carmen's lover. I didn't even care if he killed David. The money-grubbing bastard had it coming. I had to tell him that.

I sloshed back to the courthouse. Then I stood in the downpour, soaked, staring numbly at the ugly chains that held the doors closed. I heard sirens, police sirens, maybe a block away. The office building. My stomach took another flip-flop. I felt a chill colder than the rain. Come on, legs. I couldn't make them speed up. It was like being the Six Million Dollar man, running in slow motion. The rain spattered my glasses. My shoes bogged down in the mud.

By the time I got there the police cordon was up, but almost unnecessary. The rain was awful and it was Queens, after all. It took a pretty persistent gawker to be out for the sight of an ambulance and a few police cars parked in a haphazard fashion along the street.

I ducked under the police barricade. No one stopped me. I peered into the back of the ambulance. Empty. I saw the secretary from Cooperman's office with a uniformed cop who was trying to write down her hysterical babble.

"What the hell is going on around here?" I screamed, only to be drowned out by the wind and the rain.

The cop and the secretary were forced to come out into the rain to make way for the boys in white with the stretcher. They didn't seem to be moving terribly fast. There was no sense of urgency. The cop followed the stretcher to the ambulance and exchanged a look with the EMTs.

I took off my glasses just as the cop lifted the sheet. Even with my crummy eyesight, it was a gruesome spectacle. The assistant D.A. wouldn't be making Carmen Price laugh anymore. Kenneth Cooperman had put a gun to one side of his head and blown his brains out.

This was bad. This was the fuckup to end all fuckups.

I felt painful humiliation burning through me with the added edge of some barely remembered wound being reopened. One of the cops finally noticed me.

"Hey, you don't belong here."

Another brilliant conclusion from our law-enforcement personnel, I thought, running away from the scene like a bat out of hell, albeit one laden with water and guilt. A nice guy had been driven over the edge and the steering wheel was covered with my prints.

At least Catholics had confession. All I had was a need to unburden myself and no one to listen. I couldn't tell Karl. That would be like telling dad you'd crashed the family car. Doug would be worse. That would be like telling Dad you were knocked up. I would have called Jana, if I had any idea where to reach her. I felt completely alone.

I was starting to shiver. There had to be someone I could talk to. I thought of Jerry. He seemed to be a good listener. What the hell. I was practically in Brooklyn anyway.

It took another three blocks to find a pay phone. I remembered the phone number. Now, if I could just manage a coherent sentence.

"Hello?"

I couldn't control the words and I was still half crying.

"Jerry, oh my god, it's awful."

"What? Who is this?"

"It's Marti, he killed himself."

"Marti, please try and calm down. Are you O.K.?"

"How can I be O.K. when the poor yutz killed himself on my account?" I screamed.

"Right, but are you O.K.?"

Maybe he used the same technique to calm down hysterical eight-year-olds.

"More or less," I sniffed. His voice had a soothing effect on me, traces of Brooklyn and all.

"Where are you?"

"I'm in Queens."

"Why?"

"Don't ask."

"Should I come get you?"

"No, you don't have to do that, but could I come over for a while?"

He told me the address.

"That's your mom's house, isn't it?"

"I've taken the plastic off the couch."

"Put it back on, I'm soaked."

"I've got towels. Come on over, before you catch cold."

He was just like a Jewish mother, only this one was male and a great dancer. Maybe that was just what I needed.

15

I sat in the back of a cab, feeling wet and miserable. Would the death of an assistant D.A. make the news? I didn't have the nerve to ask the surly-looking driver to turn on the radio. I wound up overtipping him to compensate for the big wet spot I left on the seat.

Williamsburg didn't seem so bad. It felt safer than Queens. It felt like home. Jerry lived in a one-story house, in the nicer section.

He met me at the door with a big, fluffy towel and a small yapping Dachshund. I instantly fell in love (with the dog, not with Jerry). While Jerry tried to dry my hair with the towel, I crouched down to make squeegee noises at the brick-colored cutie. I was already an accessory to suicide. How many more years could they tack on for dog-napping?

"What happened?" Jerry asked.

"What's the dog's name. Oh, he's so cute."

The dog went running into the house and I followed.

"It's a she. Her name is Strudel. What did you mean when you said 'He killed himself'?"

"Why Strudel?"

"I got her from the German baker down the street. Marti, you are going to get pneumonia if you don't get into something dry. Debbie left some clothes in the closet. It's in that room over there."

I hesitated, not wanting to be away from the dog for a

second. I needed the distraction or I would fall apart from the weight of guilt and shame.

"O.K.," I said reluctantly. I really was starting to sniffle. Great detectives have no time for head colds. I walked slowly, trying to case the apartment. Mrs. Barlow was in Florida and the plastic slipcovers were gone, but the place still had a time-warp ambiance of Fifties warmth.

The bedroom told me little, except that Jerry watched TV in bed. I had a feeling he wasn't doing much else there but sleeping. I peeled the soaked dress from my body and looked in the closet. A blue cotton shirtdress caught my eye. My memory of Debbie was blurred with jealousy. From putting on her dress, I could tell she was both taller and more *zaftig* than I was. The dress fit me like a tent, coming down past my knees. I liked it. It would cover the fact that my bra and panties were a loss for a while.

I found my way to the bathroom and left my clothes draped over the shower-curtain rod so they could drip into the tub. I sat down on the toilet. I had to pee so badly, it was as if I'd absorbed some of the rain through my skin. It was the kind of urinary experience after which one can only say, "For this relief, much thanks."

I caught a glimmer of a smile on my face in the bathroom mirror. The medicine chest was heavy on Band-Aids, cotton, and shaving stuff, low on anything else, except on the top shelf, where there was a small prescription medicine bottle for Deborah Barlow, with quite a few pills left. Valium according to the label. I pocketed the bottle.

When I came back out, Jerry got this sort of weird, rueful look on his face. At first I thought he was reacting to the fact that my hair was drying in an ungodly mess. Then I decided it was the dress. I was going to tell him that if he couldn't stand the sight of his ex-wife's garments, he should have gotten rid of them after she split.

That would have been too obnoxious to say to someone who was waiting for me with a cup of tea and an afghan that I could imagine Mrs. Barlow crocheting back in 1949.

Jerry waited until I was curled up on the couch, under the afghan, with Strudel on my lap.

"Now, will you please tell me what happened?"

He listened, just as I had hoped he would, even to the parts he already knew. When I got to Kenny Cooperman, I started crying again. Jerry put his arms around me, without any hesitation or awkwardness, and held me to his chest while I told him how badly I had fucked up, and what an idiot I was, and what the hell was I going to do now?

It was the second time in one week that I'd sobbed all over him, but his arms were so comforting and his white flannel shirt was so soft that I pushed the thought aside. Maybe this was the friend I should have had for all those years, instead of putting my faith in a narcissistic bitch like Jana Crowley.

The crying stopped. My jaws felt exhausted from the strain. All of me felt exhausted. Jerry made room on the couch so that I could stretch my legs out. Strudel hopped down off the couch and went into the kitchen. I was still talking.

"If Jana did know that David was a blackmailer, how could she stay with him?"

Jerry didn't have an answer. All he could do was keep listening and looking at me intensely. I felt so tired. If I just let go, I knew I would drift away. I was dimly aware of Jerry taking one of my feet in his hands and starting to knead the bottom of it. That was a pretty intimate gesture for someone I barely knew. I would have said something about it, if it hadn't felt so good, and if I hadn't fallen asleep first.

The rats, the roaches, and the bees were all chasing me down the tunnel. I knew they were gaining on me, but I couldn't stop to see how closely. There were stairs in front of me. I tried to run toward them, but I was stopped by a blast of heat that could have come from the hottest corner of hell. I couldn't move and they were coming. It was all over. I couldn't fight anymore. I sat down on the bottom stair and prepared myself for verminous destruction. I felt the first bite, but I couldn't tell if it was a rat, a roach, or a bee. I looked down to check and saw a raindrop land on a rat's head. Suddenly the stairway was flooded and the vicious little critters were running in the opposite direction. I sat in the rain, in danger of drowning like a turkey, with my face turned up to an unseen sky.

I woke up soaked in sweat. Nothing had changed. I was still lying on the couch. Jerry was still at the end of the couch. Strudel was sitting at his feet. Everything was the same, but something seemed different.

Jerry's white shirt and pants looked looser. Had the cuffs and the top button been open before? I couldn't remember. He wasn't as sweaty as I was, but there were beads on his upper lip. Maybe my vision was just blurry. I had left my glasses in the bathroom. He had to clear his throat to get his voice to work, and I even got the impression that he was out of breath.

"Are you hungry? I could make some soup. It's just Lipton's, but . . ." he trailed off awkwardly.

"Why are you being so nice to me?"

I meant it as a throwaway line to thank him. He considered it seriously. Whatever was going through his head bothered him. I sat up and moved closer.

"Hey, Jerry what is it? You've been wonderful, don't get all moody on me now. I'm feeling better, really. I can go, if you want."

"No. Don't. Please."

"So what's with you all of a sudden?"

"Do you remember *Lolita*?"

"Of course I do. 'Lolita, light of my life, fire of my loins. My sin, my soul.' " I recited mechanically. "It's my favorite book in the world."

"I mean your speech. Your book report. Senior English."

"Oh my god."

The burning, slippery feeling of public humiliation

spread over me as though I were being covered with gasoline.

Senior English. Late in the spring of 1968. A few weeks before the fateful dance. Mr. Katz innocently assigned a book report. I was in the terminal stages of my Brian obsession. I already knew *Lolita* backwards and forwards, so it was a coast. The fact that the book was still considered risqué was a plus.

I loved the book for its wit, its eroticism, and of course, the word play. Most of all, I identified with passionate, obsessed, rejected Humbert Humbert. (Another literary point of contention with Stephanie.)

The theme of my book report was that if someone loves you as much as Humbert loved Dolores, then you have an obligation to try and love them back. It might have been immature thinking, but I wanted Brian to love me so badly, it hurt.

I poured all my hurt and rejection on dear little Lolita. I blithely ignored the fact that they did sleep together continuously. My point was the unrequited love. It was a great paper. Unfortunately Mr. Katz was the only sentient being within the confines of Williamsburg High who didn't know that I was crazy about Brian. He was impressed with my writing. He was so impressed that he asked me to read it in front of the class. What was I going to do, say no?

I stood up there, shaking like a leaf, reading my manifesto. They stared at me. What were they feeling? Disgust? Horror? Shock? By the time I finished, I knew that I would never forget those faces.

Except I had. I had never mentioned the scene to Karl. I had completely forgotten the whole thing.

"Jesus on roller skates." I stood up. I was dizzy for a moment, but I felt a sudden need to pace. "Jerry, it's that post-traumatic stress stuff. I couldn't teach that class at Berkeley because of Senior English. My son-of-a-bitch shrink was right. I don't believe this. Do you believe this, Jerry?" No answer. "Jerry?"

He had picked the dog up into his lap and was petting

its back, very deliberately, but he was looking at me.

"That was the class we were in together, right?"

He nodded.

"Where you used to snoop at my writing?"

Another nod.

"Did you tell Brian about the speech?"

"No, but somebody else did."

"Of course. When that class was over, I knew there was no hope. It was the end of the ride, but I couldn't get out of the car."

He shook his head slowly. His voice was that of a man being forced to say something he had vowed never to say. It actually hurt him.

"There was never any hope. He didn't like your looks. He didn't like your attitude. He didn't like you, Marti."

"Gee, thanks." I tried to make it sound glib, but the pain was still there. I distracted myself by going over to Jerry's record player to check out what he'd been listening to lately. "Love Songs" by Neil Diamond was on the turntable. A Janis Ian record was in the first slot of the record rack. I wanted to tell him that he'd never get better listening to that stuff. He beat me to the next line.

"Do you still feel that way?"

"About Brian?"

"About *Lolita*?"

"It's still my favorite book."

"I don't mean that."

"Well, what do you . . . oh. . . . Oh!"

I turned around slowly.

"Are you saying what I think you're saying?"

"I don't know. When you gave that speech, I knew you were talking about Brian. It was the first time I ever really looked at you or thought about you. Before that I just thought you were crazy and you were hounding my friend. That day, though, I mean, you were wearing a blue dress and I thought you were brave and passionate and I liked your eyes and your hair and just the way that dress looked on you. By the time you were done, I had to use my loose-leaf to cover up my hard-on on the way out of class."

"How come you never told me?"

The Jerry of the past few days was a mask. The real man was in the knowing smile and sad eyes that I was now looking into.

"Come on, Marti. What would you have done if I had?"

"I would have used you to try and get close to Brian."

"That's what I thought."

"Well, it's nice to know that I was wanted back then, even if it was just once. I just hope you don't expect me to believe you've been carrying a torch for me through ten years and two marriages."

"I wanted to talk to you, but you didn't come to graduation. Things happened after that. I'm not the big romantic obsession type."

"Then what would you call Debbie?"

"My ex-wife."

"You were married to her before Lady of Spain, right?"

"Nicaragua, but yes."

"I don't see any clothes here from the second one."

"She didn't live here long enough to unpack."

"Easy come, easy go."

"Yeah. I'd forgotten about you, but when you walked into that room on Monday, it all came back. Mostly I felt bad that I didn't tell you."

"Now you've told me. Maybe I should leave."

"Not until you tell me if you still feel the same way."

He stood up. Light five o'clock shadow was visible on his face. I didn't want to find him attractive. He was sweet and vulnerable and I thought of myself as hard and crazy. I spoke slowly.

"If somebody loved me as much as Humbert Humbert loved Dolores Haze, and there's no way you can tell me you want me that much . . ."

"What if I did?"

"I'd have to try." He stood about a foot away, just looking at me. Had anyone ever looked at me quite so tenderly? Not that I could remember, but my memory was an unreliable source, it turned out. After a few minutes of silence, I felt myself on the verge of a smart-ass remark just to break the tension.

"Jerry . . ." I said, trying to say that we should let this thing slide before serious embarrassment set in.

Either I failed to communicate this message or he didn't pay attention. Instead he took my left hand and kissed my palm. I offered no resistance when he placed the hand on his chest. I could feel his heart beat.

I closed my eyes, thinking I'd play along for one kiss to avoid hurting his feelings, since he was such a nice guy. Then I was overwhelmed by the strength of his arms and the softness of his lips and the sudden feeling that I never wanted to be outside those arms again.

I found myself kissing back, exploring his mouth and wondering how long I could go without coming up for air. Speaking of coming up. No loose-leaf to hide behind. I heard a muffled moan and realized it was me.

I opened my eyes. My hands were in his hair, teasing the back of his neck. His hands were positioned firmly around my butt and I wasn't wearing anything under that dress. This had to stop immediately. Dry humping in the living room, for pete's sake. I was working on a gentle maneuver to push him away when he pushed me away first. That got my goat.

"Hey, what's wrong?"

"This isn't a good idea."

"Nice time to figure that out."

"I'm sorry. I told you the other day. I feel like the next girl I care about is going to get hurt, and you've been hurt enough."

"You just got me pretty hot, Jerry, and I know you were there too. If you are planning to talk your way out of this, you're going to need a better line than that."

I took a step toward him and pushed at his stomach. He did a long-legged stumble backward and ended up on the couch. I stood looking at him with my hands on my hips.

I was having a real bitch of a day, and I wasn't about to take rejection on top of it.

I kneeled across his lap, straddling him. He still wanted me and I was going to make him admit it. I started nuzzling his neck.

"Marti." I had to admire the willpower involved in forming words. "I'm still married to Anita. The divorce hasn't been finalized."

"The cop I'm seeing is married."

I went for an earlobe. I'd break him, if it killed me.

"Well, can't we go out for a drink first?"

"I told you I don't drink. Even since that spiked-punch fiasco."

"The punch wasn't spiked," he said so simply that I stopped the attack.

"Of course the punch was spiked. That's why I got sick and missed my last chance to talk to Brian."

Just remembering that awful night put a manic note in my voice. Jerry removed me from his lap. We sat side by side on the couch, with him holding on to both of my hands.

"You want the truth? If I make love to you, I have to tell you the truth."

"Well, that's a novel approach."

"It's not funny. You want to solve a murder, but you can't even be honest with yourself. Before Debbie left, I went to the therapist with her a few times. I learned how to tell the truth, even if it's the most painful thing in the world. Do you think you're tough enough to do that?"

"Of course I am."

"There was no spiked punch. You did talk to Brian. *He* talked anyway. He even danced with you."

"NO, NO, NO, NO!!!!!!" I screamed. And there I was crying again. If the gasoline had been lit and ten years of scar tissue were being torn off my body, it couldn't have been more painful.

"Debbie had already said she wouldn't marry him. He wanted to hurt somebody."

Jerry's voice was far away. What I heard up close was the music. "Nights in White Satin." Brian looked perfect in his tuxedo. I was working up the nerve to just say hello and hoping that something meaningful would follow, when he came purposefully toward me.

He asked me to dance. Yes, ladies and gentlemen, I thought at the time, look you bastards, Brian Bronstein is dancing with me. He even held me close. For a moment I felt graceful in my high heels. Then he said . . .

"Do you know what he said to me?" I asked Jerry accusingly.

"He told me."

I started screaming wordlessly.

Strudel sensibly ran into the bedroom. Jerry just kept holding my hands. No matter how long or loudly I yelled, nothing could drown out Brian whispering in my ear, "You know the best thing about graduating? I'm never going to see you again."

As the words registered, I felt pain coursing through every inch of my body, the palsied shaking, and the sure knowledge that I was going to throw up.

He had the nerve to bow before he walked away.

I relived each moment in all of its deadly awfulness. The staggering to the bathroom, and the heavy-duty vomiting as my body tried to expel the awfulness of what had just happened. The overwhelming sense of humiliation. The realization of just how much of a fool I'd been making out of myself for so long. The sure knowledge that the whole class was out there laughing at me.

It was the most horrible thing that had ever happened to me. Ten years later the pain drove me to my knees. I thought I might wind up soaking Jerry's carpet. It was the crying jag to end all crying jags. Jerry kneeled beside me, gently rubbing my back, but this time I didn't think that I'd ever be able to stop.

Of course the punch wasn't spiked. I was vaguely disappointed in my imagination. It was one thing to repress memories, but the cover story was so weak. Spiked punch?

I could have written something better than that.

Even that provoked more tears.

It felt like hours.

Finally it stopped. I felt completely drained and defeated. I had nothing left. No pride, no voice, no tears, no nothing.

"I'm sorry."

It was odd to hear Jerry's voice when I'd been listening to my own wailing for so long.

"You weren't the one who did it," I whispered.

"I should have stopped him. Or I should have been nicer to you then."

"You did what you could."

"I want to make it up to you now."

He put out a hand to help me up off the floor. He was such a nice guy.

"Jerry, this particular bout of honesty may be the answer to my crying jags, but it's not a big libido boost."

"I wasn't even thinking that."

"Whatever you say, Jerry. I really do have to go now."

"Why?"

"Because this is too heavy, man. I can't handle this. Too heavy."

"Don't start talking like a hippie just because you've had your denial broken."

"Don't regurgitate your failed therapy because you can't get what you want. I'll get through this, I think, but it'll be a whole lot easier with some drugs."

"Are you on pills?"

"Don't be silly."

"Weed?"

"No, sweetie, you're talking about a misdemeanor and I'm talking about a felony."

I got my bag from the kitchen and my shoes from the bedroom. Everything was still soggy. I knew I was going to keep Debbie's dress, so I figured I'd leave my underwear as a memento for Jerry. Maybe he could jack off over them later. Unless of course he'd already . . .

"Jerry," I said, "were you, uh . . ." None of the standard euphemisms were especially helpful. "Were you playing with yourself before I woke up?"

He gave me the most outraged, disbelieving look. Either he was offended that I would even think of such a thing or he was shocked that I had caught him.

"What about that murder? Do you think Ken Cooperman shot him?"

It hurt to think about it, but I really didn't believe that Kenny had done it. Which meant I had to keep looking for the real murderer and I felt weary, so weary.

"Right now I'm not sure I care anymore."

"You care. You have to care about something. Do you think it could be me?"

"I really like you, Jerry. You've gone above and beyond for me this week. You're a great dancer and between you, me, and the walls, it's like the Weavers once said, You've got kisses sweeter than wine. Put it all together and it might spell happily ever after. On the other hand, it might just be guilt mixed with nostalgia and rain gets in your eyes. You need to think about that. Then maybe we'll talk."

"You almost ran out of breath again."

"No breath, no voice, what's the difference. Say goodbye to Strudel for me. Tell her I'm sorry I yelled."

"I will. I feel like I should stop you."

"You can't."

"Can I kiss you good night?"

"If you kiss me again, I might never leave."

16

Remember that party I mentioned before?

It took place about a month before David died. It was at the Junebug, the same singles bar where I first saw him. I was never too clear on the purpose of the party. There were a lot of people associated with the gallery and some of the crowd from Studio 54.

Jana just called me up one day and said it was time for a party, so she was having one. She told me I could invite anyone I wanted. Since the movie date, I had been looking for a way to up the ante on a certain policeman. He wanted to flaunt me in front of his buddies? Two could play that game.

I mentioned the party to Doug and asked if he'd like to go. I assumed he would say no. He said he'd try to stop by. I assumed he wouldn't. He did.

I was part of the crowd around the piano listening to David when I saw Doug come in. Jana was standing next to me.

"That's him isn't it? He really does have big teeth."

"Well, what do you think?"

"Not bad. Very physical."

"Not as good as yours, though."

I was surprised that Doug showed up. I was flabbergasted that he appeared to have a good time. He hung around the piano with me. David was taking requests. Doug wanted to hear the Notre Dame fight song. He sang it loudly with one hand around a beer glass and the other around my shoulder.

He shook hands with Ricky Grant and didn't appear the least bit phased by Ricky's usual flouncing. I, on the other hand, was tightfisted with apprehension over making that introduction. Even worse was the moment when I had to say, "Doug, this is Jana Crowley," and wait to see if he fell for her.

He wasn't much, but he was all I had to peg my ego on. His eyes made the tour, but no special light went on in his eyes. If he had a yen for her, he hid it very well.

"So what did you think of her?" I asked him at the door.

"Who?"

"Jana Crowley."

"I was expecting a cross between Marilyn Monroe and Raquel Welch. She's a pretty girl, sure. That's it."

"Do you think she's prettier than I am?"

"That's a sucker game, babe. Come by the bar tonight. Wear that dress. I like it."

He used a police whistle to summon a cab from the crowded streets.

When I came back, Marc asked me to dance. I hadn't had a chance to introduce him to Doug, but he must have seen us making the rounds.

"Robbing the old folk's home, sweetie?"

"Don't start with me, hon."

"So is it true what they say about cops?"

"What?"

"That they have big guns."

"Just your average forty-five Magnum."

Ricky cut in. Grace wasn't there. Not her kind of gathering. Not really Ricky's either. Not enough celebrities. He must have really liked David and Jana. Where were they anyway? I looked around and found them in a corner, dancing to "Mandy." I nearly fell on Ricky.

"What's the matter?"

I didn't want to talk about it. Instead I told Ricky my

creative woes. He suggested the Ricky Grant cure for writers block or anything that couldn't be cured with cocaine: take two Quaaludes and don't talk to anyone for three days. To get me started he reached into a pocket and handed me the Quaaludes. I'd had them ever since.

I'd never done Quaaludes. I was scared. I held a certain amount of contempt for those who allowed their drug use to take over their lives. I'd seen a lot of ludites who'd long since given up control. I couldn't let that happen to me.

The two pills were sitting in the top drawer of my nightstand. Sometimes I would open it up and look at them. They reminded me of the antibiotics I'd taken when I was in the hospital with pneumonia and a broken heart. Maybe Ricky was playing a placebo trick on me.

On the other hand, I thought as I got back to my apartment from Brooklyn that night, if there was ever a time that I needed to completely destroy my consciousness, this was it.

I popped the pills along with my birth-control pill, washing the whole mess down with a Pepsi. I hoped my Ortho-Novum wouldn't be diverted from its purpose by being consumed with such naughty company. I ran a hot bath, got in, and waited.

Whatever I was waiting for didn't seem to be happening. The water felt wonderful. I let my head fall back so my hair could float freely in the water. My ears were under the surface. I was on the verge of falling asleep with just my nostril above the water, when I got the groggy notion that a bathtub wasn't the best place to be under the influence of a serious soporific. Look what happened to Jim Morrison. No, not that he got fat, but that he ended up dead in a bathtub, if in fact, he was dead.

What if David wasn't dead? Did anyone see the body? The cops? Jana? They could all be lying. I hadn't seen the body. I didn't know he was dead.

Come on, Marti. I know you're out of ideas, and writing a mystery with no ending, but the old "he's not really dead'' routine isn't going to cut it. What would you do if he wasn't dead?

I'd probably kill him.

I wanted to sing ''People Are Strange'' but the words came out of my mouth sounding like toothless garble, and my legs felt so heavy that I could barely get myself out of the tub.

I'd seen drunks at the 900 Club walk with more coordination than I displayed while staggering to my bed. Don't worry, I thought. Some people do this stuff all the time. Yeah, maybe those are the same people you see down at the Port Authority, talking to themselves. Kind of like you are right now.

Talk, shmalk. I'm going to sleep.

No rats.

No bees.

No snakes.

That was some good sleeping. It was so good that when I woke up, I had no idea what time it was or what day for that matter. Nor did I care. The phone was ringing. Maybe it had been ringing for a long time. I had no intention of answering it.

For one thing, Ricky's prescription was not to talk to anyone; and for another, it just wasn't possible. I knew I couldn't talk and I didn't think I could walk. I could barely crawl. I eased myself off the bed and crawled across the floor to get to Debbie's blue dress. Her Valiums were in the pocket and I wanted them. I wasn't ready to deal with the world yet, and the Quaaludes seemed to be wearing off. I didn't like to take pills dry, but the kitchen and bathroom were both a million miles away. I choked one down and climbed Mt. Everest to get back in bed.

The phone stopped ringing. Good. I didn't want to talk to anybody. Not Doug, not Jana, not Karl, and certainly not Jerry. Not David either. He wasn't very likely to call anyway. Neither was Brian. I wondered where he was buried. I'd have to buy a pair of tap shoes for that trip.

So there I was at the senior dance with Brian. David was playing piano. Brian started whispering.

I woke up screaming.

When my heart rate got back to normal, I decided that nothing succeeds like excess. Time to smoke some pot.

Problem. My stash was in the kitchen. The phone was in the kitchen. It might start ringing.

Well, I just wouldn't answer it. And I didn't. My legs still felt like rubber bands but functioned well enough to get me to the kitchen. I sat at my kitchen table and rolled a joint while not answering my phone. That'll show them. I took a deep hit, thinking that the people who were messing with the other stuff had it all wrong.

I had a friend at Berkeley who believed that the way to world peace was a pot-party summit. She would point out that anyone can become your soul mate of the moment if you get high together.

She was a political-science major who claimed to have gone down on Jimi Hendrix just before he played at Woodstock. Her name was Claire. I thought she looked like Jean Seberg in *Breathless*.

Before I left for Israel, she gave me a handcrafted clay hash pipe. I'd been foolish enough to leave it behind when I left the kibbutz. I'd lost touch with Claire almost as foolishly. I wondered where she was. Maybe still hanging out in Sproul Plaza.

I remembered handing out McGovern fliers while she cracked me up by doing impressions. Of course, the people in the impressions were always stoned. I once asked her why she was wasting her time with political science when she could have been an actress.

"An actress," she said, launching into a wildly exaggerated Bette Davis, holding a joint instead of a cigarette. "Why go on stage and fool a few people, when you can go into government and fool everybody?"

Good old Claire. If I ever solved the David Price murder, maybe I'd try and find her.

First the murder. It wouldn't go away.

I wondered what David was like high. Didn't he ever let himself get out of control? Probably not. Too many guilty secrets that could come out in careless euphoria. David had been a careful guy. Not careful enough. It must have been the last person he ever expected to turn violent on him.

Maybe he'd gotten away with it for so long that he started to feel invincible. No, it was women who were invincible. I started singing "I Am Woman." (Croaking was more like it.) It was dark outside. I went back to bed, wondering if there were any other songs containing the word "embryo."

I woke up thinking about David.

The late Ken Cooperman should have been number one on my hit parade of suspects. I had believed him when he told me he didn't know who killed David, but the suicide changed everything. I needed a newspaper and some oxygen. What day was it anyway? Had I spent a whole three days in a drugged stupor? How embarrassing. Of course Mike Hammer did become a lush when he thought Velda was dead. Boozing was the staple of tough-guy fiction, but doing drugs as if I were a pig-junkie burnout case was not my style.

I tried to get out of bed. My muscles launched a formal protest. Maybe it had been three days. I managed to get to the TV set and turn it on. Bob McAllister was asking if anybody had an aardvark. "Wonderama." That made it Sunday morning. I had fulfilled Ricky's prescription. "Meet the Press" would be on soon. I had no stomach for national affairs. My mind was strictly on the local. The Sunday *New York Times* would have the skinny on the Ken Cooperman suicide or as much as the reporters knew, which I was willing to bet wasn't a tenth as much as I did. Did Superman leave a note? How much did he cop to? I needed a paper. Before that, I needed to take some pity on the body I had been abusing. Claire had also been an advocate of yoga and TM. I was never much for the meditation, but I had picked up some of the exercises.

Even while doing a cobra stretch, I couldn't free my mind from the murder. The characters kept spinning in my head like a wheel of suspects. Kenny, Grace, Ricky, Jana, Hannah. It could have been any of them. It could have been none of them.

All I had were generalizations. I didn't know the terms of the blackmail. Was it all cash and carry or were there goods and services involved? I didn't know how many people were being blackmailed, much less who they were. How could I solve the puzzle when I didn't have all the pieces?

I was sitting up in bed with my back to the wall, flexing my toes, when I heard an amplified hiss through the wall. The kid next door was home. I had a feeling it was going to be a selection from "Greetings from Asbury Park, N.J." I was wrong, which was just as well, because I was in no mood for that "Nuns run bald through Vatican halls, pregnant, pleading immaculate conception" stuff.

Instead I heard something different. He was definitely listening to Bruce Springsteen. Raspy-voiced, overarranged, and unmistakable, but not anything I had heard before, and I was sure I had heard it all.

I was not quite paying attention as I continued to stretch and even attempted a few sit-ups. My body made a series of popping sounds. Toe-touches were a mistake. Blood rushing to my head made me dizzy. I just lay there curled up on my side.

Where the hell were the kid's parents? What did I want them to do, charge into the brat's room and turn down the volume? This was probably the most important thing in the little snot's life. I felt torn between a posture of parental anger or kindly social worker. Twenty-eight had never felt so old.

My train of thought was derailed by a racing drumline punctuated by glockenspiel notes. Then came the Boss himself, speaking in a nearly sexy hush, *"In Candy's room,"* and then muttering about *"pictures on the wall."*

Something icy and ugly and uncomfortable in my mind manifested itself as physical urgency, driving me out of my apartment. I leaned on the white buzzer of my next-door neighbor's apartment. I hoped the tinny sound could penetrate the sonic shield within.

Finally I banged on the door and imperiled my vocal chords all over again by shouting: "Come on, I know you're in there."

I wanted to give it up as a bad idea, but my saner half wasn't running the show. The vibrations stopped. I knew the needle had been pulled off the record abruptly. It scared me. Don't be scared, I told myself. It's just a kid.

The door opened.

"What the hell is it?"

It was definitely not a kid.

I guessed midthirties. He had an inverted triangle face with angry black eyes. His hair was dark and glossy. He was wearing nothing but a white undershirt and a pair of boxer shorts.

"That's a nice way to answer the door."

"Look who's talking."

So what if my robe wasn't covering my breasts very well and I was barefoot? I could finesse. I didn't have much choice.

"I'm sorry to bother you, but I live next door and . . ."

"If it's about the noise, I don't want to hear it."

"No, it's not about the noise. Well, it is, in a way. I need to talk to your son."

His version of the Martian look was to roll his eyes heavenward in disbelief and exasperation.

"Look, I don't know who you are or what planet you think you're on, but I'm not married and I've got no kids, so you can just . . ."

"So who's listening to the music all the time?"

"That's me, and like I said, if you got any complaints, you can tell the landlord, you can tell the super, but it won't do you any good."

"You're the kid next door?"

"I know that voice. You must be the screamer."

"The what?"

"You're the one who gives out with the banshee noises when you're going at it. You still balling that duck guy?"

"Duck guy?"

"Yeah. When you start screaming, Duck, Duck, I'm always waiting for him to say Goose."

I felt a burning blush start deep in my chest.

"Doug," I muttered. "His name is Doug."

"Not the way you say it. I've been listening to you a lot. I bet I could make you scream louder. I don't think the duck knows what he's doing."

"I'll bet you don't get a chance, and furthermore it's none of your business. So what's a grown man doing listening to that stuff anyway?"

"Don't knock it. Bruce is the greatest. I keep it on when I'm working out."

Even without my glasses I could tell that he had a taut muscularity, mostly centered in his upper body.

"Gotta stay in shape for the camera. I'm an actor."

From his tone of voice, I obviously should have known this.

"Who are you? I mean what name do you act under?"

"It's Jack. Jack Forrest."

It meant nothing to me. I ignored an impulse to ask which restaurant he worked at.

"The record you were playing. I've never heard those songs before."

"Of course not. It just came out. I picked it up this morning. Bruce has been working on this album for a year. Don't you read *Rolling Stone*?"

"Not anymore. So tell me, does the album have a lyric sheet?"

"Yeah."

"Can I see it?"

"Why?"

"I'm trying to solve a murder and something about that last song feels like a clue."

It sounded ludicrous, even to me.

"O.K., I confess, it's just a ploy to see your apartment.

I'm from *New York Magazine* and we're doing a story on studs around town.''

''So you *have* heard of me. Come on in.''

I wasn't sure if he had outsmart-assed me or if he actually thought reporters showed up in their bathrobes on a regular basis. I also wasn't sure that I wanted to be alone in my bathrobe with this man in his underwear. I was sure that I wanted to see those lyrics immediately. That settled the matter.

His bed was located directly opposite mine on the other side of the wall. It was between two behemoths. At one end was a stack of black, comprising his speaker system. On the other side, a metal contraption reminiscent of a medieval torture device, which I took to be exercise equipment. Various weights and barbells could be seen on the floor. There was no TV set. Furniture was at a minimum.

There was an album cover lying on the bed. I picked it up. The title was ''Darkness on the Edge of Town.''

''That's the Boss?'' I said in disbelief. He nodded.

I was not impresssed.

Mr. Springsteen stood in front of a large venetian blind with his hands thrust into the pockets of a black jacket over white T-shirt and had an expression made up of equal parts hurt and stupidity. The hair alone would have given Marc fits. That ''just woke up and can't be bothered with a comb'' look was not attractive in the least.

Jack defended his hero.

''I saw him play once at the Nassau Coliseum. It was incredible. He played for three hours. It was the best show I ever saw.''

''How nice.''

I took the inner lining out and looked for the lyrics to the song that had set off the sirens in my brain. ''Candy's Room.'' That was the one. I read the lyrics. '' 'In Candy's Room, there are pictures of her heroes on the wall.' '' I read it again. '' 'Pictures of her heroes on the wall.' ''

I got it. I was blinded by the light, as Bruce would say. Pellucid.

I had to go see Grace.

"I have to go see Grace."

"You should put some clothes on first."

"Yeah, put my clothes on."

The T-shirt and boxers looked more naked than they had before. He had a dangerous, full-lipped sensuality. He was giving me a man's look. I wasn't sure if I could split the difference between flattered and revolted, but I didn't have time either way.

"I still can't believe you're the kid next door. I thought you were fifteen with pimples."

"I thought you were a blonde with big tits."

"That's such a male chauvinist thing to say."

"You're not one of those are you?"

"Yeah, Jack, I am."

"Too bad. I was gonna ask you to stay awhile."

He was staring right at my breasts. Doug Kimberlin without the charm.

Pulling my robe together, I started walking quickly enough to break into a run, if necessary. He followed, but he wasn't chasing. The menace was all in his voice.

"You're just saying that stuff to get away from me."

"No, Jack. I'm a real-life, honest-to-god, diesel-dyke women's libber."

He leaned casually against the door with arms folded, making me squeeze past him to get out the door.

"You'll be back."

I had to see Grace, but I didn't have to rush.

There was time to take a shower, time to dress up enough for Park Avenue, and certainly time enough to walk.

It was a ripe summer afternoon. Lighter fluid and grilled meats flavored the air. It was one of those days when the city felt like a community and I felt like a part of it. It really was a hell of a town. The psychological mystery was solved and the murder was about to be.

Then I could settle down and write about it. I'd probably need to get a job. Without my emotional problems, the little charade with Dr. Hammerschmidt would evaporate. I wasn't worried. I could certainly find a job to pay the bills until my book hit the best-seller list.

Grace and Ricky were too far away for me to walk it all. Eventually I had to get a cab to take me away from the New York inhabited by mere mortals to that stretch of the East Side where the very rich lived in their old, beautiful apartments.

I would never belong there, even if I did write a best-seller. That was O.K. with me. I'd been an outsider all my life. My Washington Heights habitat with the kid next door and the giant martini on the corner was the most perfect home I could imagine.

The geriatric doorman told me that Miss McCoy and Mr. Grant were not at home. Maybe it was a Studio 54 night. Maybe they were having dinner at 21. For all I knew, they'd gone to the Hamptons. Whenever they came back, I'd be waiting.

It got dark. Streetlights went on. Cop cars patrolled sporadically. I leaned against a lamppost to take the pressure off my feet. Hours went by. I held my ground.

They rounded the corner hand in hand.

"Hi, Grace. Hi, Ricky."

"What brings you out this way?" asked Ricky. He sounded cheerful.

"I need to talk to you both. It's about David."

Grace frowned the way a concerned mother would.

"What more is there to say?"

"I know who did it."

"The D.A. bloke, right?"

I hadn't looked at a paper yet.

"He left a note?"

"Of course he left a note. It's been in all the papers for three days. Where the hell have you been?"

"Don't ask. What did he say in the note?"

"It was more of special pleading, really," said Grace in her gentle voice. "The poor man was horribly guilt-stricken."

"About what? The thing with Carmen isn't pretty, and it's not the kind of thing you advertise if you're an ambitious kind of guy, but it's the Seventies now. It's not that bad."

Ricky picked up the narrative.

"Have you been in a cave or something? He didn't even mention the kid. Carmen might have had him by the dick, but the big news is that the Mob had him by the balls. They put him in business here. They got him appointed assistant D.A., and they yanked the chain whenever they wanted. This one has got people shaking from Four Seasons to Gracie Mansion."

"What about Studio Fifty-four?

Grace shook her head sadly.

"They talk, but they don't care. It's not their tragedy."

"The thing that's all over the note is that he was being bled by a leech. That's a quote. Pretty colorful, huh? Doesn't say who was doing the bleeding. Gracie and I remembered what you were saying about David being blackmailed. You got it backward, didn't you?"

There was an evil glint in Ricky's eye.

"Yeah. I was a prime chump."

"No you weren't. You saw part of the truth when no one else was even looking."

"Thanks, Grace, but I was a chump nonetheless. I loved David so much that I didn't realize he was a bastard. I have seen the light."

"Praise the lord." Ricky was mocking me.

"Did Kenneth Cooperman, in his pathetic missive, admit to putting a bullet in David Price?"

"He doesn't mention being the actual killer, but he does say that he was responsible for the cover-up. The natural conclusion would be that he had a hand in the killing. I must say, there's quite a bit of egg on the faces at City Hall regarding that breaking-and-entering announcement. Heads will probably roll."

"As well they should. However, anyone who assumes

that Kenny Cooperman was the killer is wrong. He didn't do it."

There were no stars visible. They couldn't compete with the artificial light any more than I could compete with Grace's money, prestige, and sense of belonging in the world. The stars were there, though, and somewhere inside me there was the strength I needed.

"Well, if it wasn't him, and it wasn't a sneak thief, then who in the bloody hell was it?"

"Do you really want me to tell you out here?"

Ricky took a step toward me. Grace put a restraining hand on his arm.

"Why don't you come in for a while. It's getting a bit chilly out here."

Chilly? It must have been eighty degrees. It was even hotter in that stuffy rattletrap of an elevator. Ricky was humming snippets of "To Be Real" in a mindlessly off-key manner. The smell of fear was in the air and it wasn't mine for a change.

I led Grace and Ricky into their own apartment. The pictures were the way I remembered. Especially the sketch of David. I stared at it, trying to discern any trace of his real character, any touch of evil. There was none. Either Jana hadn't known or she couldn't bring herself to show it.

"Hey, Ricky."

"Yeah?'

He had lit a cigarette and was smoking it too casually. He was waiting. Grace was waiting.

I was going to have to re-create this moment of power in the book. It was a new experience.

"You ever hear of a guy named Jack Forrest? He says he's an actor."

"If you want to call that acting."

"Is he on a soap opera?"

"Loops."

"Loops?"

"Still a few things for you to learn, sweetie. Are we

talking about a lean fellow with dark hair and the charming demeanor of a serial killer?"

"That's the one."

"He's in porno films. Has a reputation for endurance and a certain God-given talent. Where did you run into him?"

"Around."

Back to the matter at hand. David Price. "Candy's Room." Pictures of her heroes on the wall. I reached up for the sketch of David.

"What the hell do you think you're doing?"

Grace McCoy says "hell," I thought. Another revelation. She was trying to be the Grace McCoy who ruled the financial world of New York City and could easily destroy a nobody like me.

She was fragile. Thin-armed. Thin-waisted. Thin-lipped. Her skin, I wasn't sure about.

"I need to make a point."

"You're going too far, missy," Ricky huffed.

"When did you get this picture?"

"I got it at the gallery the night the show opened. It captured his presence so well."

Even her voice sounded thin. Pinched, constricted, almost painful to listen to. All depth lost to stress.

I took down the framed picture. When I turned it over, the jagged edge where it had been ripped off a sketch pad was visible. I made sure they both saw it. Then I carried the picture of David into the living room. I knew they were following me.

As though it were apropos of nothing in particular, I said:

"Yeah, I'm sure Jana sells a lot of her pictures with torn edges like that. Of course, I've been to the apartment and I've seen the pad. We could go there right now and find out if the edges match up. You guys want to do that?"

I sat on the couch. They stood staring down at me.

"I didn't think so. O.K., which one of you did it?"

More staring.

"Even if you were both there, one of you had to pull the trigger."

"I need a drink," Ricky announced, and went to the kitchen to get one. Apparently whatever was in the cut-glass decanter on the table wasn't strong enough.

Grace sat down on the couch next to me, without relaxing. There was no give in her. I wondered what it was like to live under such tight control.

"What did he have on you?"

"What do you mean?"

"Come on, Grace, it's over. David wasn't just blackmailing Ken Cooperman. He was burning everyone he could. I'd love to get a look at his bankbook. You are one of the richest women in New York, if the papers are to be believed."

"Reports are greatly exaggerated."

"Sure they are. Maybe you've got billions instead of zillions. You have it. David wanted it. He was charming, handsome, talented, and insidious. He found something and started bleeding you. No one does that to Grace McCoy. You showed him who was boss. I don't blame you. He was a parasite, like the rest of the cockroaches in this town. I'm not interested in justice. I just want a complete accounting. What did he have on you?"

She smiled. That was good. I didn't want to hurt her. Grace was my hero.

"You might really be a good writer."

"Gee, thanks."

"It does get in the way of your little detective game, though."

"What's that supposed to mean?"

"The truth stares you right in the face and you can't see it. I think your mind is looking for something more dramatic. You need a satisfying conclusion instead of mere reality. Good writing, bad crime-solving. You ask what David had on me in that pseudo-tough way because you expect the answer to be some page-turner of a secret. It's really nothing of the kind. All David had on me was what he had on you.''

''David didn't have anything on me but my heart. . . .''

I felt sick. It wasn't nausea or dizziness, just a solid sense of all around rottenness.

Grace was a self-made, self-assured, self-sufficient feminist heroine. She was someone I could emulate, even if I kept falling short, and here she was telling me that she'd fallen head over heels for the same gorgeous charmer who'd broken my heart.

''I thought you were . . .''

''Yes, dear, so did I. Amazing what one thinks until one finds out otherwise. Your great good fortune was not having anything he wanted. That allowed him to merely reject you.''

''Merely? I've been on the verge of a nervous breakdown.''

''What's that compared to a constant torrent of teasing and taunting and innuendo and broken promises? David wanted so much, but was willing to give up so little. It finally turned out that he wasn't willing to give me the one night I wanted. I made the mistake of pushing him the night of the engagement party. If he was going to marry Jana, I wanted to have it before then. I wouldn't want to threaten the marriage. I would have given him whatever he wanted. I would have subsidized a group, given him the best contract of any studio musician in the country, taken care of Jana's Middle Eastern affair, but I wanted what I wanted first.''

Her logic was mind-boggling, but I knew exactly how she felt.

''You gave him an ultimatum?''

''Yes. And do you know what he did? He just smiled. You know what he could do with that smile. Then he said, 'Not tonight, I've got a headache,' and went home. Ricky told me to let it go. He said he knew prettier boys who came at less cost. It didn't matter. It wasn't Jana who went upstairs. It was me. Maybe he was expecting me. He didn't look like he had a headache. I asked him point-blank when I could expect him to hold up his end of the bargain."

"What did he say?"

"He laughed."

"Laughed?"

"An ugly sound. It stopped when he saw the gun."

Santa Claus hadn't been a big star in the Hirsch house, so I'd never experienced that particular *goyisher* heartbreak. If I had, it couldn't have been a worse disillusionment than finding out that Grace McCoy had shot David Price because he wouldn't fuck her.

"I wish I were dead," I said slowly.

"This must be your lucky night."

Ricky had a drink in one hand and a gun in the other.

A logical reaction would have been fear. All I felt was another wave of disappointment.

"Oh come on, Ricky, I thought we were friends."

"I can't let that matter right now."

"Ricky, dear, do you really think this is necessary?"

Grace seemed genuinely perturbed. She rose and stood alongside her husband.

"You know I'm not going to tell anybody. David was scum. He had it coming. Justice is done. Have a nice day."

"It's not that easy. Grace will have my head if I mess up the rugs, so we're going for a ride."

"Going for a ride? What is this . . . an old gangster movie?"

"It's a bloody tragedy is what it is. Now get up and get moving."

I thought about it.

Ricky pointed the gun at me and did something that made a clicking sound. Fear started to break through the gloom of disillusionment.

I thought about it some more. The getting up part seemed reasonable. Getting moving I wasn't so sure about. I figured that Ricky had every intention of killing me but no intention of soiling Grace's carpets with my blood. Therefore it seemed prudent to stay in the apartment as long as possible.

I was depressed, but I didn't want to die. There had to be a way to finesse, and I was going to think of it in just a second.

I never got a chance.

There was a great ruckus in the hallway. Doug came barreling into the living room with his weapon drawn. His big gun was a lot more impressive than the thing that Ricky had been scaring me with. Behind him was the petulant doorman whose word was supposed to be law when it came to Mr. Grant and Miss McCoy not being bothered.

"What the hell are you doing here, Doug?"

"Rescuing you from the looks of it, babe. Put that thing down, you idiot," he said almost as an aside to Ricky, who immediately and somewhat sheepishly complied.

I was royally pissed off.

Rescued, like some damsel in distress, by Doug Kimberlin of all people. Drat and double drat. Ricky looked embarrassed. Grace wouldn't meet my eyes.

Doug stood there looking tough, but didn't instigate any further action. It was Johnny who actually removed the gun from Ricky's limp hand.

There was a conspicuous lack of handcuffs and Miranda laws. Doug took my arm a bit roughly and escorted me out of the McCoy domain. I didn't get a chance to thank Grace and Ricky for a lovely evening.

"How did you know where I was?"

"Figure it out yourself, Nancy Drew."

"You've been following me?"

"I've had you tailed."

"And you just happened to pick that moment to come galumphing in?"

"A little more traffic and there'd have been one less pushy broad in this town. I didn't think they'd do something that stupid. I just wanted to get you out of there before you could get yourself arrested for harassing one of our town's most prominent citizens. What the hell were you thinking? Christ almighty!"

"You know what I've been doing?"

"Mostly. Come on."

He pulled my arm roughly.

"Would you mind not manhandling me?"

"You always liked it before."

"Very funny."

"Get in the car."

There was a deadly quiet in the big old sedan. I couldn't stand it.

"Why?"

"Why what?"

"Why follow me? Did you think I might find something that would break open this whole dirty mess? Was the New York City Police Department afraid that their little cover-up might be exposed, so they decided to keep an eye on me? Is that what's going on?"

Whining. Clear diction gone in favor of a sound as ugly as David's laughter must have been to Grace.

"Shut up."

I fumed the rest of the way back to my place, but I did it silently. I tried to figure out how angry he was, compared to his usual level of rage. I guessed somewhere between pissed off and livid. I was surprised when he put a protective arm around my shoulder and used one hand to steer the car into a cozy double-park in front of my apartment house.

He lit a cigarette and killed the lights of the car. The pinpoint glow of the Camel was the only illumination.

"Did it ever occur to you that I was trying to keep you safe?"

"Not for a minute."

"Don't let it go to your head, babe, but I've been worried about you."

"I can take care of myself."

"You were doing a real good job tonight. Not to mention doing a real number on the assistant D.A. in Queens. I don't know what you said to him, but if anyone with a big mouth places you there, you've got a whole lot to answer for."

"But I solved the murder. Grace McCoy did it. She told me."

"Maybe."

"Maybe nothing."

"You got this on tape? Anybody else hear her say it?"

"No. Just Ricky."

"And I figure him for accessory or accomplice. You got nothing and you're up against big-league power. You're lucky they ain't pressing some kind of harassment charges against you."

"It doesn't matter. I just wanted an answer so I could write a book about it."

"You do that, babe. Put it in a book. Then I can stop wasting taxpayer money to keep an eye on you."

"Were you really worried?"

He flicked the half-smoked cigarette out the window.

"I'd hate to lose you." He kissed the top of my head. It felt like a father kissing a daughter before bed. "Now, get out of here. I've got a ton of work waiting for me at the station."

I went upstairs in a bit of a daze. Doug's tender side left me confused. Especially since I still wasn't sure he knew my name.

I made a mental note to get typewriter ribbons and paper in the morning. I had a book to write.

17

Guess what? I couldn't do it.

I had a new ribbon and white bond paper to spare. The whole book was laid out in my mind. The names were cunningly changed to protect the guilty. I just couldn't do it.

I was not haunted by the ghosts of mediocrity. Every word would be a gem. It was a great story. I just couldn't face the ending.

Grace and David. Brian and me. Jerry and Debbie. No hope for any of us. Only for people like Jana who could survive anything. I wasn't crying anymore, but David Price still made me sick.

I did everything I could think of not to write. I went grocery shopping. I watched television. I thought about writing. I smoked some pot. I watched more television. That was the morning of the first day.

A soap opera was getting engrossing when the phone rang.

"Don't you know 'Ryan's Hope' is on?"

"S-s-sorry. I can call back later."

"I solved the mystery. Grace McCoy killed David. She wanted him and he was stringing her along. When she couldn't take it anymore, she shot him."

"Congratulations."

"I feel awful."

"Are you c-c-crying?"

"No. I keep expecting to, but I don't. I think it's over. That mystery got solved too. It was all about Brian and high school and repressed trauma."

"Was it rape?"

"Get your mind out of the gutter. I almost wish it had been rape. So much more dramatic. It was just good, old-fashioned rejection. He told me what I knew all along and did it in the most painful way possible. It's pretty pathetic. It won't make much of a case study for your next book. I kind of lost it when I found out, but I seem to be fine now."

"Trauma is trauma whether it happens in a j-j-ungle or in a high-school gym. Whatever happened was very damaging to you. I've been concerned by you're c-c-condition. I was thinking you might need inpatient care."

"You were going to commit me to Bellevue?"

"P-p-payne Whitney."

"Whew. For a moment there, I was worried."

"I still need an assistant."

"But I'm not a psych patient anymore. I'm all better, Doc. Besides I'm writing a book. The one that's going to make me rich and famous."

"How is it going."

"I wanted David as much as Grace did. It's as if she killed him for me. How can I write a story like that? I have a compulsion to write it and I'm paralyzed with loathing at the idea."

"Yes, I can tell you're c-c-completely cured. Maybe you should come in so we can talk about it."

"I don't think so. I have to write the book."

I knew there was so much more I needed to say to Karl, but I wasn't ready to say it. I said good-bye and went back to my soap operas.

All week I kept up a busy schedule of pointless shopping, visits with the dogs in the park, "Ryan's Hope," "All My Children," "General Hospital," "Edge of Night," "Mike Douglas," "Dinah Shore." Then came the awful moment each day when there was nothing to distract me from trying to write.

By Friday I had ground out ten brilliant pages, every one of which I hated with a passion. Getting the words from my head to the paper was so grueling that it required frequent periods of rest.

Meanwhile I had to deal with the outside world via my telephone. There was something about the noon hour that made it especially attractive for people to call. On Tuesday, it was Jerry. I knew it was him as soon as the phone rang, maybe a second before.

"Marti, it's Jerry."

"Hi, Jerry."

"Are you O.K.?"

"You're always asking me that."

"I worry about people I . . . care for."

"You were going to say 'love.' "

"Maybe. Things were really confusing when you left."

"Things are still confusing. I don't know what to say to you."

"I can't believe that."

"I need a script and right now I'm working on the book . . ."

"The one about David Price?"

"Yeah."

"You solved the murder?"

He sounded more excited about it than I felt. Of course he didn't know what I knew.

"That's great."

"No, it isn't"

"So who is the killer?"

"Can't you wait until the book comes out?"

"Marti, I helped you do the detective work, right? I deserve to know."

I went through it again, feeling like the Ancient Mariner. There was a stunned silence on the other end of the line.

"You still there, Jer?"

"Are you sure? Grace McCoy? That sweet, gentle

woman . . . I know she's a sharp business lady, but . . . It doesn't make sense. Not for David Price."

"You think I'm happy about this?"

"But, are you sure she did it?"

"She confessed, goddammit!"

"You don't have to yell at me. It's just wrong."

"Morally? Maybe he had it coming."

"Just wrong. It doesn't work. It's like an unresolved chord."

"How so?"

"I'm thinking."

"That's great, Watson. Write if you get work. How's Strudel?"

"Who went upstairs?"

"Huh?"

"Upstairs to the apartment?"

"Earth to Jerry."

"It's a timing problem."

"Yeah, like it's almost time for 'All My Children,' and if I miss it there's going to be a problem."

"The night of the murder . . ."

"Yeah."

"Jana told you that she found the body and that's what Derek, the security guy, said, right? But you're telling me that Grace went upstairs and killed him. They both can't be true."

Maybe there was hope.

"Obviously somebody is lying. That would have to include our friend Derek or . . ."

"Or maybe Grace didn't do it."

"I like it, Jerry, but why would she say she did it, if she didn't?"

"To protect someone."

"Who?" I asked, hoping he had an answer that would make everything better.

"How should I know? They're your friends. It's your case."

"Well, let me think about it."

"Do you want to come out here? Maybe we could think about it together."

"That's sweet, but I don't think so. Not right now."

"You know, you left some stuff here." I refrained from asking if he had a good time with my panties. "Are you mad at me about the other night?"

Did I hear palpable yearning or just whining.

"I'm not mad at you, Jerry. I don't know how I feel."

"Well, I know how I feel. This may sound crazy, but I feel like I'm ready to take a chance . . ."

"Slow down, kiddo," I quickly interjected. "You may be ready to take a chance. I'm not so sure. Everything is on ice until I finish the book, and if Grace didn't do it, then I can't even do that, so messing with my solution to the murder is not particularly helpful, if you know what I mean."

"Breathe."

I took a breath.

"You think I'm a bitch, don't you?"

"Sometimes."

"Good."

I was out of witty repartee so I begged off. I tried to concentrate on "All My Children," but now I had too many other things to think about.

Jerry getting mushy on me was bad enough, but the timing problem was a nightmare. Who went upstairs? Who was lying? Who could I ask? The only person I could think of was Jana, and no matter how many mental messages I tried to send or how many times I tried to use a pen to open channel one, she wasn't anywhere that I could reach her.

I forced myself to face the typewriter. Everything that wasn't about Grace ran smoothly. The red herrings, the assistant D.A., the drugs. Great scenes. I hated every one of them.

When I wrote about David, my fingers clenched on the keys. David Price, the blackmailer. Why couldn't he have wanted me? The same question Grace must have asked herself.

It was time for a walk.

I went to the children's zoo at Central Park to watch the seals and hear the clock-tower bells. Unfortunately the children's zoo was full of children. I left and wandered aimlessly through the park, vaguely aware that it was getting late and the park was dangerous.

I thought of going to the Museum of Natural History. That was Holden Caulfield country. Not the safest place for my psyche.

The sad fact was that it was a warm night in the most exciting city in the world and I had no place to go. Even though I came out of the park on the west side, I wasn't going to cry on Dr. Hammerschmidt's analytical shoulder. I didn't even know if I could cry. It went without saying that I wasn't on the list at Studio 54. The martini at the 900 Club wasn't beckoning me.

All I could do was go home and suffer alternating bouts of bad television and painful writing. I fell asleep with Johnny Carson and woke up with the doorbell ringing. I nearly broke my neck tripping over the cord from the typewriter to the plug. The intercom button was close to Gloria Steinem.

"Yeah."

"It's me."

It was Jana through the sputter and static.

"Get your ass up here," I screamed, buzzing her in.

I was so desperate to see her that I waited by the elevator in my bare feet and the previous day's slept-in clothes.

The elevator door framed her like a picture. Mourning was no longer the order of the day. She wore a white halter and shorts that set off her dark brown hair and the tan she'd managed to pick up. She was showing enough skin to catch anybody's eye.

I wanted to ask her about David, about Grace, about blackmail and murder.

"I missed you," I said.

"You would have loved the funeral."

"What do these *goyim* know from fancy funerals? Do you want to get some breakfast?"

"No, I've already eaten, but we do have to get out of this hallway."

"You're not still afraid of roving Arabs, are you?"

She shook her head.

"Were you ever?"

She didn't answer. She did look me in the eye, maybe looking to see how much I knew.

"Jana, we have got to talk."

"I know. I'm sorry."

"Don't apologize. Just come in and tell me what the hell is or has been going on."

We sat at the kitchen table. I picked mushrooms from a slice of leftover pizza. She managed to sip a Pepsi without messing up her lipstick. There was no nice way to say it.

"Did you know about the blackmail?"

"Yes."

"Why didn't you tell me?"

"Well, it's not the kind of thing you go around talking about."

"This is me you're talking to, Jana. Don't even think of doing the Daisy Mae routine."

"Sorry, just a habit."

"There I was running around like an idiot, asking people questions, when I didn't even know the most important thing about the whole case. You should have told me."

"It didn't seem important."

"The love of your life is shot dead and the fact that he is extorting money from rich, influential people, including the assistant D.A. of Queens County, doesn't strike you as relevant?" I screamed.

"Stop screaming."

"I'm freaking out."

"Well, don't. Here's what I know. It started a long time before he met me. He told me about it the same night we first made love. He just opened up and told me. I didn't approve or anything. I didn't want to know too much. He said that now it would be for both of us. So we could have everything we wanted."

"You were doing just fine."

"It wasn't enough."

"For you or for David? Was it so you would finally be free of your father?"

"It just wasn't enough for either of us."

"Were you involved?"

"Certainly not."

"Where's the money now?"

"I've got it."

"You don't call that being involved?"

She shrugged.

"Did you know what he was doing to Grace?"

"Kind of."

"Kind of?"

"I didn't want to know that stuff."

"I would have been dying of curiosity."

"I'm not a snoop like you are. You should have stopped. Grace is pretty upset."

"So I'm persona non grata in the spinning social circle of Grace McCoy?"

"It's worse than that."

"And her publishing company won't be so hot for my book about the murder."

"Marti, you can't write that."

"I'll disguise everything."

"That's not a nice thing to do to your friends."

"Blackmailing them is?"

"That was different."

"Who went upstairs?"

"What?" she asked, looking confused, caught off guard.

"The night of the murder. You told me you went up and found the body, but your description was vague at best. Derek confirmed your story. He said you went up and ran out."

"He's a nice guy."

"Not too bright."

"Bright enough to keep his mouth shut."

"Not quite. He's the one who first mentioned blackmail, almost in passing. Was he being blackmailed."

"Bribed is more like it."

"How?"

"I smiled at him a lot."

"That would do it. Who went upstairs?"

She looked down and shook her head. It had to be tough for her. Grace was still her meal ticket. Jana was a better person than David, though. She had faith in her talent. If Grace withdrew sponsorship, she'd survive. For two years we had told each other everything. Keeping things from me was unnatural.

"Grace."

It was what I expected, but not what I wanted to hear. It put me right back in the same bind.

"Then she really did kill him?"

"I guess so."

"Did you know all along."

"I suspected. She came down from the apartment and told me he was dead and that I should get out of town. She pretended to believe it was Akhmad, and I pretended to believe that she believed me."

"Didn't you care?"

"Of course. I loved David. We were perfect together. But I never thought he was more or better than what he was. You know the real reason I never told you the truth? For one thing, you wouldn't have believed me; and for another thing, once you did, I'd have to look at that shattered expression I'm seeing right now. You can't write people as if they were characters in a story. David wasn't your Golden Boy, Grace isn't the Queen of the Amazons, and whatever you think I am, I'm probably not that either."

The mask had cracked. For a second I thought she was going to cry. I couldn't have handled that.

"I've got to write this book."

"You make it sound like a sickness."

"It's worse." I outlined the preceding days of angst and ennui and soap operas. "What am I going to do?"

"At the risk of sounding crude, it sounds to me like you could use a good lay."

"That is crude. Major Crowley would be shocked."

"I doubt it. He used to be a drill instructor."

"Now what?"

"He's going to retire next year."

"I meant you."

"Grace thinks I can do a tour with the show."

"I don't believe this."

"Well she's not mad at me."

"Where are you staying?"

"At the Sherry, for a while."

"The Sherry Netherland?"

"Uh-huh."

"Who's paying?"

"David."

She smiled. I smiled back.

"Can I crash with you at the Sherry sometime?"

"Sure. Bring the typewriter. Maybe you need a better place to write."

"Maybe. Maybe I need to get out of town."

Jana made Scarlett O'Hara swooning gestures.

"You are thinking of leaving this thriving metropolis from which all literature must spring? I am shocked."

"I'm not getting anything accomplished here."

"Where are you going to go?"

"I don't know. Pine Valley, Salem, some place like that."

"The boonies?"

"Television land."

"Los Angeles?"

"Perish forbid. Sorry, hon, I'm just drifting. I don't know where I'm going and I don't know what I'm doing."

"Do you want me to stay here with you?"
"Nah. You know how I get when I'm like this."
She got up to leave.
I didn't see her out.

18

After Jana left, the crazies really set in.

I couldn't stomach the thought of her condoning David's blackmail, especially his manipulation of Grace's infatuation. When I tried to put that out of my head, I was haunted by flickering images of my own obsessions. I told myself I was cured, but visions of David and Brian continued to alternate in my mind, both of them brutally rejecting me.

No crying, thank god.

Writing was out of the question.

On top of that, Jana's words had put a spell on me. I was horny as hell.

I could always put on something slinky and stake out a bar stool at the 900 Club. Doug had to show up sooner or later. I wasn't sure we still had enough anger between us to create the kind of sex that had put a bounce in my walk and a light in my eye. I couldn't take any more disappointments. Maybe it was time to see what Johnny, his partner, had behind those blue eyes. Maybe it was time to go to the Village and finish what I started at Quincy U. I wondered if I should call Dr. Hammerschmidt and ask if I could still get myself checked into Payne Whitney or Sloan Kettering or Cedars of Sinai. It was obvious that I was one sick chick.

I decided on a plan of action: get some weed and go to the movies.

It was broiling out. A perfect day to escape into an air-conditioned theater. I didn't know what was playing. I stopped at a newsstand to buy a *New York Post*. My world had been shattered, but it was comforting to know there would always be a headless corpse in a topless bar on the front page of the *Post*.

There was also a Suzy column on page six. The name Grace McCoy jumped out at me in bold print. Suzy said that both the financial and social communities of the city were shocked by the announcement that Grace McCoy was suffering from exhaustion and was taking a year off to travel around the world with her husband, noted photographer Richard Grant. They were leaving that afternoon on a cruise ship. I tried not to be disappointed that I hadn't been invited to the bon-voyage party. I wondered if Jana had.

According to Suzy, Grace's business holdings would be managed by her close business associate, Nicholas Perrino. It was hard to imagine Grace being so tired she couldn't run her own business. New York must have gotten too hot for her, in one way or another.

I looked for the movie listings. I decided to skip all the contemporary sturm und drang and go to a double feature of Fred Astaire movies at the Theater 80 St. Marks, with a stop in Times Square to see my buddies Matt and Gary for some weed.

They weren't on the corner. I walked up and down the street looking for them. Someone watching me might think I was auditioning for Hannah's job.

It turned out that someone was watching me. A lanky frame was leaning against the building, holding a bunch of those familiar fliers. Any attempt to actually distribute them to passersby was imperceptible. He was more involved in watching my bloodhoundlike pursuit through blue-mirrored sunglasses. There was a mixture of amusement and confusion on his face, as if he thought he recognized me but couldn't figured out exactly who I was or what the hell I thought I was doing.

I got the oddest feeling that I knew him too. He smiled, revealing a mouthful of big, white teeth. Lord save me from men with big teeth, I thought. Then came the déjà vu boomerang feeling of the last time I had thought the same thing. It was at Jana and David's housewarming party. He was the drummer I had been getting high with just before Jana gave me the key.

"Holy shit! Keith?"

"Yeah."

He nodded his head, causing shoulder-length hair to bounce up and down. His teeth were less uniformly perfect then Doug's. There was a slight hint of buck teeth in the front, giving him a larger range of expression. There was a pleasant wolfishness in his grin, without the blinding shark-attack look I knew so well.

He still didn't know who I was.

"It's Marti. I'm a friend of Jana's. We met at the housewarming."

"Yeah." The light was dawning. "Wow. Marti. Good to see you. What's the word?"

"The word is, what the hell are you doing this for?"

"Gotta eat. I'm between gigs."

"You could get sessions."

"That's what David used to say. I didn't feel like selling my soul."

"Did David sell his soul?"

"You gotta have one first."

"Were you on the blackmail list."

"A lot of my friends. Hey, how do you know about this stuff?"

"I've been turning over rocks. It's amazing what crawls out."

"How much do you know?"

I couldn't resist. How often do you get to be that smug?"

"I know who killed David."

"The broad in Brooklyn?"

"Nope."

"The Mob?"

"Try again."

"The butler did it."

"They didn't have a butler."

"Who did it? Who killed that no good piece of shit?"

"I thought you were his friend?"

"That's how I know."

"I really shouldn't tell you."

"But you really want to."

"Promise you won't tell anybody else."

"I can keep a secret as well as you can."

"Which isn't saying much."

"Exactly."

"Amazing Grace."

" 'How sweet the sound that saved a wretch like me.' What are you trying to say?"

"Grace McCoy killed David."

He took off his sunglasses. He wanted to look in my eyes to make sure I was telling the truth.

"Wow. That is so heavy."

In Keith's personal corner of the "Twilight Zone," the idea that Grace McCoy had bumped off our mutual friend, was heavy but not implausible. He didn't demand proof or an explanation.

"Yeah. Heavy." I muttered, disappointed not to be able to show off my brilliance.

"She must have balls that go clank in the night."

"Because she killed somebody?"

"And then showed up at the funeral."

"Wait a minute. You were at the funeral? In Chicago? Didn't that cost a lot of money?"

"Jana fronted me the dough. I wouldn't have missed it. I love guinea funerals. Great food."

"You go to funerals to scarf?"

"Why not? Big munchies. Big goombas."

"And Grace? Grace and goombas?"

"That's how I got this job."

"You call this a job?"

It was a snotty thing to say, but it didn't seem to bother him.

"Pays the bills, and it never hurts to make buddy-buddy with the big guys. At the funeral I was talking to Jana and she introduced me to Grace McCoy. Then this goomba named Nick comes over and starts talking about David. He seems to know a little about jazz. I mention that the town is bone dry for gigs, and he asked if I could use a job. I said who couldn't. For a couple of days I was keeping an eye on things inside. Recently this job opened up."

"What happened to your predecessors?"

"I hear one got busted and one left town."

I wondered which was which. I hoped it wasn't Matt who had been arrested.

"Are you taking over the other job opportunity out here?"

He didn't get it. I didn't want to spell it out. We stared at each other with no information passing until I broke down and made the smoke sign.

"Oh no. This is a clean street now."

"Says who?"

"The man."

"Is that Nick the man or a certain narcotics detective by the name of Kimberlin."

He shook his head in disbelief. He was wearing a denim jacket with the arms cut off over a bare torso. The arms were muscular. He wasn't particularly my type, but I was in a state to be attracted to anything in pants and maybe anything in skirts. I pushed the thought away.

He was smiling again. What big teeth you have.

"You should write a book."

He was flirting with me.

"If they asked me, I could. Gotta go. See you around." I was getting ready to set off for the Regency sans pot when a new level of deceit came into focus. "Hey, Keith, when exactly was that funeral?"

"Let me see. About a week ago . . . it was last Friday. It was Friday night."

"A funeral at night?"

"Actually the wake. When else can you get a bunch of musicians and gangsters to show up? We had a great jam session."

"Yeah, right."

Grace had called me Friday morning to tell me about Akhmad. She had told me to tell Jana. And then she got on a plane and went to Chicago to a funeral where she knew she would see Jana. She was a master of misdirection. Balls that go clank in the night.

I missed the first ten minutes of *The Bandwagon*. It didn't matter because I stayed to see the double feature twice in a nearly empty theater. My mind kept straying from the happiness and glamour on the screen. The case was closed, but it wouldn't stay shut.

It seemed as if I hated the truth so much that I was unearthing a different solution by force of will. If the Nick that Keith had met at the funeral was the same Nicholas Perrino who was handling Grace McCoy's business affairs in her absence, then Grace was involved with organized crime right up to her pert, freckled nose. That made her one cunning liar. Maybe David was using that as his blackmail weapon. Grace would still be a killer, but she wouldn't be pathetic.

Who was I to call anyone pathetic? Grace might have been run out of town, but she still had Ricky and oodles of money. I had nothing and no one. I felt very lonely in the crowd. On top of that, I was still hot to trot and thinking of Doug. It was his big teeth and strong arms I wanted to feel.

The book was still waiting for me at the apartment, so I went back to 42nd Street.

I walked along porno row, wondering if any of the epics being screened included a performance by my next-door neighbor. Maybe he was waiting for me too. I stopped in front of a bookstore with a window display full of dildoes and vibrators. My eye settled on the biggest one. It had to be at least eight inches long and backlit so as to appear both throbbing and glowing. Soon I was throbbing too.

I took the subway home. The humid air and the bouncing of the train aggravated the sense of anxiety and deprivation. I tried not to catch anyone's eye. I didn't want them to read my mind.

At home I turned on the radio and listened to the Cousin Brucie show. All those oldies. All those memories, all of them miserable. High school. Brian. *Lolita.* Senior dance.

Oh Jerry, I thought, you should have told me. Brian, you stupid son of a bitch. Joining the army? Because a girl wouldn't marry you right away? As always, there was David. What did I want to say to him? Maybe you sold your soul before you ever played a session.

At midnight a mental alarm went off. It was two weeks to the day and close to the hour that David had been killed.

That did it. Passion overcame passivity. I wanted Doug Kimberlin and I was going to have him.

I was on my way out the door, when I remembered that it was Saturday night. His home night. He was home with his wife and kids.

Time for a little fun. I didn't know where Doug lived. It was somewhere close to the other side of that bridge that glowed outside my window. I made a list of towns and started annoying operators in Northern New Jersey. I also woke up a few Kimberlins of the non-Doug variety. He wasn't in Fort Lee, Secaucus, Clifton, Englewood, Teaneck, or Paramus. Then I tried Ridgewood, Glen Rock, Paterson, and River Edge.

My hands were starting to sweat and I was tense with fear that he might be unlisted. Maybe it was safer for cops that way. They never knew when some crazy woman might be looking for them.

I stared out the window at the bridge. I couldn't really be thinking of leaving New York. How could I give up that view? New Jersey had no real form. I couldn't imagine what the towns looked like or what it would be like to live there.

I knew there were swamps. The gospel according to Bruce Springsteen. "*My machine she's a dud, all stuck in the mud, somewhere in the swamps of Jersey.''* I asked the Boss where Detective Kimberlin resided. Asbury Park? Too far away. How about Fairview. *''I hear she's got a house up in Fairview, in a style she's trying to maintain.''* I couldn't find a Fairview, but there was a town called Fair Lawn.

What a perfect, boring suburban name. In Fair Lawn, New Jersey, there was a Douglas Kimberlin. I had it. I knew I had it. I smiled my best approximation of the Kimberlin grin and dialed with my heart pounding. It rang six times. Come on Doug, get to the phone.

''Yes. Hello?'' It was a sleepy sounding woman. I must have woken up Laura (or whatever her name was).

''Detective Kimberlin, please.''

''You're from the precinct?''

''That's right.''

''You must be new.'' She sounded aggravated as well as tired. ''He's at Dutch House. Hold on. I'll get the number.''

''That's O.K., ma'am. I've got it here. Sorry to disturb you.''

''Sure.''

I didn't have any such number, but I wanted Mrs. Kimberlin to go back to sleep without thinking there was anything odd about my call. Let her think I was some incompetent rookie at the police station. One more call to information for Dutch House in Fair Lawn, N.J. What the hell was Dutch House anyway?

The answer came as soon as the phone was picked up. I could hear voices and music. There was probably a pinball machine too.

''Dutch House.''

I imagined a bartender similar to the one at the 900 Club. I decided not to play cop. I started chewing an imaginary piece of gum.

''Is Doug Kimberlin there?''

There was a pause through which I heard more bar noises.

"He can't come to the phone right now."

"What's that supposed to mean?"

"It means he's in the can. O.K., lady?"

"So I hold."

"Not on my line." "I ain't that far away. I'm in Clifton. I'll just come over."

"You don't want to do that, lady."

"He's not there, is he?" I asked in my normal voice.

The connection was broken on the other end along with another piece of my heart. I wasn't a singular babe. I was one of many. He had the system down to an art with everybody playing along. I wanted to feel pain. I even wanted to cry. Instead I found myself giggling.

It was brilliant. Doug Kimberlin was a genius, maybe even a magician. He could be in two places at the same time. He could defy time and space.

I turned to my tarot cards, which were lying on the windowsill. A thin layer of dust had settled on them. It had been a long time since I had consulted with the occult. I shuffled while telling the cards what I thought. I asked them to tell me who killed David. The first card to come up was The Heirophant. Symbol of rules, regulations, and the constraints of society. In the reversed position a symbol of hypocrisy.

The murder was solved.

19

On Monday morning, my hand was steady on the telephone.

I called the homicide division and asked for Captain Morrison. I was told to wait. I was ready for that. I had my bread pudding and my coffee. I could wait for Captain Morrison for as long as it took.

I imagined his jowly face, scowling over industrial-strength coffee, wondering what the hell Marti Hirsch wanted with him. That was assuming he knew who I was. I had finished the bread pudding before he came on the line, sounding both brisk and brusque.

"Captain Morrison here. What is it?"

"Hi. This is Marti Hirsch. Doug Kimberlin's friend from the 900 Club."

"I know who you are. What do you want?"

"It's about the David Price murder."

"For the love of Mike, that thing is closed. What do you want me to do, have a squad car chase Grace McCoy across the ocean?"

"Grace didn't do it."

"Then why are you bothering me?"

"Because I know who did, and with the cover-up people no longer involved, I had the crazy idea that the homicide department might just be interested in knowing about it before I call the *New York Post*, but obviously I was mistaken. Sorry to have taken your time. Good day."

"Wait. You know, if you were my daughter . . ."

"Well, I'm not, so let's both be thankful for small favors."

"Get down here in half an hour. This had better be good so that I don't regret wasting any part of my day on some loony-tune with a bug up her ass."

"I'm leaving now. And don't tell Doug I called. This is for homicide, not narcotics."

I tried to dress myself in the garb of respectability. I put on one of my old office outfits. The reaction when I got there was staggering. Had they never seen a woman in a miniskirt before? What about Pepper Anderson and Christie Love? One of the less-than-stunning policewomen gave me a fishy look when I asked for Captain Morrison.

I was left to cool my heels until he was ready to see me. I took the time to run through the spiel in my head again and again. The same uptight chick came to usher me into the captain's office.

He didn't get up to greet me. He didn't seem to like what he saw when I walked in.

"Well, go ahead and tell me who blew away the piano player."

"Can I sit down?"

"You won't be here that long. Get on with it."

I took a breath and laid it out for him. The killer, the opportunity, the motive. I watched it hit him. The color drained from his face. His jowls shook. I casually perched myself on a corner of his desk and slowly crossed my legs while I waited for the explosion.

"Jesus mother-fucking Christ. I don't fucking believe it."

"That's no way to talk to a lady."

"You don't look like a lady. You look like a whore."

"Gee, now I'm upset."

"How the hell can you come in here and tell me something like that?"

"Because it's the truth. Do you think I'm happy about this?"

"I don't know what to think about you, lady. I know you got no great love for cops."

"Come on, Tommy."

"What goes on with you and Doug ain't love."

"I never said it was."

"Personally, I don't think a man should run around on his wife, but seeing as he's a friend and a fellow cop, I just say well, that's Doug. There usually ain't much to say. They come and they go. They're all pretty and young. The only time I've ever said anything was the first time he brought you around to show off. You know what I told him?"

"What?"

"I said to him, 'You be careful Doug, because this one is smart.' "

"Why are you telling me this? You don't even like me."

"You're damn right, I don't. I sure don't like what you just told me, but I think you're too smart to march into my office with a story like that unless you got a way to prove it. Am I right?"

Behind the tired eyes and the cranky demeanor was a very sharp cop.

"Well, yeah." I said hesitantly. I was rock solid on the basic premise. My plan for proving it was less so. "I've got a plan, but I'm going to need some help."

"Great. That's just great," he growled, picking up the phone. I heard him ask for the narcotics department. For a moment of terror, I thought that he was calling Doug. I leaned across his desk, trying to catch his eyes with a desperate, pleading look. He waved me off. I abandoned the desk and took up fervent pacing until I heard him say, "Give me Detective Rostelli." I didn't think that was such a hot idea either, but it was out of my hands. "Johnny, it's Captain Morrison. I need you to get over here right away . . . Not Doug, just you . . . Yes, it's important . . . No, don't tell him. Good. I'm waiting for you."

It was a long, stuffy, sweaty wait in Captain Morrison's office. When Johnny came in, he found me slouched in a chair. I was glaring at Captain Morrison. Captain Morrison was shuffling papers in a studied effort to ignore me. Johnny entered the room wearing jeans and a leather jacket along with his usual quota of attitude. He went from strutting to deeply confused to infuriated in the amount of time it took for him to wonder what I was doing there and for Tommy to tell him.

I couldn't watch. It was hard enough to listen as Captain Morrison repeated my theory. Corroborating evidence included my observations of how business was being conducted along a certain stretch of 42nd Street, including the fact that two drug dealers were being overlooked to keep them as snitches. It didn't reflect well on Johnny, even though he wasn't implicated in the murder.

"You goddamn bitch!"

"She may be that," said Captain Morrison, coolly, "but is she a lying bitch?"

"Captain . . ."

"Answer my question, boy, is she a lying bitch?"

I couldn't keep my eyes down anymore. The tension in the room compelled me to look up. Johnny looked at me. His hands were jammed tightly into the pockets of his jacket. I thought I knew hatred until I saw the look in his eyes. He was more frightening than Gary. Johnny Rostelli was totally sane and he hated my guts.

"We got snitches out there, just like every other cop on the street. I don't know about the other stuff. You gonna call Internal Affairs?"

"What you guys have to do to make the bust is your business and your captain's. This is homicide. There's this stiff named David Price. I never took too kindly to the way that case got slammed shut on us. I ain't saying I'm going along for the whole ride with her, but if she is right, we gotta prove it. She's got a plan, but she says she needs help. Either it's you, or I get someone else. Do you want me to get someone else involved in this?"

"No. Just me."

"Yeah, that's what I thought. O.K., missy," he said, turning to me," what exactly is the plan?"

"Well, I figure what we need is a confession, and we have to have it on tape as evidence. The thing is, you can't wire me, and a bug inside my apartment might still be too risky, but I have really thin walls. We need to talk to my next door neighbor. I hope he's home."

We got to Washington Heights around half past two.

I had no contingency plan for the kid next door not being home. Luckily I didn't need one. "Candy's Room" blasted assertively down the hallway. Bruce, I thought, you led me astray. Of course it hadn't been Bruce doing the leading. For a well-known smart person, I had managed to act like a total idiot. As always, it took serious door-banging to get a response.

"Come on out, Jack," I yelled, "it's me, the screamer."

He must not have checked the peephole before opening the door. The two men with me were obviously a surprise, even more so when they flashed badges. His pointy features rearranged themselves into an ingratiating smirk.

"Look officers, if it's about the noise . . ."

He wore jeans with a tan jacket. He wasn't bad-looking, but the traces of acne scars on his cheeks and the mean-looking eyes made me wonder how he could be in dirty movies. Then I remembered something Ricky had said about endurance and "talent." I tried to check him out, but the cut of his jeans wasn't giving anything away. The matter remained unsettled and I filed it away for possible future research.

Captain Morrison was doing the talking.

"No, it ain't about the noise, but it's going to be about the noise and a whole lot more if you don't cooperate. Am I making myself clear?"

"Yes sir, crystal clear. Anything I can do to help."

"Start by turning off that noise and letting us inside."

Johnny started sizing up the apartment, making sure it

would be suitable for the purpose. Tommy told Jack and me to go into my apartment and talk near the wall. Naturally that meant talking near my bed, a fact that Jack glommed onto immediately.

"So, that's where you and Duck go at it, huh?"

"Doug. His name is Doug."

"Where is he?"

"I guess he's working. How about you? Have you done any serious acting lately?"

"I'm always up for parts."

"I know what parts you're up for and what parts of you are up for them. I think it's disgusting."

"No, you don't. You just want to find out how talented I am."

"All right, you two. That's enough." Tommy Morrison's voice came booming through the wall.

Gloria Steinem looked at me on the way out. I promised her I would never, ever sleep with Jack Forrest. Jack caught me looking at Gloria. I got the idea that he knew who she was. He gave me one of those snorting eyeball rolls of derision. In an arrogant act of mock gallantry, he held my own door open for me. What a creep!

Such a creep, in fact, that in exchange for use of his apartment, he extorted permission to be there during the event. I could have throttled Captain Morrison. He wasn't too thrilled about it either, but he was operating on the edge and doing the best he could. He had to run to a friendly judge for a warrant. He had to order Johnny to call in sick for the rest of the day. Then he realized that he would have to baby-sit a seething, brooding cop. On top of that, his old Irish heart still hoped I was wrong.

I was left alone in my apartment to wait and worry. If I was wrong, I was going to die from embarrassment. If I was right, I could get myself killed. I felt small and scared and vulnerable. I hated feeling that way.

I tried humming a few bars of "I Am Woman." I tried to call Jana at the Sherry Netherland. She wasn't there. I turned on Channel 13, hoping for the soothing presence of

"Mister Rogers." Instead there was the "Galloping Gourmet," flouncing around with cherries flambé. I marched back to the kitchen. I opened my fridge and stared at the food, telling myself that I wasn't going to start crying. Then I slammed the door shut, grabbed the phone, and dialed the number that my fingers had already memorized.

The bugs were set up next door to pick up sound from the bed. I called from the kitchen and spoke as quietly as I could.

"Hi, Jerry, it's Marti. Can you talk to me for a while? I'm really scared. Oh god, I hate myself when I whine like this."

"Whoa. Time out. Breathe. Please don't be scared. It's going to be O.K. What are you scared of?"

"I've got the killer coming over here tonight and I've got to get him to confess."

"Wait a minute. I thought you said it was Grace McCoy."

"I haven't talked to you lately, have I? Hold on to your hat, sweetheart. Big news flash. Yours truly was wrong, wrong, wrong. Grace McCoy didn't do it."

"I tried to tell you that I didn't think she did."

"Well, I wouldn't listen. So, go ahead and be smug. I have it coming."

"So, one more time, who killed David?"

I told him who. I told him how I was going to prove it. (Most of it anyway. He was better off not knowing all the details.)

"Are you sure?"

"Pretty sure."

"Do you have to do this tonight? It sounds dangerous."

"I felt big and brave this morning. Now I want to just run like hell. Maybe go to Palm Beach and mooch off my parents for a while. I don't think I can do it."

"If you don't, what happens?"

"He gets away with it."

"And you don't write your book."

"No, not that one."

"Then you've got to do it."

"I don't think I can."

"You can do it. You're from Brooklyn."

"What's that got to do with it?"

"It means you're tough. It means you keep going when you don't think you can go on anymore. You can give in, you can give out, but you never give up."

"That's so dumb, it's brilliant. Can I use it in the book?"

"Will you dedicate it to me?"

"Sure. To Jerry Barlow, who has the most oddly soothing effect on me."

"Come here when it's over, O.K.?"

"I'll try."

I didn't want to make any promises I couldn't keep. I wasn't sure it would ever be over. I didn't even know when it had started. When David was killed? When I started crying? When Brian broke my heart?

I tried to wash away the morbid moping in a long, hot bath. I washed my hair. I reminded myself that I was 140 pounds of female brilliance. I was from Brooklyn. I could do it. Piece of cake.

I had some quick shopping to do around the corner, and then there was nothing to do but wait some more.

The shift ended at 11:30. I made the call at 11:15. I phoned from Jack's apartment. He had his hair slicked back and was wearing glasses. Maybe it was his idea of looking like an intellectual. The glasses were probably fake.

I didn't look at him or Johnny or Tommy. I closed my eyes and concentrated on putting a bright, seductive note into my voice.

I twitched as I heard his voice for the first time in what felt like a very long time. It had only been a week.

"Detective Kimberlin speaking."

"Hi, Doug. Guess who?"

"Babe." Same old Doug.

"Long time, no see."

"It's been a zoo here."

"I missed you."

"You know I can't talk here."

"Can you come over tonight?"

"Yeah. Why?"

"Because I'd really like to see you."

"I'm up to my ass in paperwork. Johnny called in sick today."

"Come over. I'll make it worth your while."

"How." He was getting interested.

"I'll tell you who killed David Price."

"I've heard this before."

"But this time I really know," I said meaningfully.

There was a thoughtful pause.

"I'll see you later."

The thud echoed in my ears as well as those of Captain Morrison, who was listening on headphones. He gave me a perfunctory nod as I went back to my apartment. I fixed my hair and put on makeup. I turned on the radio as much for time checks as for music.

I'd stumbled through this whole case like a blind fool, and now I was getting ready to put everything on the line to prove that I was right, because more than anything, I had to be right. And yet some small traitorous part of me voiced a hope that I might be wrong. I told that part to shut up.

At 11:43 the buzzer went off rudely. Either he left early or he had the best luck in the history of New York City traffic. I took a minute to turn off the radio and light a candle before pushing the button that would let him in the front door.

I stood in the foyer feeling my heart pound. I still wasn't sure I could do it, even if it was the only way. I told myself I was doing it for David and Jana and Kenny Cooperman, and even for Brian who had nothing to do with it and everything to do with it. I was even doing it for Gloria Steinem. Doug had been a big step off the road to liberation. I had to get back on.

I heard the footsteps down the hall, but I waited until he had tapped out "shave and a haircut, two bits" before I opened the door. All six feet five inches of him were framed in my doorway, wearing his old suit. He needed a shave. His tie was loose and his shirtsleeves rolled up. One hand held the jacket over his shoulder; the other, a cigarette.

He scowled at me. I knew why. I was wearing my comfy, ratty robe, which he hated. I let it fall off my body to show him the black, silk nightgown that he had given me.

His toothy, lewd grin had once made my toes curl with lust. This time it was for the cause that I glued myself to his body and reached up for a kiss. The door shut behind him.

"Can we talk now?"

"Not now."

"Do you want a drink?"

"Nope."

I tugged gently on his tie and led him to the bed. Normally Doug and I had sex with all the finesse and sensitivity of Rockem-Sockem Robots, but that night's agenda called for something different.

I made love to him in a way I never had to anyone else, man or woman, because it had never been so important for me to control the action. I used every little touch I had ever picked up from a book or made up for one of my unpublished scorchers. I wasn't sure my big, strong, macho cop would play along with my more aggressive approach, but when I started unbuttoning his shirt and running my fingers through his thick, salt-and-pepper chest hair, I felt him relax.

He tensed up again when I started playing with his nipples, but wasn't making any complaints. I paid attention to every part of his body, even massaging his feet. I used my mouth in a way that made him moan and start saying, "Babe, babe, babe," almost like a chant.

I peeled myself out of the nightgown, which was now clinging to me, damp with sweat from nerves and exertion. I wondered how this scene was playing next door. Could they hear every "ooh" and "aah"? Did anyone have to take a trip to the loo for a little hard-on relief?

I had thought it would be cold and clinical at best, repulsive at worst. I was having sex with a man who I was sure was a murderer and three other men were listening in. I should have been nauseated.

My body had other ideas. Exhibitionism, added to the complex mixture of heat and hate I'd had for Doug from the beginning, especially now that I was in charge of the action. On top of that was the culmination of the odyssey that had started when Doug called to tell me David Price was dead. It all seemed to be coming down to one moment.

There's always something special about a first time and a last time. This particular last time left me laughing and crying and gasping for breath all at the same time. I knew I was saying good-bye.

My first thought upon return to planet earth was that it was actually a good thing that Jack Forrest was there. Otherwise the police might have thought that I was being killed and they would have burst through the door at just the wrong moment. That reminded me that it was time to get down to business and commence the second part of the evening's festivities.

I detached myself from the rapidly shrinking Mt. Kimberlin and fetched a damp towel from the bathroom. I fought an impulse to get into my robe.

My next stop was the kitchen for a bottle of Jim Beam and a Dixie cup. I found Doug lying on one side, facing the wall. That meant he was going to doze off. I wanted him out of it, but not unconscious. I reached over with the towel to clean him off. That caused a luxurious, low-throated groan of contentment. Then I poured a drink and held it under his nose. He lumbered to an upright position with his back against the wall. I handed him the cup. He downed the booze and held the cup out for a refill.

I continued playing the cheap floozy by going to his jacket and fishing out his cigarettes. They were in a side pocket, but I felt something heavy on the inside that put knots in my stomach. I lit a cigarette for him. A man with a drink, a cigarette, and a naked woman catering to him. Stephanie would puke.

I went as wide-eyed and coquettish as I knew how.

"Please, Doug."

He spoke as an indulgent father would to a whining daughter.

"O.K. I know you're dying to tell me your latest hare-brained theory. Go ahead. Who killed David Price?"

In all my mental rehearsals, it had come out in a perfectly modulated husky contralto. Faced with reality, I produced a strangled whisper.

"You did."

I watched his face. The jaw dropped but recovered before it could be described as having hit the floor. His eyes narrowed slightly. He was good, damned good, but I had the son of a bitch. He just didn't know it yet. He thought it was a game.

"What makes you say that?"

"Because I know that sometimes when you're home with your wife and kids, you're really out drinking at Dutch House. And sometimes, when you're out drinking at Dutch House, you're not there either. It's a great system, Doug. It gives you freedom from your wife and anybody else you want to cheat on."

"I never said I wouldn't."

"Nor would I want you to. I'm not, repeat not, jealous. I'm just saying that the system gives you a perfect alibi. The precinct says you're home, your wife says you're out with the boys, and the bartender never opens his mouth except to call you and sound the alarm.

The night of the murder, you drove to New York, shot David, drove back, and downed a few shots of bourbon or went to the home of one of your Jersey sweeties. You told me they called you at home. Which they did, thereby setting off the system. Brilliant."

He finished off the bourbon and crushed the paper cup. The cigarette got stubbed out in the ashtray that held one lonely roach. He noticed and gave me a look of disapproval.

"That stuff makes you stupid, kid. Why the hell would I want to shoot some piano player that I barely knew."

"I suppose you knew I was madly infatuated with him and you could never truly possess me until he was out of the way."

His grin was big enough to fill the room.

"You don't really believe that, do you?"

"Of course not. He was blackmailing you."

The great beast lost some of his bluster. He lay down on his back with his hands cradled behind his head.

"Tommy told me to watch out for you. He said you were smart."

"Are you going to kill me?"

"Only if I have to. Is the place bugged?"

I turned around slowly to remind him that I was buck naked.

"I'm not wired. Check the place out if you want. No bugs. I haven't told anybody. I'm not going to tell anybody. I'm not even writing about it. This is just between you and me. I'm glad you killed him. He was slime. I'm only sorry I didn't do it myself."

He patted the bed next to him and crooked a finger for me to join him. We cuddled like real lovers. His New England–tinged voice insinuated itself into my ear.

"Then maybe this'll make you feel better. You did kill him."

"Huh?"

"You got him knocked off. Does that make you happy?"

"Slightly. What happened?"

"That was a great party you took me to. Except your pal Price turned out to be a real rat-bastard. He calls me a week later at the station and tries to squeeze me."

"About what? Corruption?"

"Hey, there ain't no damn corruption."

"I've spoken to Matt and Gary."

"That's different. Your pal . . ."

"He wasn't my pal."

"You gonna let me finish?"

He was cupping my left breast in a proprietary way that I found very annoying.

"Yeah. Fine. What did he have on you?"

"He had you and me. He threatened to tell Cathy."

"Who's Cathy?"

"Mrs. Kimberlin."

"I've always thought of her as Laura."

"Well, she's Cathy."

"Cathy would have to be a total idiot to think you've been true blue all these years."

"Don't talk about her like that. What she does or doesn't know is between me and her. No one tries to blackmail me. No way. I started doing a little research on this David Price guy. Not such a sterling character, not to mention the fact that he was trying to work on my turf. Very stupid."

"You found out about the Chicago connection and that he was pumping Hannah for information and using the drugs as party favors."

"You might make a good cop yourself."

"I hate cops."

"I know you do."

"So what happened?"

"The more I found out about David Price the more I wanted him out of the picture. I couldn't bust him on extortion or drugs. I got to thinking that killing him would be good for everyone involved."

"Especially you."

"I told him I'd pay off. I set up the meeting, and the bastard went for it because he thought he'd have a witness to keep him safe."

I had to think about that. What witness? Not Jana. Oh . . .

"Grace?"

"Yeah. He tells me to come to his apartment. But I smelled a big rat, so I got there a little early and decided to wait in the closet. He's noodling away on the piano when who comes knocking on the door but Grace McCoy, and it's pretty obvious they were keeping a previous appointment.

I hear her yelling at him about how much longer does he think she's gonna stand for this. He starts laughing."

"Was it because she loved him or because he was using the Mob stuff against her?"

"Loved him? Come on, babe."

Doug looked at me with the utmost contempt.

"She wasn't pulling that gun because of love. The bum was gonna let the papers know exactly who she was in bed with, and I don't mean this kind of bed. He just kept laughing. Right then I really knew the little pissant had it coming."

I'd been right about Doug's anger. And who would have pissed him off more than a good-looking, smooth-talking, blackmailing son-of-a-bitch like David?

Doug seemed completely relaxed as he told me about it. There was even a hint of braggadocio. The plan was working perfectly.

"I could tell that Miss McCoy didn't have the guts and that I'd have to do it myself after all. I just strolled out and took the gun from her."

"Prints?"

"Gloves."

"So you shot David, point-black, in front of Grace McCoy, and she covered up for you?"

"She had to."

"Because you knew that she was involved with the bad guys and she couldn't have that come out. So you took up where David left off. That's pretty sick."

"She wouldn't have had to do much if you hadn't been poking your nose around. The Queens thing took us all by surprise. We didn't know why that guy was killing the investigation."

"Kenny was his own worst enemy."

"But you are one pushy broad. After Cooperman offed himself, we all figured you'd end up back with Grace, so she agreed to confess for your benefit."

"The whole gun scene was a setup?"

"Yeah. It was Grace who came up with the idea of telling you she shot him because he wouldn't screw her. I told her you'd never fall for that in a million years, but she figured you would since you wanted him yourself. Smart lady."

"Obviously smarter than me."

He put my hand on top of his dick, apparently planning on round two. I knew I couldn't do it again. Not knowing what I did. Not realizing how much of a sucker I'd been played for. Not knowing that he really was a cold-blooded murderer. His dick stayed limp. I stifled a sigh of relief. I figured he'd roll over and go to sleep, but I had to know a few more things.

"How'd you know when I'd show up at Grace's, much less when you should come prancing in for the big rescue?"

"You were being shadowed the whole time. As soon as you got near the McCoy place, I was on the way. Grant signaled from the kitchen window. We were ready for you, babe."

"O.K., Doug, you had me blindsided three ways from Sunday, but what made you think I'd stop there? There were inconsistencies, holes a mile wide. Why didn't you think I would keep going?"

"You're a quitter. You quit Berkeley, you quit Israel, you quit your job, you don't follow up on your writing."

"Did I tell you all that?"

"Some. Some I found out. I knew you were a quitter that first night when I came up in back of you. You didn't even play your last ball. You're smart, babe," he yawned, "but you're a quitter."

"Not this time."

While he was sleeping, I went into the bathroom to throw up and take another bath.

He was dressing when I came out. Going home to Cathy. I watched him put on his jacket.

"Do you have your gun with you?"

"I never bring a piece on a social call. If you got a death wish, do it yourself."

"Maybe I will," I mumbled, trying to project suicidal despair. He wouldn't kill me if he thought I would do it to myself first. "So what's so heavy in your jacket."

He pulled out a wrapped package with a ribbon on it. Probably perfume.

"Tomorrow's my wedding anniversary."

"*Mazel tov.*"

"What?"

"Congratulations."

"Thanks. Let me give you some advice."

"Whatever."

"Go back to school. Do something with your life."

"Maybe I will, or maybe I'll just go out there and jump off that bridge."

He was leaving.

"Doug."

"Yeah?"

"Do you know my name?"

"Martha Evelyn Hirsch. Usually called Marti. But who could call a girl Marti? So long, babe."

I didn't bother to watch him walk away.

After giving my stomach and tear ducts time to settle down, I put on my robe and went next door. I found two glum cops and one smirking porn star. I felt a rush of panic.

"Don't tell me you didn't get that."

"Oh we got it," said Captain Morrison, "we got it right here." He had a reel-to-reel tape in his hands.

"So why don't you go get him. Chase him. Arrest him."

"You watch too much TV," snarled Johnny from across the room. At least he was talking to me. He was dismantling the recording equipment.

Jack was leaning against his windowsill. He gave me the usual look.

"What is it with you and that robe?"

I ignored him.

"Excuse me for breaking up this wake. You just heard

Doug Kimberlin fess up to murder one. I was right."

"*Mazel tov,*" said Tommy dryly. "Believe it or not, we follow due process in the New York Police Department. The same judge who got me a warrant to legally bug this joint will get me a warrant to legally arrest Detective Kimberlin. He will show up for work and I will stop by to personally present it to him over his first cup of coffee. Will that be satisfactory, Miss Hirsch?"

"Yes. That's fine."

"Good. Thank you for your cooperation. Now get out of town."

"What?"

"Get out of town. Get lost. Be where no one can find you. Call me when you're far, far away. We'll bring you back when we need you."

"Aren't you supposed to tell me not to leave town. Don't I have to give a statement. What about testifying?"

"You can't testify if you're ten feet under."

He jerked his head in Johnny's direction. I had seen hatred in his eyes. Captain Morrison saw death. Since he was the head of the homicide squad, I decided to take his word for it.

Before I could leave, Jack had a last shot for me.

"You know, you sounded pretty good. Maybe I could get you into the business. Of course, you'd need a boob job first."

"Jack, could you come here a minute?"

He sauntered to where I was standing by the door. I opened my robe so that he could see my body. I ran my hands down my sides as sensuously as I could. I had his undivided attention. If the others were watching, so much the better. He raised his eyebrows suggestively. I looked down. Signs of talent were making an appearance. I licked my lips.

"Hey Jack," I said seductively.

"Yeah?" He looked eager.

"Suck my dick."

I walked out.

20

It didn't take long to pack. I threw all the important stuff into my El Al flight bag. My Gloria Steinem picture, my tarot cards, my Toodleloop, my ratty robe, other articles of clothing. The bag started to overflow, so I put some things in a Channel 13 tote bag. I left behind *The Female Eunuch*, but took *Lolita*.

I knew the cops were gone when the music started coming through the wall. Bruce serenaded me with "Born to Run." Thanks, Jack. I caught myself singing along. Man, did I need a change of scene.

"The highway's jammed with broken heroes on a last chance power drive. Everybody's out on the run tonight, but there's nowhere left to hide."

Home is where you go when you run out of places, which I emphatically had. Brooklyn felt safe as long as Jerry was there, but I wasn't sure about loving him, much less with all the madness in my soul.

Speaking of madness, I decided to call my shrink. I dialed his home line, knowing full well I would wake him up.

"H-h-hello."

"Hi, Karl."

"Marti. Why are you c-c-calling so late. Is everything all right?"

"Everything's fine. Doug Kimberlin just confessed to killing David."

"What? Didn't you tell me that Grace McCoy confessed to the same thing?"

"I don't really have time for the whole story, Doc. Take my word for it. It was Doug."

There was a long pause.

"You're quite amazing."

"Nah, I've been a schmuck on this thing from the get-go. They've all been jerking me around. Grace, Ricky, Doug, even my best friend, Jana Crowley, the queen of manipulation."

"But you did what you set out to do. Very few people ever accomplish that. You could be a good therapist yourself."

"Why is everybody giving me career advice all of a sudden? Right now all I'm planning to do is get out of town."

"Do you need anything?"

"I've got a little money and a copy of *Steal This Book* lying around here somewhere. I'll be fine."

"You still need help with your emotional problems."

"Oh, no I don't. I remembered what happened at the dance, I had the *uber*-crying jag. It's all over."

"C-c-catharsis is the beginning of healing, Marti, not the end."

"I'm hitting the road, Jack. I just wanted to call and say good-bye. You've done so much for me. If it wasn't for you, I might really have gone over the edge. I'll always be grateful. You're a hell of a shrink, Karl. I hope you do get that lousy book published."

"You're going to need help someday, Marti. Remember, you can always call me. Even at this kind of ungodly hour."

"Any more of this and I'll start crying again. Good-bye, Karl."

"G-g-good-bye."

For a moment I considered making a call to the Sherry

Netherland. Then I realized that even if Jana was there, I didn't want to talk to her. What I'd told Karl was true. She had been as manipulative and calculating as Doug himself. David was dead. Kenny Cooperman was dead. Doug was going to jail. Grace and Ricky had troubles of their own. I was running scared. Meanwhile, Jana Crowley was smelling like a rose. That was really amazing. I'd call her later.

Maybe.

I took my bags and went out to say to good-bye to the martini. It glowed and shimmered as beautifully as ever. I might not miss the city, but I would definitely miss the damn martini.

I went to the Fort Washington Avenue bus station. So many options. There was a row of yellow cabs. I could go to the airport and get on a plane to Florida. Mom and Dad would be thrilled to see me. I would get a tan and hide out among the hurricanes and mosquitoes.

The station was full of buses; I could jump on any of them. See America.

I had to do something. Captain Morrison had put the fear of God, or at least Johnny Rostelli, into me. He hadn't even mentioned the fact that Doug could get out on bail. That idea really gave me the heebie-jeebies.

"Get out of town," Tommy had said.

I went to Brooklyn.

Not a creature was stirring in Williamsburg, except maybe a small, yapping dachshund. I woke up Strudel and maybe the whole neighborhood.

Jerry came to the door wearing pajamas, with hair askew and visible beard-growth. For the first time I really saw a grown man instead of a boy from high school.

"Hi, Jerry."

"Hi, Marti."

He smiled and I could see the boy again.

"It's over."

"Are you going to write the book?"

"I'm going to try."

"Do you want to come inside or did you plan to stand out there all night?"

The words started spilling out in a breathless burble that I couldn't stand, but couldn't stop.

"Oh my god. I was thinking about this all the way over here. You are so sweet and I love being with you and maybe I do love you, but I know it'll never work out. It would make a great ending for the book. The heroine solves the murder and gets together with swell guy who has cute dog. Play 'We'll Meet Again.' Fade out. The end. But this is real life. I'm a women's libber and I'm impossible to live with and I'm probably crazy. I was seeing a shrink, you know?"

I stopped for breath.

"Marti, I was just asking you to come inside."

I held my breath. One more embarrassing humiliation? I couldn't take it.

He sighed and took a step forward. Suddenly his arms were around me and we're kissing. His lips were so soft.

I followed him into the house. Soon we were lying together on the couch. I knew he wanted me. I knew it wasn't such a good idea right then, but I didn't want to use the phrase "sloppy seconds." After a few more of those kisses, I didn't care.

Making love with Jerry was all warmth and melting sweetness. There was urgency but no desperation, and certainly no anger. It was like dancing.

Lying in his arms felt perfectly comfortable. I wanted to stay there forever. I dozed off, dreaming of something vague and happy. A passing police siren jolted me back into the reality of terror. Doug had been having me followed. He probably knew all about Brooklyn and Jerry. Johnny might know too.

I sat up gasping. Strudel came running out of the kitchen, yelping and whining like a frightened child. She jumped up on the couch and nestled herself between us. Jerry patted the dog's head and held me against his surprisingly muscular chest, trying to calm both of us at the same time.

"Jerry, this is serious. The hungry and the hunted. Jungleland. I have to get out of town."

"I'll go with you," he said without hesitation, almost casually.

"You are stark, raving crazy."

"I guess that makes two of us."

"What about your life here?"

"I'm in a rut. I want to write music instead of grading spelling tests."

"I didn't know you wrote music."

"We've got a lot to learn about each other."

"Wait a minute. Did you hear all that stuff I said before? It's important."

"Yes, I heard you. Now listen to me. You want liberation? As long as we're together, you'll always know where the door is and I'll never stand in your way. And after Debbie and Anita, I'm ready to tolerate any *mislegas* you've got to throw at me."

I tried to think of something really awful to tell him.

"I'm not on the list at Studio Fifty-four anymore."

"It's O.K."

"So I'm supposed to let you hurt me and do all the things you said you were going to do to get over your ex and almost ex-wives?"

He shook his head, almost exasperated.

"Do you really think I could hurt you?"

I felt a terror that had nothing to do with Johnny or Doug or crazy Arabs or anything I had ever been scared of before.

"Why should I take that chance?" I demanded.

He shook his head again. The long hair looked so soft, even in a tangle.

I looked at Strudel. Her eyes were fixed on mine. Come on, Marti, I thought, this is too important to let yourself be influenced by puppy-dog eyes, no matter how adorable they are.

I reminded myself that I was twenty-eight years old and every man I had ever idolized had broken my heart. I wasn't about to give any man that chance again—even if he did have soft lips, fluffy hair, and dancing feet.

I was getting ready to extricate myself when I heard him say:

"There's always *Lolita.*"

That was so low and manipulative I couldn't believe it. I was about to tell him off, but I found myself smiling in admiration. He grinned back.

My kind of guy.

By daybreak we were on the road, heading in a direction opposite that of Florida. Strudel was perched on my lap in the front seat of the Mercury Cougar.

We were looking for a safe place. Someplace where he could write the music that he felt inside. A place where I could write the book that I had to write. A place where I could find out if I loved Jerry Barlow as much as he said he loved me.

Preferably someplace with a disco. I had learned that love is eternal only as long as it lasts, but I knew that disco would last forever.